FAILURE

F-BOMB: SEALS LOVE CURVES, BOOK 4

MARY E THOMPSON

F-BOMB: SEALS LOVE CURVES

Welcome to the world of F-BOMB where a group of former SEALs have come together to protect the curvy women they love and the country they call home from the dangers of the world. They have the training and the knowledge, and they have the ability to kick some ass when needed. And it'll be needed.

F-BOMB: SEALs LOVE CURVES

Freedom

Fiancée (subscriber exclusive)

Forgotten

First

Failure

Friends

Family

Forbidden

Future

Finally

SUBSCRIBE NOW AT MARYETHOMPSON.COM

For second chances, and third chances, and love that never ends...

1

———

Ashleigh Edwards was exhausted. It had been a long trip, and she was ready to collapse into bed and sleep until morning, or longer if she had her way.

She was almost up to her room when she heard the front door open and close. She went to call out to Frederick, but she heard his sharp tone before she opened her mouth.

"What do you mean you don't know what happened?" he asked.

Ashleigh hated that tone. She wasn't afraid of her husband, but he was the kind of guy who didn't take shit from people. If he wasn't happy, he wasn't likely to be happy without some serious changes.

"I'm sorry, sir," a woman's voice said, capturing Ashleigh's attention. She didn't recognize the voice.

"Is someone going to fix this?" he barked.

"Yes, sir. They're on their way now. I've spoken to our contact within the police department, and they're aware of the situation. No questions will be asked."

What?

"Good," he said. "And what about me?"

"Sir?" she asked.

"I have fifteen minutes."

"Yes, sir. Shall we go into your office?"

"Smart woman."

Ashleigh crept down the stairs until she could see them walking away from her. His office was straight back at the end of the hallway. Her husband had his hand on the woman's lower back, guiding her. She had long, dark hair and wore heels and a dark dress over her slim figure. *What was he doing?*

Ashleigh tiptoed down the hall once they disappeared, her ears straining to hear sounds. She wasn't sure she wanted to look, but she had to see what was going on. If he saw her, she could just say she got home early and thought she heard him, but when she got to the door, his back was to her. Bent over his desk was the woman he'd been speaking to, her dress pulled up to her waist. His hips pumped, his bare, hairy ass clenched tight as he grunted and groaned.

Ashleigh almost threw up. She almost screamed. She wanted to kill him, but more than anything, she just wanted to get out. She was supposed to be gone for another day, so she could leave and figure out what she wanted to do before she had to return and face her cheating bastard of a husband.

She was almost to the stairs when a sheet of paper fluttered to the floor. She glanced back, but the grunting hadn't stopped so she knew he wasn't done.

Ashleigh bent to pick up the paper. It was a missing child report. A three month old. She remembered the story. Her heart broke for the parents when they went on TV to plea for anyone to offer information about their son.

Why does Frederick have this?

An open file was on the hall table, and Ashleigh

assumed that was where the paper came from. She went to put it back and saw another sheet, with a picture of the same child, but this was an adoption docket.

Ashleigh's heart sank. *No.*

She wanted to look through the rest of it, but she heard the jangle of Frederick's belt as he pulled up his pants. She dropped the sheet on top and raced to the stairs, climbing as fast as she could so she would be out of sight.

Frederick and the woman came back out of the office and paused in the hallway. He grabbed the file off the table and straightened the pages. "Is the boy ready to move tonight?"

"Yes, sir. He will be with his new family early next week."

"Good. Another successful adoption."

"Yes, sir."

Ashleigh clamped a hand over her mouth as tears ran down her face.

"Good. My wife will be home tomorrow by four. I need to be back by then."

"You will be, sir. Not a problem at all."

Ashleigh squeezed her eyes shut and pressed her hand into her stomach. The front door opened again, then closed and locked. Ashleigh opened her eyes and peeked around. She was alone.

Terrified to move in case they came back, Ashleigh stayed on the dark staircase for close to an hour. Only once she was sure they were truly gone did she dare move. She went to her bedroom and keyed in the code for the safe behind the original Monet and waited for the locks to disengage. When it opened, she reached inside for her passport, just in case, but more than one fell out.

She picked them up and opened the first one. Frederick's face smiled back at her. She met her husband through work.

She was working at the local bank processing business loans, and he came in for one. They started talking and hit it off. When he asked her out, she wasn't surprised at all, and she said yes without hesitation. They were married within a year, and he convinced her to quit her job so she could do something else, something she enjoyed.

Ashleigh volunteered with numerous organizations that helped place children for adoption. Her degree in accounting was a benefit to the companies that couldn't afford their own accountant on retainer. The trip she just got back from was a conference about the dangers of private, domestic adoptions because many times the children were kidnapped and positioned as orphans.

It was on her mind. That was the only reason she was even considering what she thought she saw. And thinking Frederick had anything to do with it. He was a good man. He volunteered at church and he had a lot of connections in his business. He was good.

Ashleigh went to fold the passport and return it when she scanned the page and gasped. The name on the passport was not Frederick Edwards. It was Jonathan Moreau. She opened the next one. Albert Fordham. With shaky hands, Ashleigh reached inside and pulled out more passports. More names. More people. All with her husband's face.

She had to be wrong, but she wasn't sure how she was.

She stuffed everything back into the safe and locked it. She swung the painting over the safe and looked around the room. She hadn't touched anything else. She grabbed her small suitcase and raced back down the stairs and out the front door. She half expected to find him waiting for her, but all that greeted her was the cool night air and darkness.

Ashleigh walked down her street and around the corner.

She knew there was a bus stop a few blocks away, and if she could get on it, she could get away before he even realized she had been home.

She kept to the shadows, praying no one would recognize her. Her feet ached and her arms screamed in protest at carrying the suitcase while half-running. Ashleigh wasn't the kind of woman who ran. She carried a few extra pounds and a few extra curves, much to her husband's dismay. He constantly encouraged her to eat healthier and frequently ordered her clothes that were a size too small.

She told herself all along that he was trying to help her. He wanted her healthy, because if she was healthy, she'd be around longer. For their children, if they had children one day.

She couldn't believe him anymore, though. She wasn't sure what to think. His words hurt her, but she told herself he loved her. She told herself that about a lot of things Frederick did and said.

Bile rose in her throat as the picture of the child came back to her mind. He mentioned the child being delivered to his new home. There was no mistaking that. He never mentioned adoption being one of the industries he had a hand in, and with her work in the same business, it would have definitely come up over the last seven years.

If it was legitimate.

She couldn't help the whisper of doubt. How many times had she questioned her husband's motives? His actions and words. He always explained everything away, but there was no way to explain this away.

A child was in danger, and Ashleigh couldn't sit back and let it happen.

She knew what she had to do, where she needed to turn. She hated the thought of seeing him again. The last time she saw him, he ripped the rug out from under her. She thought she was going to spend her life with him, but he chose another life. A life that didn't include her.

Ashleigh never wanted to see him again, but she knew if she needed help, he not only could provide it, but he would do it in a heartbeat. Because that was just the kind of man he was.

THE LAST THING Daniel Dunn wanted to do was run one more mile. His lungs were screaming at him to stop, his muscles begging him, but he couldn't outrun his demons if he didn't run. So he kept going. He pushed himself harder and faster, praying it would be enough to keep the nightmares away for a few hours. It never kept them away all night, but he could get a few hours of peace if he was lucky.

The lights of his house came into view, but he didn't want to go home. He knew he needed to, but he wasn't worn out enough. He would toss and turn half the night, and then he would be pissed off the next day.

But he couldn't run any longer. His lungs ached for a big gulp of fresh air, but the damp chill of the autumn night made it impossible to fill them. He slowed his pace and panted, trying to bring his breathing down to normal as quickly as possible. After sixteen years as a SEAL, he knew how long it should take him to recover from a punishing run. The longer he was out of the service, the longer it took for his breath to catch up.

He was almost to his front porch when movement to the side of the door caught his attention. At first, he thought it was an animal, but the noise was too big to be an animal.

He drew his gun from the holster on his hip and pointed it at the noise. "Get the fuck out here, asshole."

Instead of a slow movement, the woman jumped and scampered back. She fell on her ass in the mud from the recent rain and squealed.

Dunn's dick twitched at the sound, something that hadn't happened in far too long.

"Get up," he demanded, both pissed off at himself for responding to her and at her for being there in the first place.

"I'm trying," she spat. "Why the hell did you pull a gun on me?"

Dunn's eyes narrowed as he tried to see through the darkness. "Ashleigh?"

"Yes. What is wrong with you?"

"Why the hell are you at my house? And how did you find me?"

"I need your help, Daniel." She finally stepped into the light. "Please."

Ashleigh Connors. Holy shit. Daniel couldn't have been more surprised. He hadn't seen Ashleigh in years, but she still had the ability to turn him inside out with just a look. One look, and he couldn't say no to her. There was fear in her green eyes.

He nodded and looked around, then let them inside. He turned on the lights and locked the door behind them. Whatever happened, she was running from something. Or someone. Anger churned in Dunn's gut thinking about Ashleigh being in danger. She was always so smart and strong and good.

She looked around as she walked through his home and he wondered what she saw. He lived like a bachelor with a small house in the woods, secluded and dark. He had lots of wood and dark furniture. He hadn't bothered to decorate because he didn't have anything to hang on the walls except his TV. His couch and his TV were really all he needed. And a kitchen so he could eat, and a fridge to hold his beer.

But what did Ashleigh see? Did she see a man she was happy she didn't spend her life with? A part of him hoped so, and a part of him hoped she wished things had turned out differently.

He thought about her more than a man should be allowed to think about his ex. On nights when he wasn't sure how he would survive BUD/s, Ashleigh was on his mind. On nights overseas when he wasn't sure if he was going to live, Ashleigh was on his mind. He regretted the way he treated her, which was why seeing her again was a shock.

Dunn couldn't believe she was standing in his house. The years had been kind to Ashleigh. Kinder than he would have been. He knew the toll being a military wife took on some women. Ashleigh was the kind of woman who would have wanted him home, but he'd always wanted to fight for his country. He was willing to die for his country, and to do so, he had to give her up.

But staring at her from across the room, he could tell her life hadn't gone exactly as planned either. The clothes she wore were not cheap, but her hair was matted on one side and her makeup was smudged. He wanted to pry, but he wasn't sure where the line was. Yeah, she said she wanted his help, but did that give him any rights? He didn't think it did.

She looked up and caught him staring at her. She didn't even bother hiding her disdain for him. He couldn't blame her. She had every right to hate him. When he broke up with her, she found out that he'd never intended to spend his life with her, even though he'd said he would. He always said it in the moment, when he tried to pretend he was a regular guy. But he wasn't. And she was destroyed by it.

"I have a good life," she finally said, her voice rough like she'd been chewing glass. She cleared her throat and drew in a breath. "I had a good life. I've never wanted for anything. It's all over now."

"Why?" Dunn asked. Rule number one of an interrogation was to keep the subject talking. The only way he'd find out why she was there was if she told him, and when dealing with a caged animal, the only choice was to let her come to him.

"I saw something. My husband... he's not the man I thought he was. He's... I guess I don't know who he is. But I couldn't stay there. I couldn't..."

She put her hand on her stomach and drew in a breath. Her exhale shuddered through her and shook the room. Dunn acted on instinct, letting it lead his feet across the room to where she stood, looking out the window into his dark backyard. When he reached her, he didn't hesitate, just pulled her into his arms and held her.

Peace settled over him. Ashleigh. The one woman he'd have given it all up for. The one woman he wanted to give it all up for. The one woman who...

"Ow!"

Slapped him. She actually slapped him.

Well, guess she didn't feel the same about him anymore.

"I'm married, Daniel! And you have no right to touch me," she spat. She shook all over at the feel of his hands on her. Rage from watching her husband fuck another woman. Fear from wondering what he was really involved with. Excitement from being in Daniel's arms again.

But she wasn't allowed to feel that last one. The last one was dangerous. She was married, or at least, she thought she was married. She wasn't going to cheat on her husband just because he had a few extra passports and slept with someone else. That wasn't who she was. Her marriage was over as far as she was concerned, but she wasn't a cheater.

"I'm sorry," he mumbled. "I wasn't trying to do anything."

She drew in a shaky breath and tried to push all her feelings away. Being in Daniel's arms, even just for a second, brought back too many memories. He was her first love, and the first man she made love to. She gave herself to him, thinking they were building something together. She wanted to be with him forever, but he never had that intention. And it hurt when he finally told her the truth. More than anything she'd ever been through in her life.

"Why don't we sit," he offered. "And you can tell me what's going on."

She hesitated, not ready to talk yet. It had been a day since she snuck away from her own home and vanished. She didn't know if someone was watching her, so she took multiple trains and buses to get from Detroit to Niagara Falls. The fastest way would have been to go through Canada, but it wasn't until she was in Ohio that she found out where Daniel was. She hated going to him, but she didn't know where else to go, so she was stuck begging the man who destroyed her for help.

"Or you can take a shower," he said when she didn't respond. "And we can talk after that."

She nodded. "That sounds good."

2

───────

Dunn showed Ashleigh where the bathroom was and instructed her on how to use his shower. He could have sent her to his guest bathroom, but he wanted her in his shower. In his room. Hot water sliding down her naked body in the same room where he would strip naked later.

He was a fucking idiot. Fantasizing about Ashleigh was as dumb as falling for Ashaki. Two women who nearly ruined him. But like everything else in his life, he picked the wrong one to trust.

A part of him always wondered if he and Ashleigh could have been happy if he'd been honest with her from the start. If he'd told her he planned to become a SEAL. Would she have been okay with it, or would she have run the other way? He'd never know the answer to that question.

He had a lifetime of regrets, and Ashleigh was simply one in a string of many.

Dunn wanted to strip off his sweaty clothes and join Ashleigh in the shower, but she was a married woman and not his, so he told his dick to shut the fuck up and went to the kitchen to find something to eat.

He tossed a frozen pizza in the oven, just in case Ashleigh was hungry, and twisted open a beer. He tipped it up to his lips and gulped down the cold liquid, hoping it would help to clear his muddled mind.

He tried running through reasons of why she was at his home instead of her own. She said she was married, and that her husband wasn't who she thought he was. Dunn wanted to grab his phone and order English, his computer whiz and all around tech genius, to find out who her husband was and what he'd done. And the guy could do it, too. It wouldn't take long for English, also known as Liam Johnson, to find her and learn everything there was to know about her and her husband. But if Dunn was going to get her to trust him, he had to let her tell him what happened and what was going on.

He checked on the pizza and decided it needed another couple of minutes when the door to his room opened. His entire body tightened as he waited for her to walk into the kitchen. He tried to act casual, like he wasn't painfully aware of her presence, but his gaze locked on hers the second she stepped into view and gave him away.

Ashleigh was still as stunning as ever. With her dirty blonde hair wet, it looked brown. She brushed it back from her face which made her green eyes look huge. She looked around warily, but her gaze settled on him. She chewed on her cheek like she always did when she wasn't sure of herself.

"What is it?" he asked, his voice a little more than gruff.

He was grateful for the peninsula between them so she couldn't see the effect her curves had on him. She was always a woman who could fill out a dress with her hour-glass figure, but the years had added a few more pounds in all the right places. She was softer, more feminine, with her full breasts and rounded hips. Her belly was full, but narrower than her hips, giving her a shape he wanted to run his hands over. She was the sexiest woman he'd ever seen, and by far the most beautiful one he'd ever had in his bed.

But he'd never have that chance again.

"Thank you for the shower. And for letting me in," she said softly.

Dunn nodded. "Of course. Are you hungry? I have pizza in the oven."

She smiled, that tentative smile that lit him up inside. "You're always hungry. I don't know how you haven't gained any weight. It's not fair that I've blown up and you still look like a statue."

"You're fucking gorgeous," he blurted without thinking. They were the same words he'd said to her over and over again when they were together. She never believed him, but he would tell her that when he was buried deep inside her, when he watched her get dressed, when she was having a tough day. He wanted her to always know that no matter how she thought about herself and no matter what anyone else ever said, he thought she was the most beautiful woman around. Now he knew that was only part of it. She was the most beautiful woman in the world.

Her cheeks turned scarlet. He had to close his eyes, but that just allowed him to picture exactly how far down her body that blush went. He could see all of her vividly, like it was yesterday that he'd last been with her.

"I don't remember the last time I had something to eat," she finally said.

He nodded and grunted, then bent to get the pizza out of the oven. He set it on the stove and busied himself getting the pizza cutter out of the dishwasher and washing it, then grabbing plates and napkins before he cut the pizza and handed her three slices.

"It's hot," he reminded her before she took a bite.

She smiled and nodded, pursing her lips to blow on the pizza.

Jesus, he needed to get laid. Just watching Ashleigh had him ready to fucking blow.

He stared at his own pizza and took the chance that it wouldn't burn his mouth. He took a huge bite and regretted it as soon as the hot cheese melted to the roof of his mouth. He hissed and sucked in a breath, but the damage was done.

Ashleigh stared at him for a second, then burst out laughing.

Dunn tried to choke down the scalding hot pizza, but it still burned. He sucked in cold air and chewed until it was small enough to go down his throat and stop burning.

Ashleigh laughed the whole time.

"What's so funny?" he finally asked her.

She grinned and rolled her eyes. "You used to do that all the time in college. You would burn your mouth because you were too hungry to wait for your food to cool down. I really thought you would have gotten smarter by now."

He shook his head. "Nope. I'm still the same dumbass who let you go."

She glared at him. That was definitely the wrong thing to say.

SHE SHOOK her head and wanted to walk out the door. If she had anywhere else to go, she would, but she knew her husband would never look for her with her ex. He didn't even know who Daniel was. She mentioned a guy she dated in college, but she underplayed it when she realized how jealous Frederick got when she talked about other men, or talked to other men. She didn't think Frederick would do anything to Daniel, but she also never imagined her husband could be involved in something like kidnapping or human trafficking.

The pizza lost its appeal when she thought about what she saw in her house the night before. She set the plate down and stepped back, breathing through her mouth so she didn't vomit.

"Why don't we sit," Daniel suggested.

He walked around the peninsula and over to her like he was going to guide her to the couch, but he backed away at the last second so he didn't touch her. She missed his touch like a physical thing, wishing she hadn't pushed him off the first time. She could really use a hug, someone to hold her and tell her everything would be okay. Her dad always gave her the best hugs, warm and comforting. With his arms around her, she felt like nothing bad could ever happen.

But her dad had been gone for eight years. He died shortly after she and Frederick started dating. Ever since then, she felt like she was missing a piece of herself.

Ashleigh walked over to Daniel's couch and sank down into the cool leather. The couch threatened to swallow her, which was almost as good as a hug. He passed her a blanket, and Ashleigh curled up in the corner and spread the blanket over her lap.

"What are you doing here, Ash?" he asked.

Ash. Daniel was the only one who ever called her that. Frederick called her Ash once, and she told him she didn't like the nickname. In truth, it felt like something that belonged to Daniel. She didn't want to share that part of herself with anyone else.

She finally looked at him and admitted the truth. "I needed to get away from my husband."

"Did he hurt you?" Daniel growled.

Ashleigh shook her head. "Not physically, no. I saw him having sex with someone else."

"Ah, fuck, Ash. I'm sorry."

She nodded. Daniel was a good man. The best. He was looking at her like she was a wounded woman, but when she told him the rest, he'd look at her like she was a victim.

They were walking through campus one night when a woman came running toward them. She was looking back and barely cared what was in front of her as long as she got away from whoever was chasing her. She plowed into Daniel and Ashleigh, nearly knocking them over, but Daniel caught the woman.

She fell into his arms and told him a man just attacked her and was chasing her. Daniel had murder in his eyes when he went after the guy. It was the first and only time Ashleigh saw him look like that. He was in charge and determined to make it right.

As a twenty-two year old in love, she was jealous of the way Daniel protected that other woman. He checked in with her regularly until she transferred to another college. Ashleigh couldn't tell him she didn't want him to reach out to the other woman, but she hated whenever he did.

She was about to be that woman.

"When I was leaving, I saw a picture of a boy. He was a few months old and had been taken from his parents. Kidnapped. I went to set the page down and I saw another paper that looked like something you would have for an adoption, a docket with details about the child and the birth parents." Her cheeks heated when he narrowed his gaze, silently asking how she knew what that looked like. "Frederick and I have been talking about adoption. We've had trouble getting pregnant for years, and we thought adoption would be a good idea. Take the stress off me, and thirty-nine is pretty old to have a baby."

Daniel nodded with his jaw clenched tight.

"Anyway, the boy wasn't adopted. It was a current picture, and it looked like he was going to be adopted."

Daniel narrowed his gaze. "What are you saying, Ash?"

She took a deep breath. "I think my husband is involved in kidnapping and human trafficking of an infant boy in Detroit."

"Well, fuck me," Daniel said.

Ashleigh nodded. Her thoughts exactly.

DUNN WAS PARALYZED for the first time since he saw his boss and mentor with a gun to another man's head. For all the shit he'd seen in his life and his career as a SEAL, he was rarely surprised. People were vicious, horrible pieces of shit. But as a SEAL, the people he encountered were fighting for their lives. Right and wrong didn't matter as much as survival, so people did horrible things all in the name of saving their own ass.

But the real world was different. He didn't expect to see the same inhumanity in the real world. Having Williams turn on them was the shock of Dunn's life. Ashaki betraying him and the rest of the Team hurt, but that was more of a prideful thing. He didn't see it coming and felt like an idiot. But Williams had been stringing them all along for years. He made them believe he was on their side, but he wasn't.

He got that Ashleigh was feeling the same way. Her husband was not the man she thought he was. He should have been keeping her safe, and instead he was involved with people who were stealing children. Dunn's mind spun with the possibility of her husband taking that child for himself and Ashleigh, of adopting him as their own, but his gut told him that wasn't the case.

Too bad he didn't trust his gut anymore. But his team? He trusted them.

Dunn stood and pulled out his phone.

Ashleigh shouted, "No. You can't call anyone."

Dunn looked down at her. She was shaking again, her eyes wild with fear. "Why can't I call anyone?"

"He could find me," she said.

Dunn sat back down. "Why would he expect you to come here? He would probably think you'd go to your dad's or to see a friend."

Ashleigh shook her head again. "Dad died a few years ago. And I'm still not speaking to my mom. All my friends are his friends."

"Okay, so if he doesn't know you're here, how will he find you?"

She drew in a shaky breath. "I... I don't know. Don't people have ways to find people? He's a very powerful man."

Dunn nodded. "I understand, Ash, but I'm not going to let him get to you. I need to call my team, though. So they can start to figure out what's going on."

"Are you sure none of them are working for him?"

She asked the one question he couldn't answer. The one question that rubbed a raw nerve with sandpaper. A couple of years ago, he never would have thought twice about the men he considered his brothers, but after Williams, Dunn wasn't sure of anything.

"They're good men, Ash. You'll see," was all he said.

Dunn sent out a group text asking everyone available to

meet at his house immediately. All of them responded that they were on their way.

"They'll be here soon," he told Ashleigh. "I need to take a quick shower."

"I—" She stopped herself.

"What?"

She looked around the room and stared out through the sliding glass door. It was one of the reasons Dunn bought the house, for the big doors so he could open up his house and move between the two spaces. And she was afraid of it.

"Do you want me to close the curtains?" he asked.

She hesitated, then nodded. "Yeah. I guess I'll be okay like that."

Dunn tugged the curtains closed and checked that the doors were locked, then handed Ash the remote and went to his room. He left the bedroom door open in case she needed something, but closed the bathroom door. He tossed his sweaty running clothes into the hamper and jumped in the shower, washing himself quickly so he was out before any of the guys showed up and scared the shit out of Ashleigh.

He dried off and cracked the bathroom door to let the steam out. Once he was mostly dry, he wrapped his towel around his waist and went into his room.

Where Ashleigh was sitting on his bed.

Her gaze dropped like a stone, falling to where his dick hid beneath his towel. So much for keeping him under wraps. He responded instantly to her gaze, even though there was a towel there, and pulsed against the cotton. Her eyes widened, and she trailed them up his chest slowly.

Dunn knew he should get dressed and tell her to wait for him in the other room, but Ash had seen him naked more times than he could count. It had been almost two decades, but he hadn't changed that much.

"Why are you in here, Ash?" he finally managed to ask.

She looked up and met his gaze. "I didn't want to be in the other room alone. I'm sorry. I'll close my eyes or something so you can get dressed."

She clamped her eyes shut. Dunn sighed. She was terrified, and he couldn't just toss her out.

Checking again to make sure her eyes were closed, Dunn went to his dresser and grabbed a green tee and a pair of black shorts. He pulled the tee on, then dropped his towel and pulled on boxer briefs and shorts. When he turned back to Ashleigh, she was watching him.

"Sorry," she said, her cheeks turning pink again.

"Of all the places you could have gone, why did you come here?" he asked her.

She looked up at him, likely surprised he didn't say anything about her checking him out naked. Then she smiled sadly and said, "I knew you'd do anything to keep me safe. Even though you don't love me anymore, I knew you'd protect me with your life. It's who you are, Daniel."

3

―――――

ASHLEIGH WONDERED WHAT CAUSED THE SHADOWS IN Daniel's eyes at her words. She wanted to ask him about it, about the losses she knew he'd been through, but she couldn't. She lost any chance at that right when she married another man. Daniel wasn't hers.

Before he could respond to what she said, someone pounded on the door. Ashleigh jumped off the bed and leaped at Daniel. "He's here. He found me. Help me."

Daniel held her, wrapping his arms around her and holding her close. "Ash, that's my team. I told them to come here. It's not your husband."

"But what if he's with them? Or what if he got into your group somehow?"

"He never knew about me. You said you didn't tell him, so there's no reason he ever would have bothered with me. Right?"

She finally nodded, but she wasn't ready to let go of him yet.

He was a big guy in college. Tall and built, but with eyes that said he was really a teddy bear underneath. Those soft eyes were mostly gone, and the tall, built guy was even wider, with more muscles covering his body. When he walked out of the bathroom, Ashleigh couldn't speak. He was simply stunning. All that dark, smooth skin drew her gaze. And when his towel twitched, she nearly moaned.

Her sex life was relatively good with Frederick, but it was exceptional with Daniel. She'd never been loved by a man the way he loved her. Seeing him mostly naked again was a reminder of the way he made her feel beautiful and desirable and sexy. She promised she would close her eyes, but she couldn't resist getting a peek at him. And he was still the most beautiful man she'd ever seen.

The pounding on the door started up again, and Daniel pulled away from her just enough to push her behind his back. He kept his hand on her as he moved down the hallway toward the front of his house. When he got to the door, he tapped on it. Someone tapped on the other side, and Daniel stepped back and opened the door.

"What the hell took you so long?" asked the first guy through the door.

"We were out there for five fucking minutes," said the next guy.

"What's going on?" said the third.

Then they all stopped. The first guy looked at Ashleigh, clutching the back of Daniel's shirt, then looked at Daniel. He shook his head. "It's not what you think. She needs our help."

One guy stepped forward and offered her his hand. "I'm Jack. It's so nice to meet you…"

"Ashleigh."

His eyebrows went up, and he glanced at Daniel. Obviously, Jack knew who she was. "Ashleigh," he repeated. "Forgive me, but I didn't realize you two were in touch."

"We're not," Daniel said firmly. "Move along."

Jack held Ashleigh's hand for another moment, then let go and moved to the dining room table.

She was introduced to the rest of them in succession. Archer, Jaymes, English, Slade, Mason, Dex, and Rocky. Once they were all inside, they circled around the table and asked Daniel what was going on.

"I'll let Ashleigh explain why she's here, and why you're all here. Hands fucking off," Daniel said, glaring at them each in turn.

Jack smirked at him, and Rocky looked like he couldn't care less what Daniel said, but the rest of them nodded. Then Daniel turned to her and nodded for her to begin.

She told them about finding the picture and the adoption docket in her house, and her assumption her husband had something to do with it. They all waited patiently for her to finish telling her side of the story, then jumped in with more questions.

"Did he see you? Does he know you know?"

"When were you supposed to be home?"

"What was he doing that he didn't know you were there?"

"What do you know about the child?"

"Why did you come here?"

Ashleigh's head spun with all the questions. She wasn't sure who to answer first, or what they really needed to know. She opened and closed her mouth, but every time she started to answer, another question was thrown at her.

"All right, stop. Let's do this the right way so she can actually tell us what we need to know. Ash, start at the beginning. What were you doing yesterday before you went home?" Daniel asked calmly.

"I was out of town," Ashleigh replied.

"Doing what?" She thought that was Dex.

"I volunteer with adoption agencies. I have a degree in accounting, so I work with them to help set up systems to track their finances. Since most organizations are stretched thin, they rarely hire enough people or the right people to monitor their income and expenses. My husband..." She drew in a shaky breath. "He's very successful, so I work as a volunteer so these companies can get the help they need without an added expense. I was at a conference, networking and learning more about the adoption process, but I ended up home a day early."

"Why did you go home early?" Archer, she thought, asked.

"The conference was supposed to end with a dinner the last night, but it was canceled since most of the attendees booked flights to leave instead of staying one more night in the hotel. Most of them are extremely budget-conscious," Ashleigh explained.

"So you changed your flight and went home?"

Ashleigh nodded.

"Was your husband home when you got home?"

Ashleigh shook her head. "I was dropped off shortly before he came home. I was heading upstairs when he came in the door with a woman I didn't recognize."

The men exchanged a glance. Ashleigh's cheeks heated as they all pieced together exactly what happened. Instead of making them ask, she blurted out that part of the story.

"They were talking about something I didn't understand, but it was clearly work. I've met his assistant, but this woman... I don't know who she is. He told her he had fifteen minutes, and they went into his office. I crept down the stairs and followed them. They were having sex, just like all of you suspected. My husband of almost seven years was screwing another woman on his desk in my house. A skinny, perfect, cute woman. Did that answer all the questions you needed answers to?" Ashleigh was breathing heavy and flustered. She struggled to meet the eyes of the men around the room, but she did. All except Daniel's. She couldn't look at him. She already told him Frederick fucked someone else. She couldn't look at him again.

"Then you found the paperwork?" Daniel provided for her.

She nodded and wiped the tears beneath her lashes. She drew in a breath and said, "Yes. But they came back after a few minutes. I ran upstairs so they didn't see me. I just wanted to get away."

"Did you take pictures of any of this?" someone asked.

Ashleigh shook her head. "No. My phone was in my purse on the stairs, and I was in shock. I went upstairs to get my passport and found others with my husband's picture but different names. I was scared, and I just left."

"And you came here," Jack said. His arms were crossed over his chest. His gaze locked on Ashleigh's, seeing more than she wanted him to. He obviously knew who she was, and exactly what happened between her and Daniel.

"Frederick doesn't know anything about Daniel. He's a very jealous man. He never liked me talking about other men, and I never told him about Daniel or our relationship."

"So Dunn was the safe choice? Is that why you came here?" Dex asked.

Ashleigh shrugged and nodded at the same time. "I guess. Daniel has always been the kind of man who protects others. I knew he would help me. And if I'm right about Frederick, I needed somewhere to go until I figured out what to do."

"You weren't worried about bringing hell to Dunn's front door?" Jack asked.

Ashleigh knew he wasn't just asking about Frederick showing up, but about Ashleigh herself being there. Daniel was the one who ended things. He was the one who made plans that didn't include her and forgot to tell her about them. She thought they were building a future together. He was planning all along to walk away.

"No," she said firmly, glaring at Jack. "I wasn't worried about that. Daniel has always been able to take care of himself and everyone around him. And I was confident I would be another job for him. Nothing more."

Jack glared right back for a long moment. Ashleigh didn't back down. He might know Daniel's side of the story, but he obviously didn't know everything that happened between them.

"How did you know where Dunn lived?" the guy at the computer asked, breaking the spell between Ashleigh and Jack.

Ashleigh looked at him. "I looked him up online."

"Where? He doesn't have any social media profiles. None of us do. His address is unlisted. How did you find the house?"

Ashleigh looked around at the room full of men who were far smarter and craftier than she was. If she figured out how to find a man who didn't want to be found, they could find someone who didn't want to be found.

"I know about F-BOMB. I've read about it. And I know Daniel. I figured he was in a place like this. Out of the way and private. I asked around."

"You asked around?" Daniel blurted. "Who the hell told you where I live?"

Ashleigh shrugged. "A few people said there were always

a bunch of black SUVs at this house. I figured it was a good bet that it was yours or someone you knew."

"Jesus, Ash. You could have gotten killed. If you ended up at someone else's house, they might not have asked questions," Daniel said.

The enormity of Ashleigh's situation finally hit her. The risks she took to get somewhere she felt safe. The danger she was truly in. The threat she brought to Daniel's door. She couldn't handle it.

She pushed to her feet and mumbled that she needed a minute, then rushed down the hall and closed out the group of men who were questioning her every move. Especially the one man she'd ached to see for years and regretted ever laying eyes on again.

As soon as the door closed behind Ashleigh, everyone turned to Dunn.

"What the fuck is going on?" Jack asked, his voice low.

"Who the hell is she?" Archer demanded.

"She's his ex," Jack answered. "They went to college together and would have gotten married if he hadn't joined the Teams. Once she found out he planned to leave, they ended things. It fucking destroyed him. He is who he is because of that woman. Because she hurt him."

"Enough," Dunn barked. "What happened between Ashleigh and me is ancient history. She's married, and she's here because she needs our help."

"It looks like she wants your help," Dex said. "I'm not buying her story about asking around. Something's not adding up with her."

"You think she's lying?" Dunn asked. His head spun with

the possibility. He believed her without question. She was shaken when he found her outside his house. But she was Ashleigh. He couldn't be objective about her. Hell, at that point, he wasn't sure he could be objective about anyone. His instincts were always reliable, but he hadn't been able to trust himself since he found out Williams was really using him and the others to get revenge on his wife and the Navy, who he blamed for the end of his marriage.

"I don't trust her," Jack said.

"Neither do I," Dex agreed.

"She's scared. I think everything up to how she found you makes sense. Have you checked her for a phone?" Slade asked.

Dunn shook his head. Fuck. The simplest of things. She could have a phone on her, recording everything they said. She could bring anyone she wanted to his house, to all of them. He hadn't seen her in more than eighteen years. He had no idea who she was or what she was capable of.

"We need to search her things and make sure she's not working for someone else. Then we need to dig into her story. Find out everything we can about her and her husband, and try to find out if the story about the kid is true," Dex said, looking around the room.

Everyone nodded along. Dunn watched numbly as his team jumped to follow Dex's orders. Rocky and Mason went down the hall. Archer and Jack went to her suitcase next to the couch. English and Jaymes set up computers and started typing, mumbling softly to each other.

Slade and Dex approached Dunn.

"You okay?" Slade asked calmly.

Dunn shook his head.

"You want me to take lead on this one?" Dex asked.

Dunn glared at him. "She's married."

Dex glared right back. "I'm not trying to fuck her. I'm trying not to let you get fucked, boss."

Dunn shook his head and ran his hands over his shaved head. Ashleigh Connors. He never thought he'd see her again. He thought about her more than he should have, and he concocted a story in his mind about the happy life she was living without him. He told himself she was better off without him. Recent history proved that should have been the case. Ashaki was killed by the men she betrayed Dunn to help. Ashleigh should have been safe. Happy.

"She's not going to fuck me. She's not going to do anything. We're going to help her, then she's going to move on with her life," Dunn said.

"With a kidnapping, human trafficking husband?" Slade said.

Dunn just glared in response.

"Okay, let's calm down," Dex said. "We're not helping anything by arguing. Tell us everything you know about her."

Dunn shrugged. "I haven't seen her since college."

"You didn't keep in touch at all?" Dex asked.

Dunn shook his head. "No. She had no interest in talking to me again. And I don't blame her. We were together for two years. I never told her I planned to go into the Navy, to become a SEAL. When we'd talk about the future, I let her talk. I knew I was going to walk away from her, and I let her think I'd be there through all the things she wanted to do."

"Shit," Slade breathed. "That's..."

"Fucked up?" Dunn provided.

Slade met his gaze and nodded. "Yeah, boss. Why couldn't you be together? It's not easy, but you could have been a husband and a SEAL."

"Yeah, and turn out like Williams?" Dunn spat.

Dex shook his head. "Not everyone is like him. There are men who have successful relationships. You have to want both. Williams never made time for his family, so they weren't there for him when he was willing to reach out. But look at Rodney. He—"

"Got killed for being what Williams couldn't be," Dunn said.

Dex and Slade sucked in sharp breaths. It was the first time Dunn voiced that thought, but it made sense to him. Rodney was a good man. He got too close to Williams, but he was also the only one of all of them that was married. Williams played everyone, but Rodney had something Williams didn't. A happy fiancée and a life waiting for him at home.

"Do you think…?" Slade asked.

Dunn shrugged. "It's hard to believe that wasn't part of it. Williams was jealous, and if he thought Rodney knew something, maybe that took over. Rodney never said anything to any of us about Williams. If he was really that suspicious, I have a hard time believing he wouldn't have told someone."

"Fuck," Dex breathed. "Williams went after Lily, too. Just when she and Archer were getting together."

"It all adds up," Dunn said.

The others shook their heads. Dunn had a year to come up with his theory that Williams would go after any of them who managed to do what he couldn't. They had surveillance on Williams' family, but so far, he'd been a ghost. It was only a matter of time before he came back.

And with Ashleigh in his house, and three of the guys in happy relationships, Dunn was sure it wouldn't be long before Williams tried to kill them all again.

4

———————

ASHLEIGH SPLASHED COLD WATER ON HER FACE AND TOOK A breath. She tried to tell herself she wasn't overreacting, but every step she took seemed to be in the wrong direction. She showed up early to surprise her husband and found him screwing someone else and uncovered... something. She ran, assuming the worst, and ran straight to her ex. Now, his group of friends was drilling her with questions and making her feel like she was the guilty one.

Why did I come?

As soon as the question whispered through her mind, she knew the answer. She came because she was scared. Because she had an active imagination and immediately jumped to conclusions. And because the last time she truly felt safe and loved was when she was with Daniel.

She told herself she loved her husband, but Frederick was different. There were times he drew her close and made her feel like she was special, but he was all about appearances. She couldn't kick her shoes off and tuck her feet under her on the couch. She couldn't kiss him in public. And she definitely couldn't make noise during sex. None of it was appropriate, although who would know she liked to make noise during sex was beyond her.

It didn't matter, though. She was not going back to Frederick. She couldn't stay married to a cheater. And now that every man in the house knew she couldn't keep her husband happy, she was ready to get the hell away from Daniel and all his friends as quickly as possible.

A knock on the door startled her. Ashleigh took a breath and opened the door, coming face to face with two of the men. She couldn't remember their names, but it didn't matter.

"Sorry, gentlemen. I'm done. I'll get out of the way for you."

"Ms. Connors, we need to ask you some questions," one of them said as she pushed by them.

"Mrs. Edwards, although not for long."

"Are you going through a divorce?" one asked, the taller one. He was older than the others and definitely more dangerous if looks told her anything.

She smiled at him. "Well, my husband was fucking another woman, so yeah, I'll be going through a divorce. As soon as I get back there."

The men exchanged a glance, then moved quickly to block her way.

She stepped back and glared at them. She didn't look like the badass she usually was, but she had a stare that could scare most grown men.

Apparently not them.

"Excuse me, gentlemen."

"We can't let you leave, Mrs. Edwards. You need to answer a few questions for us."

Ashleigh drew in a breath and gathered up all her resolve. "Fine."

"How long have you been married?" the Black guy asked.

Ashleigh sighed and crossed her arms over her chest. "Eight years."

"And how long did you know your husband before you got married?"

"Just under a year."

"How did you meet?"

"Would you like my entire dating history?" Ashleigh asked, already annoyed.

The guys exchanged a look, and the white guy stepped forward. "May I call you Ashleigh?"

She shrugged.

"I'm Mason. I know there are a lot of us, but we're here to help you. If Dunn trusts you, the rest of us do. Rocky isn't asking these questions because we think you did something. We need to get an idea of who your husband is, and knowing how long you've known him and how well you knew him before will start to paint a picture for us. It's intrusive, and I get that. I know intrusive, Ashleigh, trust me."

She tilted her head and examined him closely. She didn't expect him to be willing to take a minute and explain to her what was going on, but he obviously had some wounds in his past. A darkness nothing had touched.

"I'm sorry. I am a very private person. Well, my husband is private. I've grown accustomed to it. It's hard to share this with strangers. Almost as hard as it is to tell the last man who didn't want me that he started a trend." She sighed heavily. "I met Frederick at work. I was working at a bank processing business loans. He came in and needed a loan. We hit it off. We were married in less than a year."

"What bank was it?"

"It's a small, local bank. Detroit First Union."

"How long did you work there before you met him?"

"Just a few months. My previous job ended when the facility where I was closed. The bank was hiring, and it was something that paid the bills."

Rocky took notes while she talked. "Do you remember what company his loan was for?"

Ashleigh nodded. "The only company I've ever known him to work for is Edwards Unlimited, Inc."

"You said he's a private person," Mason said.

Ashleigh nodded again. "Yes. He always has been. He doesn't like going out and we rarely have people over."

"Who are your close friends? The people you spend time with?"

Ashleigh thought about it for a minute, then shrugged. "We don't really have close friends. We'll go to parties for work, and I have some people from the companies I volunteer with, but there's no one I could call to help me bury a body."

"Excuse me?" Rocky blurted.

Ashleigh gave him a funny look. "You know, that loyal, dedicated friend you could call who would do anything you asked without question."

Rocky and Mason exchanged another glance.

"Did you kill your husband?" Mason asked after a moment.

Ashleigh snorted and shook her head. The two men stared at her, obviously not trusting her. Her snort turned to a full out hysterical laughter, and she had to lean against the wall to keep from falling over.

"Um, are you okay?"

Ashleigh nodded. "Yeah, it's just funny that you guys think I killed my husband and the first place I'm going to go is to a former SEAL's house and confess to his friends."

Laughter kept bubbling up. Ashleigh smiled up at them. "Thanks, guys. I needed that."

"Um, okay, so you don't have any close friends. You do volunteer work, so you don't have any coworkers you see regularly. Family?"

Ashleigh shook her head, the pain spearing through her heart. "My dad died shortly after Frederick and I started dating. I haven't spoken to my mother in years."

"What about your husband? Does he have any friends or family?"

She shook her head. "No. He works all the time. His employees are the only people he spends time with."

Rocky nodded and wrote it down. He showed something to Mason, who nodded.

"What?" Ashleigh asked.

"Rocky, Mason," someone called down the hall. "We need Ashleigh."

Rocky and Mason nodded to her and moved to the side so she could pass. Ashleigh went back to the living room where the rest of the men were crowded around the two computers on the dining room table.

"Ashleigh, we need you to look at a few things. First, is this your husband?" one of the guys asked her.

He turned his computer around, and Frederick stared back at her. The picture wasn't familiar, but it was definitely him. Ashleigh nodded. "Yes. That photo was taken a couple of years ago, though. His hair is a little gray on his temples now. Otherwise, he looks mostly the same."

The other guy cleared his throat. "There are a few different kidnapping cases in the Detroit area that we found reports of. We don't have access to FBI files, but using public information reported through the media, there are three we think might be the one you saw."

Ashleigh nodded. "Let me see them."

He pulled up the first one, but Ashleigh shook her head. They moved on to the second kid, and she nodded. "That's him. I remember him. His parents offered a reward for any information that led to finding him. I should have called the police."

The guy at the computer shook his head. "No, it's good you came to us. We can contact the FBI and you can give them all the information you have in a safe place. Especially if your husband has contacts in the police department like the woman said."

Ashleigh chewed on her nail. "I don't really have any information. I mean, I don't know what I saw."

"You saw an adoption docket and overheard your husband talking about an adoption for a child who has been kidnapped. If he's transported over state lines, it's harder to track because the kidnapping is big news in Detroit but not so much if they go to Seattle or Dallas or somewhere outside the immediate area," Daniel said calmly.

Ashleigh never thought she'd be having a conversation about kidnapping. A calm, peaceful, accusatory conversation with the man who left her behind in college.

Ashleigh drew in a breath and nodded. "Okay. If you think it could help, I'll tell them everything."

"Do you remember any of the names on the passports?" another guy asked. Dex?

Ashleigh nodded. "There were five. All US passports, but I didn't dig through so maybe there were more. Jonathan Moreau, Albert Fordham, Ricardo Juarez, Anderson... something. I'm sorry, I don't remember that one. Um, and York. Something York. I'm sorry."

Daniel reached for her hand but pulled back before he

touched her. She wished he would wrap her up and hold her close. "It's okay, Ash. You did great. And it's not easy to go through what you went through. We'll run the names and see what we can find."

"Got one," one of the computer guys said.

"What is it, English?" Dex asked him.

"Moreau. Lots on international travel. About once a month," English said.

"Juarez is only about once a year," the other guy said.

"Let's see, Jaymes," Dunn said, moving to look over Jaymes's shoulder.

"It looks like he goes to Mexico every spring."

All eyes swung to Ashleigh. "Does that ring a bell?"

Ashleigh's head spun as she processed everything. Her husband wasn't just cheating on her. He really was the guy on the other passports. Which meant the kidnapping was that much more likely, too.

Who the hell did she marry?

DANIEL WATCHED Ashleigh as she absorbed what they were telling her. He knew there was a part of her that hoped she overreacted to what she found, but they proved it wrong. There was no doubt that Ashleigh's husband was not the man she thought he was.

She dropped into the chair next to Jaymes and drew in a shaky breath. She stared at the table, and everyone around her was silent, waiting for her to answer the question. Dunn already knew her answer. But she wasn't his to answer for. Not anymore.

Finally, Ashleigh nodded. "He told me he goes there to check in on one of his factories. His company does a lot of different things. They're a conglomerate and buy up failing businesses. Sometimes they keep them running, but sometimes they have to close them. That's one that's still running."

"Do you know the name of the factory?" Dunn asked her.

He caught English's eye when Ashleigh shook her head and nodded for English to dig into it. A few clicks later, and English had the answers they needed.

"Purchased four years ago and shut down three months after it was bought." He clicked a few more times, then turned the screen so everyone could see the satellite view of the location. "It doesn't look like it's shut down, though."

The screen showed a still shot, but there were clearly people there and heavy equipment. "Any idea when this was taken?"

English said, "All satellite imagery is updated at least every two years, so no more than two years old."

Ashleigh gasped. "What else is he lying to me about? Who is he?"

She asked the questions aloud, but she wasn't asking any of them. She was confused and scared and just found out the man she put her trust in was a monster. Dunn knew how painful that was. He'd done it twice.

Dunn looked at the clock on the stove and stood. "Let's meet up in the morning. Ashleigh needs some sleep. English and Jaymes, keep digging. Everyone else, get some rest. Between the concert next week and this, I have a feeling we need to rest now or we won't get any."

The others nodded in agreement, then stood. Ashleigh stayed at the table while the team filtered out the door. Dex was the last one to leave and stopped next to Dunn with Slade right in front of him.

"Want me to take her with me?" Dex asked.

Dunn shook his head.

"I can take her," Slade offered.

Dunn shook his head again.

"Are you sure this is a good idea?" Dex asked.

Dunn huffed a laugh and shook his head a third time. "I know it's not, but I can't turn her away."

"It's been eighteen years, boss. Do you even know who she is? Do you know she's not involved in all this, too? Maybe they had a fight, and she's here to get him busted and she comes out rosy," Slade said.

Dunn shrugged. "Won't be the first or the second time I trusted someone who was fucking me over. I'm sure it won't be the last." He ran a hand down his face and breathed deep. "You guys didn't see her face when I first got here. She was terrified. Maybe she's lying, but if she is, she's developed some serious acting skills."

Slade and Dex exchanged a look. "Be careful, boss," Slade said, dragging Dex toward the door.

Dunn nodded and locked the door behind them.

He turned back to Ashleigh, but she was still at the table with her head in her hands. "Want a drink?" he offered.

She nodded.

Dunn went to the kitchen and grabbed a bottle of whiskey from above the fridge. He didn't drink much, but when he really needed a drink, he always went for the good stuff. He poured two glasses and added a couple of ice cubes, just the way they drank it in college, and set one in front of Ashleigh.

She smiled at the glass and laughed. "I haven't had whiskey since you left. I couldn't bring myself to drink it."

Dunn winced. "Sorry, Ash."

She shrugged and brought the glass to her lips. She

inhaled, then tipped the glass up and swallowed the amber liquid. She cringed, then set the glass down. "Gah. I don't remember it tasting like this."

Dunn smiled and sat across the table from her. Too far away to touch, but close enough that he could look at her. Her hair was dry and back to its usual dirty blonde color he remembered so well. He loved to wrap it around his hand when she took his cock into her mouth. The honey color against his dark skin reminded him of how many people said they shouldn't be together. They didn't blend. But they never cared what other people said. They loved each other, and Dunn would have died for her. He would have done anything for her. But she never asked him for the one thing that would have kept them together.

Her lips pursed together before she brought the whiskey back to her lips. Her tongue slicked along the edge of the glass, catching the liquid before it poured into her mouth. She drew in a breath, then swallowed the whiskey. Ashleigh did everything in a way that turned him on. Even drinking whiskey had him hard, thinking about the first time they got drunk together. They'd been dating for a few months, but they hadn't slept together yet. She said she always wanted to try whiskey, so Dunn bought a bottle for them to share.

They got drunk on the whiskey and drunk on each other and fumbled through sex. When Dunn woke up the next morning with a naked Ashleigh in his bed, he felt like an ass, but she confessed she was afraid to be with him. Not because she was afraid of him but because of her curves. She didn't know what he would think of her naked body.

He made sure she didn't worry about that ever again.

"Do you remember the first time we drank whiskey?" Ashleigh asked softly.

Dunn smiled and nodded, not admitting he was just thinking about the same thing.

"I was so sure you were going to run. I hated being naked next to you."

Dunn adjusted himself and shook his head. "You were the most beautiful woman I'd ever seen."

Her gaze snapped to his. Dunn felt that same connection all over again. Desire stretched thin between them, pulling them toward each other. He hadn't been with many women since leaving the SEALs. He didn't trust himself to pick someone who wouldn't try to kill him when his guard was down.

The first time he saw Ashleigh, she was walking across campus, her long hair flowing behind her as she walked with purpose. He had to know who she was, but he was going the other way. For weeks, he tried to find her again, but she never reappeared. Until one day she walked into the dining hall. She was talking to a friend and smiling, and Dunn was nearly knocked on his ass.

He marched up to her and introduced himself. She told him her name, then ignored him for her friend. He didn't let her get away, though. He sat with them for lunch and invited her to dinner. Her friend urged her to agree, and Ashleigh and he were nearly inseparable after that.

Until he broke both their hearts and told her his plans for his future. Plans that didn't include her.

Dunn finally broke the connection between Ashleigh and himself. He drained the rest of his whiskey and went to the kitchen to put the bottle away and put his glass in the dishwasher. He felt Ashleigh's eyes on him, but he couldn't look at her again. Not if he was going to keep his hands to himself.

Ashleigh squeezed her thighs together and closed her eyes. She had no right to be lusting over her ex. She was a married woman, and Daniel was... She had no idea.

"Are you married?" she blurted out.

He finally turned and looked at her. He shook his head. "No."

"Engaged? Dating? Involved?"

He shook his head again. "None of the above."

"Ever been?" she asked, even though she already knew the answer to that one.

"No."

"Why not?"

He pressed his lips together. He always did that when he wanted to buy time before answering a question. She wondered why he didn't want to just tell her the truth, but they weren't friends. They were never friends. They went from strangers to lovers, then back to strangers.

"I never met anyone I wanted to spend my life with."

Ouch. That hurt. Never meant he included her on that

list. She wanted to spend her life with him, but he never saw her that way.

She was surprised by it, but it still stung. If he did imagine his life with her, they would have built a life together. Instead, she let him walk away. She told him to go. She couldn't compete with what he wanted to do. And if she asked him to stay, it would have been worse. He either would have stayed and resented her for making him give up his dream, or he would have left anyway and reminded her she wasn't that important.

It was better to remember the pain. Then she could resist the man she'd never been able to resist.

"Sorry. I just wanted to make sure someone wasn't going to show up and scratch my eyes out."

Daniel shook his head. "Nothing to worry about." He moved away from the sink and went straight to her suitcase.

She noticed it had been moved and asked, "Did you search my suitcase?"

Daniel nodded. "Yes. We had to make sure you didn't have anything that could harm us."

"Like?"

He turned back to her and crossed his arms over his chest. How many nights had she fallen asleep with her head on his chest and those arms wrapped around her? She felt safe with him. Nothing could ever hurt her with Daniel on her side. Until Daniel did.

"You could have a bomb, or some other kind of explosive. You could have a gun. And since you're running from your husband, you could easily have a phone that he could track and lead him right here to you. If he's as dangerous as he seems, that would be bad."

Ashleigh's anger dissipated as she realized what he was telling her. He didn't trust her.

"I'm sorry. I didn't think about what me coming here would mean to you. I never should have come." Ashleigh stood and went to grab her suitcase so she could leave. She already had one man she thought she loved hurt her. She couldn't handle a second one in as many days.

"Ashleigh, sit down."

She shook her head, fighting the tears in her eyes. "Let me go, Daniel."

He rolled his eyes like she was being a child. "Just stop. You're not going anywhere. It's my job to make sure people are who they say they are. I can't blindly trust people. Not anymore. I have to make sure."

"But you've known me forever."

Daniel shook his head. "I knew you eighteen years ago. I don't know you now."

"And you think I could have turned into some criminal mastermind?" She scoffed.

But Daniel didn't reply. He didn't move. He just watched her.

"Seriously?" she asked. "You really think I could be messing with you?"

"How did you find me, Ashleigh?"

She threw her hands up and sighed. "This again? Are you kidding me?"

He just raised an eyebrow. She wondered how she never noticed his stoic, alpha behavior when they were in college. He would ask a question and let the other person hang themselves as they rushed to fill the silence.

Ashleigh found herself doing the same thing. "I still talk to your grandmother. She tells me what you're doing. She told me where you live."

"You talked to my grandmother?" Daniel blurted.

Ashleigh nodded. "I'm sorry. I loved her. She was always so nice to me, and when you went to BUD/s, I called her to ask how you were. We kept in touch after that, talking every few months."

"Did you call her on your personal phone? The one I'm assuming your criminal husband gave you?" he spat.

Ashleigh shook her head. "No. He reviewed all my calls and would have asked, so I always called her from public places or from jobs I was working on. She had my number in case of an emergency, but she never called me."

"Do you have your phone now?"

Ashleigh shook her head again. "I turned it off and put it in a trash can before I left Detroit. I didn't want Frederick to know where I was going, and I know he can track the phone. He's done it before."

"Who the hell is this guy, Ash? And why are you still married to him?"

Ashleigh glared at him. "You have no right to ask me that. Like you just pointed out to me, we don't know each other. Not anymore. I'm not going to question your life choices, and you have no right to question mine."

Ashleigh walked around him and grabbed her suitcase, intending to take it and leave. She yanked the handle up and he said, "Please don't go."

Daniel Dunn never said please. She turned back to him. "Why not?"

He drew in a breath and blew it out slowly. "Because I'll never forgive myself if something happens to you. Your husband... there's no way around it. He's a dangerous man, Ash. I can't stop you from leaving, but I really hope you don't. I'd never forgive myself if something happened to you."

She saw the truth in his eyes. He meant every word. He was worried about her. Scared for her safety. There was something about Frederick he wasn't telling her, but she didn't know if she could handle hearing it yet.

"There's more, isn't there?" she asked.

He shook his head. "I don't know. We've told you everything we've found, but I don't like it, Ash. I feel like there's more, and I don't want you to get hurt."

She inhaled deeply and nodded. Daniel always had good instincts. She clearly couldn't trust her own, but she could trust his. "I'm scared."

Daniel nodded. "I know. But for now, I think you need to sleep. You'll feel better in the morning. Come on."

He nodded his head toward the hallway where his bedroom was. She didn't notice any other bedrooms down the hall. "I'm not sleeping with you, Daniel."

"I never suggested it. I'm sleeping on the couch. You're going to sleep in my bed. With the door locked. But I need to get my gun. I put it away earlier."

Ashleigh nodded and led the way down the hall. She sat on his bed while he rolled her suitcase to the corner of the room and retrieved his gun. She smiled at him when he said goodnight and pulled the door closed behind himself.

Ashleigh got up and locked it, then went back to his bed. She needed to brush her teeth and change, but she decided to lie down for just a minute first.

DUNN FLIPPED on the TV in the living room, knowing he wasn't going to get any sleep. Even before Ashleigh showed up, he wasn't likely to sleep, but with her in his bed and everything going on, he knew there was no chance he'd sleep.

He'd gotten used to functioning with little sleep as a SEAL. It trained him well for guilt and anger to keep him up all night.

He grabbed his laptop and sat on the couch. He wasn't nearly as proficient as English or Jaymes on the computer, but he could figure out how to search things. He started by searching up Ashleigh's husband and reading everything he could about the man. Aside from an extensive bio and accolades about awards he'd won, there wasn't much. No pictures and no personal information. If that wasn't strange enough, there was no mention of him outside his company website.

Dunn searched the aliases Ashleigh remembered and read the limited information about both men. Again, there were no pictures, but each man had a little more information. One mentioned he lived in Detroit with his wife. Another mentioned his love of traveling. Nothing significant, but for a man who was otherwise invisible, it mattered.

Dunn kept notes on everything he read, from the minor details that lined up across all the profiles and the ones that were specific to each. Then he did a search on Ashleigh.

There was a little more information on her since she was a volunteer and had profiles done for different companies and websites. He made notes on what information was public and refrained from adding his own details. Like she always wanted to see the Grand Canyon and would never pass up a bowl of pasta.

Ashleigh had an old social media account that hadn't been touched in years. It was still under her maiden name, Ashleigh Connors. One of the last posts she made was one of her and Frederick with the caption that he was helping her heal after the loss of her father. Comments were mixed, mostly sympathetic to her father dying, but a few asked about Frederick. She didn't reply to any of them.

In college, Ashleigh was very social. She had a ton of friends. Not all of them liked Dunn, but she always told him she'd rather have him in her life than people who were going to pass judgement on him when they didn't take the time to get to know him. For her, the differences between them made them stronger, not weaker, and the similarities between them made it easier for them to understand each other.

Ashleigh's mom wasn't in the picture but she had her dad. Dunn's father wasn't around, and his mom was career military, so he was raised by her and his grandmother. Both Ashleigh and Dunn knew what it was like to take care of themselves at a young age, and both always felt older than their ages. They connected, and they clicked, and that was the most important thing.

Dunn really thought Ashleigh would find someone else who understood her like he did. If he'd known she'd end up with a man who didn't let her be who she was, he would have...

He didn't have an answer. She didn't ask him to stay, and it was too late to know if he would have been okay if she had. They'd lived their lives, and regretting the choices they didn't make wouldn't solve anything.

Dunn copied the picture and sent it to English with a link to Ashleigh's old account so he could look into it. Then Dunn went searching for anything else. He found the article about her father dying. He was in a car accident that was ruled a true accident since it was a single car incident. The article said the police assumed he swerved to avoid an animal and went off the road and hit a tree. He died on impact.

Ashleigh's mother was still out there, but a search on her name didn't reveal anything. Dunn turned his attention to the missing child next. Since it was current news, there were numerous articles about the boy and his family. Dunn dug into the parents and their history. He was almost ready to give up and try to sleep when he saw a brief mention in one of the articles. The mom was a custodian at Edwards Unlimited, Inc. Ashleigh's husband's company. That couldn't be a coincidence.

The curtains in his living room glowed with the early morning light. He was going to meet his team in less than two hours, but he couldn't sit on the info. If there was something to it, English needed to know so he could dig into it.

Dunn called English before he could second guess himself.

"I'm already on it," English said as a greeting. "I wasn't looking for Ashleigh Connors, but I guess I should have been. We can run facial rec on the husband and see what we find in the system."

"Yeah, good, but I have something else. The mom of the missing kid works for Edwards Unlimited, Inc."

"What?" English blurted. "Are you kidding me?"

Dunn shook his head. "No. I saw it in one of the articles. It's buried, not important info, but it's there."

"There's a connection. Shit. Does Ashleigh know if they know each other?"

"She's asleep. I haven't asked her."

English was silent for a long moment.

"What?" Dunn barked.

"Nothing, boss. I'll do some digging."

Dunn grunted and hung up. It was bad enough he was doubting his every move. Now his team was, too.

Dunn slapped the laptop closed and tossed it onto the coffee table. He leaned back on the couch and closed his eyes. He needed to think. He really needed to go for a run, but if Ashleigh woke up and he was gone, she might lose it.

The other thing Dunn did to clear his head was off the table, too, since Ashleigh was married to someone else, and hated him, which left him with option three.

He pushed himself off the couch with a sigh and headed to the kitchen. He opened the fridge and started pulling things out. He didn't know what he was going to make, but that was the magic of cooking. All he needed to do was try something and hope it was good enough to be edible.

Dunn set a frying pan on the stovetop and grabbed a cutting board. He grabbed fresh vegetables from the fridge and started dicing them. An omelet sounded like a good idea for breakfast, and it would hold him for a while, which was always good when he had a busy day.

Peppers, onions, mushrooms, and broccoli went into the frying pan on low heat. He added a pat of butter and stirred everything up. While the vegetables cooked, Dunn put away the items he didn't use and grabbed the eggs. Ashleigh was a fan of bread, which gave Dunn a good idea. He didn't eat cornbread often, but he had everything he needed to make it, and Ashleigh always loved it.

Dunn lost himself mixing the batter and dumped it into a pan, then slid the pan in the oven. He stirred the vegetables and cracked six eggs into them. The thin layer of eggs coated the bottom of the pan and held on to the vegetables.

Dunn watched the food cook while he let his mind wander. He couldn't help but think if Ashleigh's husband was involved in the kidnapping that he was getting sloppy.

Taking a child from someone who worked for him was risky. Which meant either he wasn't involved or he thought he wouldn't ever be caught. Dunn wasn't sure which one he hoped for.

He flipped the eggs, searing the other side of the omelet. He stared at the pan, trying to decide which man Ashleigh's husband was. A part of him hoped he was not involved, but Ashleigh was a reasonable person. She wouldn't have traveled hours to his house if she didn't have a reason for being scared.

Dunn slid the omelet out of the pan onto a large plate. He cut it in half and added a generous helping of cheddar cheese to one side. He rolled both up so they looked more like omelets and checked on the cornbread. It still had a while before it was ready, so he grabbed a fork so he could eat his omelet.

"Do I have to make my own?" Ashleigh asked from behind him.

Dunn whirled around in surprise. He didn't hear her leave the bedroom or come down the hall. He didn't feel her presence. He didn't have any idea she was there until she told him she was.

"Whoa, sorry! I didn't mean to scare you."

Dunn nodded and drew in a breath. Ashleigh looked even more startled than he was. He forced a grin and waved her over. "This is yours. But you have to wait for the cornbread to finish cooking. I can't let you get sick."

She smiled and accepted the plate. "I forgot how good of a cook you are."

"You never had any trouble," Dunn said, gesturing to the table for them to sit.

She took the same seat she had the night before, so he sat across from her. "I haven't cooked in years," Ashleigh said quietly. "Frederick hires someone to cook all our meals. They drop everything off once a week and we just heat up the food for the week."

"What if you want something special? If one of your cravings hit?" Dunn asked with a grin.

Ashleigh smiled, but it didn't reach her eyes. "I eat what we have. I don't eat a lot of sweets these days. Or much pasta. Or a lot of anything I used to eat."

Dunn narrowed his eyes. Ashleigh always loved food. All food. Pasta was her favorite, but she kept a stash of chocolate in her nightstand. She loved fruits and vegetables almost as much. She made eating an erotic experience. Something Dunn never realized was possible until he had Ashleigh in his life.

"Frederick only eats certain meats and fish. He has someone who does the grocery shopping and someone who stocks the kitchen. He found my chocolate stash shortly after we were married and lost it. He said we couldn't have chocolate in the house, and definitely not in the bedroom. If I wanted food, I needed to eat in the kitchen. I just figured it wasn't worth it to have it at all if I had to go all the way to the kitchen, so I stopped eating chocolate."

Ashleigh didn't look at him while she talked, and that just killed him. Everything she told him about her husband had him ready to find the guy and choke him out for putting so many restrictions on her. She was amazing and beautiful and as close to perfect as a person could get.

Why would anyone want to change her?

"He wasn't all bad," Ashleigh said softly. "I'm sure you're wondering why I stayed with him. He's a good man. He's always taken good care of me. We went to the Grand Canyon for our honeymoon because he knew I wanted to go there. I've never needed anything. He's kind to me, Daniel. I haven't painted a very good picture of him, but he's always been good to me."

"Do you know who people say that about?" Dunn asked her.

Ashleigh shook her head.

"Psychopaths."

6

———

Ashleigh couldn't believe he said that about her husband. He wasn't a psychopath. She would have known.

Or would she?

She still didn't have enough answers to the questions she'd been asking herself. Even without all the answers, she still couldn't believe her husband was that bad.

"Listen, Ash, you're right. I don't know him. But I know something isn't right. I know you. You wouldn't have run if there wasn't a reason to. You're not an irrational person. If you were scared, and I know you are, then something is off."

Ashleigh wanted to be able to argue with him, but he was right. She went to him. She started this whole thing. Daniel wouldn't know where she was or who she married if she hadn't shown up at his house. He never made an effort to keep in touch with her. But she couldn't deny they still knew each other.

"Could I have been this wrong about him? I keep telling you this stuff and I wonder why I put up with the way he treated me, but it wasn't always like this. He was charming and kind when we met. Now, to talk about my life with him, I wonder when it all changed, and how I didn't notice," Ashleigh said.

Daniel shrugged. "People are rarely who we think they are. One minute, you think you can trust the person you're with, and the next, you find out they're not even close to who you thought you were. Sorry you're going through it, but you're hardly the first."

Ashleigh looked at him closely. He knew because he'd been there. "Who did this to you?"

Daniel shook his head and got up, carrying his plate to the sink. He rinsed it and set it in the dishwasher. "I need to take a shower and get ready for work. I won't be long, then you can have the room and bathroom."

Ashleigh nodded as Daniel walked by her. His footsteps thumped down the hallway, then the door closed and locked. He never answered her question.

Ashleigh finished her breakfast and added her dishes to the dishwasher. She noticed the stove was still on and remembered the cornbread. It was done and on its way to overdone, so she pulled it out and set it on the counter to cool.

Alone in Daniel's house gave her a peek into the man he'd become. She didn't explore his bedroom the night before, but she had no qualms about looking around the rest of his house. His kitchen was neat and organized. Even the items in his pantry were perfectly lined up. She wasn't surprised to find he had no junk food, but she looked.

His dining room had only the table and chairs. His living room looked like the room he spent the most time in. The TV was on, showing the local news with a chippy female anchor and a friendly male anchor. Daniel's computer was on the coffee table, and there was a legal pad on top. She picked it up when she noticed her name.

Ashleigh read through everything Daniel wrote about her. He made mention of her dad's death and her post that had a picture of Frederick. She'd forgotten about that. He listed some of the companies she'd worked for over the last few years. Everything he wrote was impersonal, like someone who'd never met her made the list.

Ashleigh pushed away the hurt and flipped back to the front page. Daniel did the same thing for Frederick and the other names she remembered from the passports. Lists of details about her husband. The man she thought of as her husband. She wasn't even sure. Only one name had something about her written under it. Which of them did she actually marry? Was she even married? If she married a man who didn't exist, then she wasn't.

Was that better or worse?

Ashleigh flipped to another page and saw the same slanted writing about the missing boy and his family. And at the bottom, a note about the boy's mother working for Edwards.

Ashleigh sucked in a breath. "No," she whispered.

"Are you saying that because I found the connection you didn't want me to find or because you didn't know?" Daniel asked from right behind her.

Ashleigh jumped and spun to face him. She clutched the legal pad to her chest. "Frederick knows her? She works for him?"

Daniel crossed his arms. "Does he know her? You'd be the one to answer that question."

Ashleigh shook her head and tried to recall what the woman looked like. She'd seen the family on TV, begging for information about their missing son, but she focused more on the little boy than the parents. Ashleigh ached every time she thought about that little boy being taken and the things that could have happened to him.

There was a part of her that hoped Frederick had taken him and given him to another family, because it meant the boy was safe and not abused or dead, but that didn't make it right. It would never be okay. But it could be fixed. He could be found and returned. It would destroy another family, but at least the boy would be safe. Everyone would be alive.

But could Frederick have done that? Could he have taken a child from his family? Could he have taken a child from a woman who worked for him?

"I don't know," Ashleigh admitted. "There's a holiday party every year and a company picnic every summer. All the employees are invited, but it's a big company. Almost five hundred employees locally. Frederick insists everyone is invited and both events are family friendly. But I don't know. I never paid much attention to her on the news. I was... I should have paid attention."

Ashleigh fell to the couch, berating herself for letting so much happen right under her nose. How could her husband have done all this and she never noticed? She was complicit. She let it happen because she didn't see it. She didn't see him.

"I have to help find this boy. I can't hide here and do nothing. I have to help," Ashleigh said firmly.

Daniel stared at her for a long moment, then nodded. "Good. First, go take a shower. We can leave when you're ready."

Ashleigh nodded and went to follow his orders. She squeezed her thighs together on her way to his room, remembering other times she followed his orders.

DUNN HATED that he had to question Ashleigh's word. Before Ashaki and Williams, he never would have thought twice about it, but he couldn't risk it again.

He reviewed the notes Ashleigh was reading and slid the pad into his bag. He added his computer and zipped the bag, setting it on the counter to grab on their way out.

Ashleigh would be awhile in the shower, so Dunn set to work cleaning up the kitchen. He was happy to see Ashleigh took out the cornbread since he'd forgotten it. He sliced it up and added a couple of pieces to a container for her and put the rest away. He washed dishes and put his kitchen back to normal.

When Ashleigh walked out of the bedroom shortly after, Dunn checked his watch. "That was fast," he teased her.

She pressed her lips into a smile. "I don't take long to get ready these days."

Dunn scowled. "Another dictate from your husband?"

Ashleigh hesitated, then nodded, avoiding his gaze.

He grabbed the cornbread and handed it to her, not letting go until she looked up at him. "There are very few things a man should demand from a woman. How fast her showers are and what she eats should never be on that list."

Ashleigh's eyes widened, and her breasts rose with her sharp inhale. Dunn was only so strong, and he was a man who hadn't been with a woman in far too long. He used to know Ashleigh's body as well as he knew his own. He could turn her on with a look or a simple touch. And he could make her come in less than a minute if he really set his mind to it.

But he couldn't do any of those things now. He had to keep his hands, and all his other parts, to himself. He wasn't a cheater, and he wasn't going to make her one either. It didn't matter that her husband really looked like the scum of the earth, he was still her husband.

Dunn broke their eye contact and grabbed his bag. "Let's go," he said gruffly, not looking back to make sure she was with him.

The drive to the F-BOMB offices was only about ten minutes, but they were the longest ten minutes of Dunn's life. Ashleigh's scent filled his SUV as they drove, messing with his head and his cock. He hadn't eaten peaches in eighteen years because they reminded him of Ashleigh. After so many years, the smell brought back memories that were better left in the past. Their first date. The second time they slept together, since the first was soaked in whiskey. The night she told him she loved him. Her meeting his mom and grandmother, and him meeting her dad.

And the night it all ended.

Dunn pulled into his parking space and got out quickly. He needed a deep breath of dirty, parking lot air to clear his mind of Ashleigh.

She was right behind him, close enough that he could touch her, as they walked across the parking lot to the elevator. Dunn pushed the button and breathed a sigh when the elevator car opened in front of them. He swiped his card inside, and the car rushed them to the F-BOMB floor.

He swiped again when they got to the secured door that separated them from the public, just in case someone got up there who shouldn't be, and let Ashleigh in.

"This is like a fortress," she breathed.

"That's the point. No one knows what we do here unless they need to know. And we make sure they don't need to know."

Ashleigh didn't say anything else as Dunn led her down

the hall. No one was in the first conference room, which didn't surprise him. He went to his office, figuring he was the first one in. English was the only one who ever beat him to work, and that was when the other man spent the night at the office.

English's office was dark, as were the rest. Dunn set his computer on his desk and led Ashleigh down to the break room. It was a full kitchen, equipped with everything they needed. All of them had spent more than a night or two at the office, and they all agreed they needed a full kitchen in order to survive.

Dunn started the coffee and made a note that they were almost out. He couldn't remember whose turn was next to do the shopping, but they all shared the responsibilities for the office. They'd talked about hiring an office manager to handle tasks like that, but they hadn't had time to do it yet.

While the coffee brewed, Dunn went back to his office, painfully aware of Ashleigh following him around. He sat at his desk and pulled out his computer. Without looking at her, he said, "You can sit in the kitchen to eat, or you can go to one of the conference rooms."

She shook her head and picked at the edge of the container holding her cornbread. "I'd rather stay close, if that's okay."

He set his computer down and looked at her. "Ash, level with me. Did he hurt you?"

She shook her head.

"Why are you so afraid of him?"

She pressed her lips together and tried to smile. "I've always defended him to the people I know. No one ever understood who he was. He isn't friendly and I've lost more than a few friends because of it. But I'd been through that before, so it didn't really phase me. If they were good friends, they would stand by me, right?"

He knew she was talking about the two of them and the friends she lost because of him. He didn't say anything to her question, and after a minute, she continued.

"Frederick is quiet and a little standoffish. He doesn't like small talk, and he doesn't get personal. I've never met his family. He doesn't have a best friend. He's just a private person. It never bothered me until I saw him with that woman. I'd never seen her before. And the way she spoke to him made me think if she didn't agree to sex with him, he would have hurt her. He didn't even ask her, just said he had fifteen minutes, and she said they should go to his office. It obviously wasn't the first time it happened, and it wasn't a passionate affair. It was impersonal... like a transaction."

"I'm sorry, Ash."

She shook her head. "The thing is, that's how it is with us. He comes home or I come home, and we just have sex because we've been away from each other. It doesn't matter how tired I am, it's what he expects."

"You should never do something because he expects it," Dunn growled.

Ashleigh nodded. "I know. Now, I know. I just... He wasn't like that when we met. He was always private and held back, but I thought the more we got to know each other, the more relaxed he would get. Instead, I just grew to accept who he is. I changed my thinking and stopped fighting with people who questioned him."

"Like you did with us," Dunn said softly. He regretted she had to make decisions between him and her friends, but she had friends who didn't trust him. They took one look at his shaved head and dark skin and thought he was going to hurt her. They didn't give him a chance and never bothered getting to know him, so she cut them out of her life.

At the time, he was indignant that people were so closed-minded. That they wouldn't give him a chance. Especially people Ash was close to. He still felt that anger at being judged because of something he couldn't change, but now he wondered if Ashleigh was too stubborn for her own good. Did she cut off the people who could have saved her from a life with a criminal?

"I don't regret my choices," she said quietly but firmly. "The people who didn't want us together were unable to see you. The people who didn't want me with Frederick... everything with him was different. You tried to get to know my friends. You gave them a chance, even when they weren't interested in giving you one. Frederick never gave anyone a chance. I always thought it was because he was so wealthy. He was successful. He told me all the time how people always wanted something from him. Money, a job, power, something. So he kept his distance. It made sense. I believed him."

"And now?"

Ashleigh's eyes snapped to Dunn's. She held his gaze and breathed. Uncertainty was written all over her face. She opened her mouth to answer, but before she could say anything, a door opened down the hall.

"Marco!" Jack shouted.

"Polo!" Dunn replied automatically. His gaze stayed on Ashleigh until Jack appeared behind her in the doorway.

"You guys are here early," Jack said with a grin. Jack was always smiling. He made some of the days bearable, but Dunn wasn't sure the next few could be. Not with the way Jack studied Ashleigh, waiting for him to blow up Dunn's life.

"We wanted to get a jump on things," Dunn said, drawing Jack's attention back to himself. "There's a connection between Ashleigh's husband and the missing boy."

Jack's eyebrows went up. After they narrowed at Dunn's subtle reminder to himself that Ashleigh was married. If he called her husband by his name, it allowed him to forget she wasn't available. Referring to him only as her husband reinforced the fact that he couldn't touch her. Ever.

"Is that what English called the meeting about?" Jack asked.

Dunn fished his phone out of his pocket. "English called a meeting?" He tapped the screen to bring it to life. He didn't have a message.

Jack shrugged and pulled out his own phone. "'Need to meet. Office. Thirty minutes.' I assumed you were on it."

Dunn's neck tingled, but he pushed the thought away. Why was English calling a meeting? And why didn't he include Dunn?

Dunn didn't have to wait long to find out. English and the rest of the team trickled in over the next five minutes. Dunn pulled him to the side and asked, "Why didn't you send me the message?"

English shrugged. "I knew you were already here. As soon as you walked in, the cameras alerted me. I figured if you were here, it made sense to get moving."

"Is that all?"

English narrowed his eyes and nodded. "Yeah, why? What did you think?"

Dunn shook his head and tried to shake the fear that English was sneaking around behind his back. He fought for years with the same team. The men he surrounded himself with every day were like brothers to him. They'd lived together, worked together, and bled together. They'd lost brothers and met new ones, and through it all, Dunn knew he could count on all of them if he ever needed anything.

Until the man who taught them all to be brothers killed one of their own and betrayed them. Then everything went sideways and Dunn didn't know who he could trust.

7

———

DUNN LISTENED TO THE REPORT FROM ENGLISH, WHICH WAS basically that Ashleigh's husband owned the company the mother worked for, but it wasn't clear if they knew each other. English could do some tech magic and try to get into company emails to see if they'd ever traded messages, but the team agreed it was best not to risk alerting him.

"At some point," Jack said, "someone is going to start looking for Ashleigh. We're going to hit twenty-four hours tonight. We may have already if the husband realized she was on an earlier flight."

Dunn nodded. He was waiting for the same thing. When Ashleigh's husband went on TV with his own plea to return his wife. No doubt he'd have a sob story about them wanting kids and how she volunteered her time to help kids find their forever homes. It was what anyone would do, but they were working against a clock before someone would start searching and Ashleigh's presence would be more of a concern.

"Have you given any thought to how we're going to handle it?" Jack asked.

"No, I haven't. English has a search on her name. He'll let us know if something comes up. So far, nothing current."

"It won't last long," Jack said.

Dunn knew. He didn't want to think about it because they didn't have any definitive answers for her. Her husband definitely was suspicious, but there was no way to prove her husband was behind the kidnapping unless they got a whole lot more information.

"We need to confirm what we know and dig deeper into him. We can't sit back and let him come for us," Dex said.

Dunn agreed with that, too. He just wasn't sure how to go about doing it. He liked the cases where they knew what the point was. The ones where they had a specific tasks. With cases like Ashleigh's, they were digging to see if there was a reason to be digging, potentially ruining her life either way.

"Let's get into the family. And search out kidnappings in the Detroit area over the last few years. See if there's any connection. If we really think her husband is involved in this, it doesn't sound like it's the first time. And if he has a local PD contact, we need to keep them out of this," Dunn said.

The others nodded, and they all got to work digging.

Hours later, Dunn was no closer to any answers, and judging by the near silence of the room, neither was anyone else.

"I'm going to pick up lunch. We have our meeting with Kate Maddox and her people in ninety minutes," Dunn said. He stood and stretched. "I'll be back in a few."

Jack nodded, but the others ignored him. Dunn went to find Ashleigh. She was in his office, spinning in his chair.

"Don't throw up on my computer."

Ashleigh stopped the spin and looked up at him with a smile. "I'm bored out of my mind."

"Sorry. We tend to get into something and forget there's a world outside. I'm running out to pick up lunch for everyone. Want to go for a ride?"

Ashleigh nodded. "God, yes. I need to get out of here."

Dunn smiled and led the way downstairs. Ashleigh chatted, asking questions about the things they do and why they needed a fortress for an office. Dunn told her what he could. They were secretive about what they did, even to people they were close to.

Dunn parked on the street in front of JB's Subs. It was a team favorite, and a place they could call with little notice and get a large order. He walked up to the register and smiled at Katie behind the counter.

"Hi, Daniel. How are you?" Katie asked. She was cute and a good decade younger than him. She flipped her braid behind her shoulder and leaned on the counter.

"Hey, Katie. Can we add one more sandwich to the order today?"

Katie nodded. "Of course. Anything for you. What do you need to add?"

"Turkey on white. Extra cheese. Mayo, pickles, spinach, tomatoes, and extra onions." Dunn turned to Ashleigh. "Is that still right?"

Ashleigh gaped at him but nodded.

Dunn turned back to Katie, who was scowling. She pasted on a grin when she saw him looking at her. "New teammate?"

"No," Dunn said, not offering any additional information. Katie was cute, but she wasn't ever going to be more than the woman who made his lunch.

Katie's smile faded. She just nodded and turned to the

next customer. Dunn nodded to a booth near the back for Ashleigh to sit, then went to grab chips and bottled drinks for everyone. When he turned back to Ashleigh, someone was sitting with her.

"Who's this?" Dunn asked, setting the bag of extras on the table.

Ashleigh looked up at him with fear in her eyes. "He said he knows you."

Dunn looked at the man and froze.

"Sit down, Dunn. Hands on the table," Williams said quietly. "I'd hate to have to paint the walls with your beautiful ex. I didn't know you two were back in touch."

Dunn lowered to the seat across from them, keeping his eyes on the man he hated more than he hated himself. "What the fuck are you doing here?"

"I just wanted to say hi. We're old friends," Williams said to Ashleigh.

"The fuck we are," Dunn growled.

Williams tsked. "Now, now, Dunn. I trained you. I spent years investing in you. I made it my mission to turn you into the best SEAL you could be. It cost me everything, but I did it. And you're going to say we're not friends."

"We're not fucking friends, you asshole. What do you want?"

Williams shrugged, shifting the gun against Ashleigh's ribs. She squeaked, and he shot her a glare. A tear ran down her cheek.

"I'll fucking kill you if you hurt her," Dunn hissed.

Williams smirked. "Isn't that sweet? Two lovebirds finding each other after all these years. Are you two going to get married?"

"I'm already married," Ashleigh said in a shaky voice.

"Ash," Dunn groaned.

Williams' eyebrows shot up. "You are? Well, isn't that interesting? Does your husband know you're hanging around with your ex? I can't imagine he'd be thrilled to hear that."

"Leave her out of this," Dunn said, trying to draw Williams' attention back to him. "What do you want?"

Williams chuckled. "I taught you how to interrogate. Do you really think I don't know you're trying to distract me?"

"I'm only trying to figure out what you want. I'd hate to have to kill you in front of all these people."

Williams chuckled. "She'd be dead before you could even get your gun out."

"Why are you here?" Dunn asked again. He was losing his patience and quickly running out of time. When Katie finished with his order, he was going to have to go to the counter and get it, or risk Katie or one of the other employees walking it over to him. He didn't want to put anyone else in danger, which meant he needed to find out what Williams wanted and get rid of him. Fast.

"I was wondering how things are going."

"Great," Dunn said. "We're kicking the ass of scumbags like you, locking people up or putting bullets in them. If we have to. But not in the back of the head. Only truly sick fucks would ever do something like that."

Williams scowled at him and pressed the gun against Ashleigh's side again. She yelped and tried to move away, but she was against the wall, pinned inside the booth.

Dunn tried to catch her gaze, but her eyes were squeezed shut. He didn't want to say anything to her. He needed Williams to tell him why he was there, and what he wanted, then leave.

"I'm really looking forward to the concert next week. Kate Maddox is my daughter's favorite singer. She has tickets. She's going with her entire family. Her mom and sister... and her father," Williams said with a glare.

Dunn's mind spun with possibilities. They were hired to run security at the show. Kate Maddox had gotten threats in the past, and while there wasn't an immediate threat, she wanted to make sure everything was secure.

Now, there was a credible threat.

"Anyway, I was hoping you could get me a ticket. Or just let me freelance with you for the night. It would be a great chance for me to make sure my family has a good time," Williams said.

"You know that'll never happen," Dunn growled. "You need to stay away from them, Williams."

"They're my family. And even if they've forgotten, I haven't."

"You need to leave them alone," Dunn said.

"Daniel!" Katie called from the counter.

Dunn looked at her, then back at Williams. He grinned at him and slid out of the booth. "Think about it, Dunn. I'll be in touch."

Dunn stood and watched his former CO and friend walk outside. He paused at the door, and Dunn waited, wanting to see which way he turned.

"Daniel," Katie said again, from right next to him. "All your food is ready." She had two large bags packed up for him.

Dunn glanced back at the door, but Williams was gone. Fuck. He turned back to Katie and forced a smile, then took the bags from her hands and set them on the table and slid into the seat next to Ashleigh. Thankfully, Katie didn't ask questions and didn't stick around.

Ashleigh was shaking and crying. She jumped when Dunn's leg brushed hers.

"It's me, Ash. He's gone."

She shook harder, and a sob broke free. Dunn wanted to wrap his arms around her and hold her, but the last time he tried, she slapped him.

Instead, he sat there, every fiber of his being hating that he put her in that position. He let his guard down, and Williams snuck in on them again. And even worse, he knew who she was.

"Daniel," she said, her voice raw and needy.

She looked up at him with fear and pain in her eyes, and he couldn't hold back any longer. He slid his arm behind her and pulled her to him. He wrapped his other arm around her and held her close. She clung to him and cried. Her body trembled, and he wanted to go back to when Dex and Jack and English asked him if he could handle her being there and admit the truth.

No. There was no way in hell he could handle Ashleigh Connors being there. Not when he still wanted her and would do anything in his power to keep her safe. She was dangerous. She split his focus. And he barely had any to start with.

"I'm sorry," she whispered after a few minutes. "I'm so sorry. I didn't know who he was. He said hello and introduced himself as a friend of yours. I didn't know."

"Shh," Dunn said. "None of this is your fault. He's a pathological liar and a murderer. I'm sorry I put you in this position."

"Why did he say you're friends?"

Dunn huffed. "Because we used to be."

ASHLEIGH COULDN'T STOP SHAKING. She had never been so scared in her life. She'd never had a gun pointed at her, but to feel the cold metal pressed against her side was even more terrifying. She didn't know if she'd ever go out in public again. Not if any random person could walk up to her and point a gun at her.

"He used to be your friend?" she blurted.

Daniel nodded, not looking any happier about it than Ashleigh was.

"Why? What happened?"

"He was my CO in the Navy. My commanding officer. I was his second in command, the executive officer, or XO. He trained me and helped me. He dedicated his life to the Navy and to being a SEAL. He gave up time with his family to go on deployments and missed birthdays and holidays and everything because he promised to serve his country. When his wife left him, he decided the Navy and the country he promised to protect were to blame and decided to get revenge. He killed one of our teammates and made it look like someone else did it. When he got out, he kidnapped one of our own and tried to blow up the city."

Ashleigh's breath was shallow. She wasn't sure how Daniel explained all that so calmly. She was either going to throw up or pass out. All she knew was she needed fresh air. Immediately.

"I need to get out of here," she said, shoving at Daniel.

He moved out of the way and stepped back while she ran through the restaurant to the front door. Ashleigh burst outside and was assaulted with the crowd. She was in the middle of an unfamiliar city, surrounded by strangers. Any one of them could try to hurt her.

She panicked and whirled around, trying to find Daniel. Where did he go? What happened?

"Ashleigh!" he called out to her.

She turned, and he was right there. Thank God. She put her hands on her knees and sucked in deep breath after deep breath.

"Ashleigh, just breathe. Are you okay?"

She shook her head. "No. None of this is okay. I'm not okay. It was bad enough I thought my husband was a criminal, but now I've had a gun jabbed in my side and talked to a murderer. Why the hell did I come here?"

"Let's go to the car, Ash. It's right here." He set the bag down and pulled out his keys. "Okay, it's unlocked. Get it."

"What if he put a bomb under the car? One of those things that goes off when you turn the key? Or a remote thing where he can wait until we're somewhere else? What if he wants to kill us?"

Ashleigh knew she was shrieking, but she couldn't seem to stop. Her mind whirred with all the terrifying ways she could die.

"Ash, get in the car. People are starting to look at us. They're going to think I'm trying to kidnap you. This will end up on the news, and your husband might see it."

The mention of Frederick woke her up. She stared at him for a second, then nodded and got in. She noticed the people watching them like he said. Daniel opened the back door and set the bags of food in the car, then jogged around the front and got in. They drove away without a word, and before she knew it, they were parking under his office again.

Daniel turned off the SUV and twisted in his seat to face her. "Ashleigh, are you okay?"

She shook her head. "No."

"What do you want to do? Do you want me to take you somewhere else?"

She shook her head again and laughed mirthlessly. "I

have nowhere else to go, Daniel. I have no family and no friends. I'm all alone."

"You have me, Ash. You always have me. I wish you didn't come here because you're scared, but you always have me."

She forced a smile and nodded. Emotion welled up in her. They hadn't seen each other in more than eighteen years. She said some pretty mean things to him the last time they spoke. But he never hesitated to let her in or help her.

"I'm sorry I dragged you into my mess," Daniel said.

She laughed. "Really? Because I think we might be even right now."

Daniel smiled. His foot tapped on the floorboards.

"You really need to get in there, don't you?" she asked.

He huffed a laugh. "Yeah, I do. But you don't have to stay here. Or you can go with one of the other guys if you'd feel safer."

"Is Williams after all of them?"

Daniel hesitated for a minute, then nodded. "Except Mason, but I wouldn't be surprised if he lumped Mason in just because he's a former SEAL and works with us now."

Ashleigh drew in a breath. "I think I'll take my chances with you. Although Katie better watch out."

"Katie?" Daniel asked.

Ashleigh smirked. "From JB's Subs? She clearly has a thing for you. If Williams is going to threaten you, she might end up on his list."

Daniel shook his head. "If I didn't know any better, I'd think you were jealous."

"Jealous? Of a child who thinks she can handle a man like you?"

Daniel puffed his chest out and winked at her. "I don't know. You're sounding a little jealous."

Ashleigh scoffed, but he was right. She was jealous. Because Katie could have him. Katie wasn't married. Katie wasn't unavailable. Katie wasn't his ex.

At least, not that Ashleigh knew.

"Did you and Katie date?"

Daniel snorted. "No."

"Sleep together?"

"Again, no."

"Kiss?"

"No."

"Anything?"

He smirked. "No. The only time I was interested in a girl her age was when *you* were her age."

Ashleigh grinned. She didn't want his words to make her so happy, but they did. She had no delusions that he'd been celibate in the last eighteen years, but she also wasn't sure she could handle coming face-to-face with his ex on day one.

"Any other questions about my sex life before we go inside?"

Ashleigh shook her head as her cheeks heated.

Daniel held her gaze for a long moment and leaned closer. Ashleigh held her breath, waiting as he moved. Closer and closer. Her eyes slid shut, and she waited.

"Ready?" he asked.

She opened her eyes. The bags of food. She felt so stupid. He wasn't leaning in to kiss her. He was reaching back to get the food.

And if the smirk on his face was any indication, he knew exactly what she thought he was doing. She was beyond mortified.

8

———

Dunn couldn't help but smile on the ride up the elevator. When Ashleigh closed her eyes and tilted her chin up, he wondered, for half a second, what she was doing. When he realized, he almost went for it and pressed his lips to hers, but he felt like an ass.

Instead, he just reached for the bags of food like he'd been doing. And grinned like a fool when she realized he wasn't trying to kiss her.

Her cheeks were pink the entire elevator ride and until they walked into the break room. Everyone was standing around and talking and rushed him when he stepped inside, and reality slammed back into Dunn.

"What took you so long?" Archer asked as he pulled wrapped subs out of the first bag. "We're starving."

"We ran into Williams," Dunn said.

The entire room went silent. No one said anything for a second, then everything exploded as they all asked questions at once.

"What do you mean you ran into Williams?"

"Where the fuck was he?"

"Did you kill him?"

"Where did he go?"

"What did he want?"

Dunn held up his hand, and they fell silent again. He relayed everything that happened, from walking over and finding him with Ashleigh to him sneaking out when Katie brought over the bags of food. They all listened closely, no one speaking until he was done.

"We have to pull surveillance in that area," English said. "Find out where he went."

"And we need to go back and talk to Katie and the others. See if they've seen him in there before," Jack added.

"I'm surprised he didn't do anything other than talk to you," Dex said.

Dunn looked at Ashleigh, who was rubbing her side. "He jabbed a gun into her side. Rocky, will you take a look? Make sure it's nothing more than sore?" Rocky nodded, and Dunn turned to Ashleigh. "He's a medic. One of the best. Let him check out your side. He can also let you know if there's something you can take to help the pain."

Ashleigh nodded.

"Our meeting is in thirty minutes," Dex said. "Eat fast, gentlemen. We need to work on a new plan since we know Williams will be there."

Dunn nodded and grabbed his sandwich and Ashleigh's. He handed hers over and sat with her at the table. His knee brushed hers when he sat, and he didn't bother to move it.

"Obviously, no one likes my new friend," Ashleigh said with a fake smile.

"Uh, no. Archer's best friend was the guy he killed. Rodney was a brother to all of us, though. We didn't know it was him until after we were out and he'd taken Archer's brother. Jaymes, you met him last night."

"He kidnapped *him*?" Ashleigh asked.

Dunn nodded. "It's how Archer and Lily, his wife, met, but that's besides the point. But Williams is a sociopath and thinks he should be thanked for giving them a reason to meet."

"That's insane."

Dunn nodded again and started in on his sandwich. They ate in silence for a few minutes, the soft sounds of murmured conversation around them their background music.

"Do you think he's going to attack Kate Maddox?" Ashleigh finally asked.

Dunn shrugged. "I don't know, but we have to prepare for it. We were looking at all possible threats, but now that he's said he's going to do something, we have to plan on something happening."

"Why would he tell you about it? It doesn't seem like a smart plan."

Dunn huffed a laugh and shook his head. "It's not. It's likely to throw us off, but we have to operate on the assumption something will happen."

"But don't you think that's what he wants? He trained you. He taught all of you how to do exactly what you're doing. If he knows what you're going to do, it's easy to throw you off. He had everything today planned, from you sending me to sit down and him having a chance to sit with me to leaving right when Katie brought out the food right. It's not a coincidence that you didn't see him leave. Or know he was there in the first place. I just don't know that it's reasonable to think he's going to tell you his plan and then follow through with it. Something else is happening."

Dunn nodded. He agreed with her completely, but what he wasn't as sure of was exactly what it all meant. Williams was smart. He never gave up more information than he had to. And if he was telling them what he was doing, it definitely meant something. They just had to figure out what.

Dunn reached over and set his hand on Ashleigh's. Just having her there made him feel better, but he didn't want her getting in the middle of their fight with Williams. "Ash, he's dangerous. I know you want to figure this out, and I do, too, but promise me you won't go digging. If you have a thought, tell us. But he's the kind of man who creates more trouble. I want you safe."

Ashleigh nodded. "Trust me, I'm not looking for more trouble."

Dunn gave her a tight grin. They were still trying to figure out what was going on with her husband, and Williams showing up right before the concert was already bad timing. Not that there was a good time, but Dunn was feeling the pressure of getting it all done.

"We gotta get on the call," Dex said, walking past their table. "We'll get it started."

Dunn nodded. The others filtered out of the break room. He balled up his trash and stood. "Finish your lunch, then you can sit in my office. We'll keep digging after this call," he told Ashleigh.

Ashleigh nodded and picked at her sandwich. "Thanks, Daniel."

He nodded and joined the others in the conference room. They had everything ready for the call from Kate Maddox. Her fiancé's family owned a vineyard in the Finger Lakes, an area Dunn hadn't visited yet, and he was even more paranoid about her safety than Kate was.

The computer beeped, alerting them to the incoming

call. English looked at Dunn, and he nodded to accept the call, standing in front of the camera so he could speak to them.

"Good afternoon," Dunn said when they came on the screen. Kate Maddox was stunning in magazines and online, but sitting across from her on a computer reminded him just how beautiful she really was. None of her pictures were altered. She was just that gorgeous.

"Afternoon," her fiancé said, moving into the shot. He was a big guy, tall and broad and definitely a suit. Dunn and the others agreed that he looked the part of a kept man, but they knew he worked hard based on their research.

"Hi, Daniel," Kate said with a smile. "How is everyone?"

Kate was the kind of person who truly seemed to care about others. She always asked how the team was before they got started and wanted to make sure everyone was doing well. One of the first calls they had with her, Dex was sporting a shiner and Jack had his shoulder in a sling. She knew right away that their job wasn't an easy one, but they would protect her.

"Healthy. Hopefully, we can stay that way. They're all here with me," Dunn replied.

"Hi, everyone," Kate said, waving.

Dunn turned the screen so she could see them all waving back. They had a large screen so everyone could watch the video chat, but they didn't have the room set up for everyone to be on camera. They wanted the option to have people in the room without whoever they were talking to aware of it. Just in case.

Dunn settled the laptop in front of himself again and said, "Everything is set for your concert."

"Good," Kate said.

"Has every threat been researched?" Dillon asked.

Dunn nodded. "Yes. We had a new one today, and we are looking into it."

Kate's smile disappeared. She reached for Dillon's hand. He held hers and slid his arm around her shoulder. "What is it?"

"We don't know if it's credible yet. We heard about it right before this meeting."

"How did you hear about it and we didn't?" Dillon asked.

Dunn glanced at the team. Dex raised his eyebrows at him, silently telling him they needed to be honest. If she didn't know the whole truth, they were deceiving her, and that made them no better than Williams. "The threat is directed at our team, not at Ms. Maddox."

"Kate, please. Or Katherine," Kate said.

Dunn nodded. "The person who made the threat is a former coworker of ours. He is after us, not Ms.— Kate. But we're treating it the same. Our priority is keeping her safe."

"Will you be distracted by this threat? If it's someone you know, it's different from a blank face," Dillon said, his brows pulled together.

Dunn nodded again. "It is different, and it is personal. I won't lie to you and say this won't affect us, but we will do our jobs. We're trained to protect people. If that means letting him go, we will. If it means we figure out something else, we will do that, too. Right now, we're unsure if the threat is real. We're investigating it."

"How long will that take?" Dillon asked.

"We should have a better idea by the end of today."

Dillon looked at Kate. "The concert is in six days. Is that enough time to deal with it?"

Dunn nodded. "We will be dealing with the authorities. We will bring in more help. This is not something that will be pushed aside. Even if this threat is not credible against Kate and a threat to the concert, we will deal with it. We will take extra precautions to make sure she is safe."

"You can guarantee that?" Dillon asked.

"Yes," Dunn said without hesitation.

The rest of the room sucked in a breath, but no one said anything.

Dillon looked at Kate and kissed her forehead. "Good. She will be my wife by the time we arrive, and if you let my wife get hurt before we have a honeymoon, I don't care if you're trained and can kick my ass without even trying, I'll kill you."

Dunn nodded, knowing the other man was as serious as a person could be. Dunn would hand him the gun if it came to that. "Congratulations. We'll get you that honeymoon."

Dillon nodded once, holding Dunn's gaze.

They talked a few more minutes about logistics and the place they were staying, then hung up with well wishes and congratulations.

Dunn clicked to end the call and slumped back in his chair.

"I found the post," English said.

Dunn didn't have to ask which post. He already knew. "And it said Williams' daughter is going to the concert?"

English nodded.

"So, we have a real threat. The whole family is going to the concert."

English nodded again.

"What are the chances he'd kill his kids?" Dunn asked the room.

Williams was messed up, they all knew that, but everything he did, he said he did for his kids. Because he wanted his kids and his wife. He tried to set his ex-wife's new husband up to take the fall when he tried to blow up the city. Would he really risk hurting his kids?

"I think we have to operate under the assumption that he's a crazy fucker who has no morals or conscious. I wouldn't put it past him to kill everyone just so he can get to the step-dad, but nothing about this feels right," Dex said.

The others nodded. "He's not this reckless," Rocky said. "He's always kept everything close to the vest. Why tell us now?"

"That's what I'm trying to figure out," Jack said. "This doesn't feel right."

Dunn agreed, but none of them could piece together what was really going on.

"No matter what, we have a job to do. We have to protect Kate Maddox. If Williams shows up, Kate's our priority," Dunn said.

"Agreed," the others said in unison.

"Can you handle that?" Jack asked, calling Dunn out.

Every fiber of Dunn's being wanted to say yes, but he knew the truth was he wanted Williams even more now than he did before. He wanted to make him pay for scaring Ashleigh, and he wanted him to suffer for what he did to Rodney and the rest of them. The man didn't deserve to walk the streets.

"Do we have any cameras in the area of JB's Subs? To see where he went?" Dunn asked instead of answering Jack's question.

English shook his head. "No. There are cameras there, but none of them picked up anything."

"So, again, we're dealing with someone who knows where the cameras are and how to avoid them. Just fucking great," Jack said. He met his fiancée when their informant, her brother, went missing. The man who took him operated the same way, avoiding cameras and eluding them for days before they caught a break and found him. Unfortunately, he'd already killed two people by that time.

Something none of them were going to forget any time soon.

"We can't let Williams hurt anyone else," Dex growled.

Everyone nodded. Going after the man who trained them was hard enough, but knowing he was toying with them just made Dunn mad. Williams already slipped through their fingers once, and now he made a fool of Dunn a second time. If anything happened at that concert, he wouldn't be able to live with himself.

They had to stop Williams. They just had to find him first.

ASHLEIGH WAS STILL SHAKING when Daniel and the others finished their meeting. She was better when she was in a room surrounded by strong, capable men, but alone in a strange office building made her more than a little anxious. If she wasn't safe in a restaurant surrounded by people, was she safe anywhere?

"Hey, you okay?" Daniel asked when he walked into the break room.

She looked up at him and smiled. He was a stranger to her. She thought she could trust him, but he brought a new devil to her doorstep. Someone who obviously knew who she was.

"Am I safe here?"

Daniel stopped on his way to the fridge and pivoted. He took three large steps across the room and slid onto the seat next to her. His knee bumped hers and she flinched. His brows tugged together in the middle, and the man she loved when she was barely a woman stared back at her.

Daniel had changed over the years. Ashleigh had changed, too, but the changes in Daniel were more obvious since she hadn't seen him in years. He was darker, harder. He was a man who'd seen things, and probably done things, she couldn't even fathom.

Did it really matter the reason, though?

"You can leave any time, Ash. If you don't feel safe, you can go."

"He knows where we are, doesn't he?"

Daniel nodded.

"Is he going to come here?"

Daniel shrugged. "We have no way of knowing that. We've been after him for more than a year. He trained us, like you said, and he knows how to hide better than all of us. It doesn't help that he hasn't been our focus. We have jobs to do and people to help. We're not after him constantly."

"Feeling that gun..." Ashleigh rubbed her side where it was sore from the end of the gun.

"I'm sorry I put you in that position, Ash," Daniel said softly.

She nodded and hugged herself. She wanted to crawl into his lap and let him hold her. He had a way of making her feel safe even when she didn't. Sitting across the table from him wasn't close enough.

"We should take you to see Rocky. Let him look at your side," Daniel said, getting to his feet.

Ashleigh stood and followed him. He knocked on a door on the other side of the hall from his and walked in.

"Can you take a look at Ashleigh's side?"

"Yeah, sorry. I forgot all about it. Have a seat, Ashleigh," Rocky said with a smile.

She walked in and sat on the chair he indicated.

"Sorry we don't have a medical facility here. We don't usually need it, and patching up all these jackasses would end up my full-time job."

Ashleigh smiled at him.

"I'll wait in my office," Daniel said, moving toward the door.

"Will you stay?" Ashleigh said quickly. "Please?"

Daniel exchanged a glance with Rocky. Rocky only shrugged. Daniel moved back into the office and closed the door. He stood with his back to it, staring above Ashleigh's head.

"Sorry, Ashleigh, but I'm going to need you to pull your shirt up on this side. I'm going to try to do this without having you remove it. If you'd rather Dunn leaves..."

"No," she said firmly. "Um, I feel better with him around."

Rocky nodded and grabbed a pair of gloves while Ashleigh pulled her shirt up to expose her left side.

Rocky shook his head. "You already have a bruise starting. You're going to feel my hands, okay?"

Ashleigh nodded.

Rocky set his hands on her skin, and she jumped. "Sorry. I know my hands are cold."

She shook her head and tried not to freak out. The only other man who'd touched her for years was her husband. As far as she was concerned, her marriage was over, but that didn't mean she was ready for another man to touch her.

Rocky dug his fingers into her flesh, and she winced. "Tell me where it hurts, Ashleigh."

"Everywhere. All of it hurts."

"Is it a dull ache or a sharp pain?"

"Mostly an ache—" she hissed "—but that's painful."

Rocky kept feeling around and sighed. "I'm really sorry, but in order to get a good look, I need you to take off your shirt and your bra. Keep yourself covered, but the bruise goes up under the band of your bra. I want to check it out."

Ashleigh nodded, but all she could think was Daniel was going to see her half-naked, and she wasn't in her twenties anymore.

9

———

Daniel wanted to break his friend's hands for touching Ashleigh, but when he said she needed to take her shirt off, he saw red. Rocky had no right to get her naked.

"Dunn, you should wait outside," Rocky said, barely acknowledging him.

"Like fucking hell," Dunn growled.

Rocky turned and stared him down. "There is a woman in here who is about to take off her shirt. She deserves some privacy."

"She asked me to stay," Dunn said firmly.

"And the situation has changed," Rocky said, equally firm. "You asked me to look at her. I'm only doing my job."

Dunn hated it, but Rocky was right. There was no reason for him to stay. "I'll be right outside. Right. Out. Side."

Rocky nodded and waited for him to leave. As soon as he was on the other side of the door, Rocky locked it.

Dunn paced in front of the door, seething the entire time. It couldn't have been more than a few minutes, but it felt like a lifetime. When the door finally opened again, Rocky stepped out and pulled the door closed.

"Nothing seems broken. Definitely a bruise, but she was lucky," Rocky said.

"That fucking psycho pressed a gun against her side. It wasn't luck," Dunn growled.

Rocky's eyebrows went up. "Nothing is broken. She's not shot. She'll be sore for a few days, but she's going to be okay. She was lucky."

Dunn finally nodded sharply, and Rocky walked away. Dunn knocked on the door and waited for Ashleigh to open it. Her eyes were red and wet.

"Did he touch you?" Dunn asked, looking to see where Rocky went.

"No," Ashleigh said softly. "It hurt, but he didn't hurt me. He was doing his job."

Dunn clenched his fists and his jaw, trying to remain calm.

"Can I sit in your office for a few minutes?"

Dunn nodded and guided her to his door. "Do you need anything?"

She looked up at him and chewed on her lip. She squeezed her eyes shut and drew in a shaky breath.

Dunn led her into the office and closed the door, then pulled her into his arms. She sagged against him and let him hold her up. She broke, the adrenaline from the day finally catching up to her. She shook as he led her to the couch in his office. He sat and pulled her onto his lap. He wrapped his arms around her, just holding her while she cried.

There was a knock on his door, but he told them to go away. Nothing was more important than Ashleigh at that moment.

She finally sucked in a breath and didn't sob. Her tears had soaked through his shirt, but he didn't care. He just held her until she leaned back and looked up at him.

Her eyes were watery and blood-shot, but she was still beautiful. She held his gaze. Desire pulsed between them. It wouldn't take much for him to lean forward and claim her lips. To take what he wanted from her.

Her gaze darted to his lips, and she licked hers. Her breasts hitched with her breath. Every inch of him tightened, preparing to kiss her again. Ashleigh. His Ashleigh. His first love.

She leaned in, and his hand slid up her back. Her hair tickled his knuckles. She slicked her tongue over her lips and drew closer. Her breath whispered over his cheeks. His cock hardened under her thigh.

"Ash," he whispered, his pulse pounding in his ears.

Nope, not his pulse. His door.

"Go away," Dunn yelled.

"We found something," Dex called from the other side. "You need to see this. Both of you."

Dunn closed his eyes and groaned. Ashleigh sighed with frustration. They looked at each other, still in each other's arms and barely a breath apart.

"I guess we need to go," Ashleigh said, pulling back first. "I, um..."

Dunn sighed. "I'm sorry. I shouldn't have done that."

She shook her head. "I'm the one who's married. I know how intoxicating you are. I could never resist you."

"Trust me, the feeling is mutual."

She gave him a sad smile and went to the door. She glanced back and shook her head, then walked out the door.

Dunn had no choice but to follow her.

"WHAT WAS SO IMPORTANT?" Daniel asked when he walked into the conference room.

Ashleigh wasn't sure why she was there, but Dex was waiting in the hallway for them and led her to the conference room.

"English found something you need to see," Dex said, taking the seat next to her. Daniel glared at him, then took the only empty seat on the other side of the table.

"I ran facial recognition on the one picture we found online, and found some interesting information. There are nine passports with the same man. Of them, three are for other countries, six for the US. The ones we looked up this morning are barely scraping the surface with this guy. He has multiple aliases, and many of them are on the no-fly list. He's a chameleon."

Ashleigh tried to understand everything English said, but she couldn't quite get it. Frederick had passports for other countries? And he was on the no-fly list?

"We've traveled together," Ashleigh said. "How could he be on a no-fly list? We went to the Caribbean last year. And Europe the year before."

"The passport for Frederick Edwards is clean. That man is a businessman who does what should be done. The other men are not the same," English explained.

"What does that mean?" Ashleigh asked.

"It means your husband is involved in a lot more than kidnapping children and putting them up for adoption. But the good news is he's also not really your husband, Ashleigh," Dex explained.

"What? But we got married."

Dex shook his head. "You married a man who doesn't actually exist. Frederick Edwards died eight years ago. Your husband assumed his identity. He's kept it clean, but the man you know as Frederick Edwards is really someone else."

"Who is he?" Daniel asked.

"We don't know yet," English said. "With this many aliases, we have to dig deeper to figure out which one came first. Chances are he's not really any of these men. But the end result is still the same. Ashleigh, you're not actually married."

Ashleigh wasn't sure if she should be relieved or not. A part of her felt married. Even though she hoped he caught some horribly painful disease from the woman he fucked in her house, she still thought she loved him at one point.

"Ashleigh, there's something else you need to know," Dex said calmly. "We looked into a few other things. We wanted to make sure we had as much information as possible when we talked to you. He has people out looking for you. Dangerous people. It doesn't appear as though he knows where you are yet, but there's no reason to assume he won't find you soon."

Ashleigh closed her eyes and tried to breathe. She fell for a man who wasn't who he said he was. She believed him. She was the one who ran his credit when they met. She agreed to a date with him. She fell for his sweet words and the way he spoiled her. She felt like she was special. Like she was important. She was just the fool who didn't see through his lies. Her friends tried to tell her something wasn't right, but she believed him over them.

And she was wrong. Just like she was wrong about Daniel. She thought he loved her and they were going to be together forever. Instead, he left her behind like she was nothing.

It was her pattern. She fell for men who lied. And she believed every word they said.

"I need... go..." Ashleigh stammered and left the room.

A part of her knew leaving the building was a bad idea, but she didn't really care. She had to get out. To get away from Daniel and Frederick and everything. She went straight to the elevator and pushed the button for it to take her downstairs.

She got out in the parking garage and looked around. She didn't know the area, but it didn't matter. She just needed to leave.

She walked up the ramp and turned left. The large building she was just inside loomed above her, casting a shadow over her and the entire sidewalk.

She walked. She didn't know where she was going or where she would end up, but she didn't care. She was alone. No family, no friends, and now, no husband. She couldn't believe she lived with him for almost a decade and never once figured out that he wasn't who he said he was.

Ashleigh tried to think back on her life with Frederick and figure out where she went wrong. Where she missed the signs.

She assumed all his quirks were because he was rich. She didn't really have an idea of how much money he had, but when they met, he was starting a new company. Even though he had plenty of money, he said he preferred to get loans so if he ever really needed one, he had a record of being a good investment. It made sense. Just like it made sense for her to move in with him when her lease expired a few months later and her rent went up.

Everything about being with Frederick made sense. They got married because she was frustrated working at the bank and wanted to do something that really helped people. He had contacts all over the country and said they could use someone with her brilliance to review their books. But she couldn't afford to do it unless he supported her, so they got married.

Every single piece of her life existed because of Frederick. And she never realized it.

She walked until she ended up in a crowd of people. Not realizing where she was, she kept moving forward, and stopped short when she saw Niagara Falls.

Ashleigh pushed her way to the rail and stared at the magnificent site. Everything in life seemed small when faced with something like Niagara Falls. She'd always wanted to see it. Growing up in Arkansas, she felt trapped most of her life. She dreamed of seeing Niagara Falls and the Eiffel Tower and the Grand Canyon. Frederick made two of those dreams come true, and they talked about traveling more, but his work always got in the way.

Ashleigh watched the water swirl and wondered where her life went so wrong. She tried to believe she made smart decisions, but she always lived with her heart instead of her head. Would she have made other choices if she hadn't fallen so hard for Daniel?

At twenty, she didn't give much thought to the rest of her life. She knew it would unfold how it was supposed to. Despite her own family history, she believed in love. She knew her father still loved her mother, and she hated her mother for hurting him, but she never questioned her father's loyalty and devotion. For him, love was forever, and he taught her the same thing.

Daniel was different from all the other boys she'd ever known. He was confident and forward. When he approached her, she was surprised because he was the kind of guy who could have asked out any girl on campus. It took her a while to believe he wanted her, and when their first date ended with a kiss instead of between his sheets, she believed that he was interested for real.

She fell hard for Daniel. Where he was confident and fearless with other people, he let her in. He told her about his dad and his mom being gone most of the time. He told her how much he adored his grandmother, but that she wasn't a pushover. And when he told her he loved her, she gave herself to him and knew she'd never love another man the way she loved Daniel.

Ashleigh told herself she loved Frederick. She thought he was a good man. But again, she fell for a man who wasn't who she thought he was. She fell for another liar.

"Ashleigh," Daniel said softly. "Are you okay?"

She whirled around and glared at him. "Did you follow me?"

He had the decency to look chagrined for about two seconds, but he still nodded. "I didn't want anything to happen to you."

She scoffed.

"Let's go," he said, glancing around.

She followed his gaze and realized just how stupid she was. She had one gun pointed at her already. She wasn't in the mood for a second.

She let him lead her back to his SUV and sat silently in the front seat as he drove them to his house. Thank God he didn't go back to his office. Not that she wanted to be in his home, but at least she didn't have to look into the eyes of the rest of his team. She couldn't handle anymore humiliation.

Daniel led her into his house, her purse slung over his shoulder. He set it down on the counter with a thud.

"Are you okay?"

She laughed mirthlessly. "Really?"

He shrugged. "I'm worried about you."

"Oh, you are? How sweet. Eighteen years ago you didn't give me a second thought and now you care?"

"I gave you a lot of second thoughts, Ash. I've always cared."

She scoffed. "You're full of shit. If you cared about me, you would have stayed in touch."

Daniel glared at her. "And who would that have helped? Because if I'd kept in touch with you, I would have left. I would have walked away so I could be with you. And then I would have hated myself for it, maybe hated you. I had to go. And I had to cut ties."

"It would have helped me, you asshole. You're only thinking about yourself. But if you'd have stayed in touch, then I would have known I was worth something. I loved you, Daniel. I fucking loved you. I died when you walked away from me. I never thought I'd find someone who made me feel the way you did. And I never did. Frederick, or whatever his name is, he's just like you. He lied to me. For years, he told me he was someone he wasn't."

"I'm not like him," Daniel growled, getting up close to her.

Ashleigh's pulse pounded in her ears, her chest heaving with each angry breath. She stared at the man she once knew like she knew herself and laughed. "Do you really believe that? Do you really think you're so different?"

"I didn't tell you I wanted to go into the Navy, but I never lied about who I was. It killed me to walk away from you."

"But you did it! You did it and never looked back!"

"Didn't you hear Williams today? He knew who you were. He saw your picture for years. I kept a photo of us with me for years. You were the reason I stayed alive. You were the way I survived. You, Ashleigh. You might have moved on and married someone else, and I have been with other women, but you were always the woman I wanted. You were the only one I ever truly loved. And that crazy fucker knows it."

Ashleigh laughed. She rolled her eyes and shook her head. "A lot of good that did either of us. I married another man who couldn't be honest with me, and you ended up working for a psycho who now wants us dead."

"I was honest with you. I loved you more than anything, Ash. I would have walked away if you asked me to. I would have done anything you asked. But you never fucking did. You just told me to get out."

"Because you would have hated me. You just said it yourself. You would have hated me."

"Dammit, Ashleigh, you didn't want me."

"I still do, you stupid ass. I've always wanted you. Why else would I have shown up here? Because of you, Daniel. Because you're the only one I trust to protect me, even though I know I'll lose my heart to you all over again."

Ashleigh realized what she admitted half a second after she said it. She closed her eyes and turned to walk away.

She didn't get very far.

10

———

Dunn grabbed her arm and yanked her back to him. Her back pressed to his front, his cock nestled between her cheeks. He groaned at the feel of her, then tightened his grip when she rocked her hips back.

He leaned down and slid his tongue over the shell of her ear. She moaned, a greedy sound that went straight to his hard cock. He wrapped their joined arms around her waist and fisted her shirt. He let go of her arm and spread his hand wide on her stomach, loving the feel of her plush body against his.

Her breathing was shallow, but so was his. He couldn't hold back another second. She wasn't married. Not legally. And if she was willing, he wasn't going to let her walk away again.

"Tell me to stop, Ash. Tell me to let you go."

"Don't. Stop."

"Fuck, Ash. I won't be able to hold back with you."

"I want to see you crazy, Daniel. I want to see you lose control. Show me what eighteen years apart did to you."

She barely got her words out before his hands went up

and down. He cupped her breast with one greedy hand and felt the heat of her core through her shorts with the other. She moaned and bucked against him, and he stroked her through her shorts.

"Do you remember the first time I touched you like this? You came so hard my neighbors were banging on the walls."

"I remember everything about being with you, Daniel."

"I love hearing you say my name. No one else calls me that."

"No one calls me 'Ash' either," she admitted.

He pressed harder against her core, letting her panties help get her off. He ground his dick against her back, barely able to keep control of himself. It had been far too long since he'd been with anyone, but no woman made him lose control the way Ashleigh did.

"Oh, God, Daniel," she moaned, rocking her hips against him.

"Come for me, Ash. Let me hear you."

"Yes," she moaned. "Oh, God. Oh, yes." She came with a shudder, but he knew her. More was in there. That was just a warmup.

"Take off your clothes," he commanded.

He let go of her so she could strip. He watched, his cock growing harder with each piece of clothing that fell to the floor. When she stood naked in front of him, he looked his fill of her.

"Jesus, you're gorgeous. I don't know how I ever walked away from you."

"Well, you did."

"Not tonight, Ash. Tonight you're all mine. Go lay down on my bed."

"You're bossy," she said, eyebrows drawing together.

He shook his head. "I know what I want."

"What's that?"

"You," he said simply.

She shivered and bit her lip.

"Go lay down Ashleigh or I'm going to fuck you over this table."

Her eyes widened. She glanced at the table and bit her lip again.

"Is that what you want?" Dunn asked her.

She nodded slowly, like she was afraid to admit it.

"Tell me, Ash. Tell me where you want me to fuck you. The first time."

"On the table."

"On your back or bent over?" Dunn asked.

She nibbled her lip again.

"Tell me, Ash. What do you want?"

She drew in a breath. "I'm not used to asking. Or any of this."

"You haven't been with a real man in far too long, Ash. Let me remind you what it's like to be fucked until you can't breathe."

ASHLEIGH WAS PRETTY sure she already knew. Watching Daniel, the fire in his eyes and the thick ridge in his jeans, she was already pretty damn breathless.

But she wasn't going to tell him that. He might stop.

Ashleigh walked over to the table and put her hands on the edge. She bent at the waist and spread her thighs, baring herself to Daniel.

She'd never been that vulnerable with Frederick. He'd never bent her over his desk, and even the thought made her think it would have been wrong. Dirty, in a bad way. But with Daniel, it felt right. She knew he would take care of her, and she never doubted that she could trust him.

"Fuck me," he growled. He crossed to her in three quick strides and bent over her back. His entire body covered hers. His hands were everywhere at once. Plucking her breasts, gliding between her thighs, pressing against her stomach. She wasn't sure she could take all of it. All of him.

He took his weight off her and slid both hands down her back. They glided over her ass and down her thighs. She shook at the feel of him, close but not quite there. When he slid his hands back up her thighs, both pressed her thighs wider.

"I love the way you smell when you're ready for me to fuck you, Ash. I've missed this." He thrust one thick finger into her and they both groaned. "Fuck, Ash. You're already ready for me."

"Yes," she moaned, rocking against his hand.

He added a second finger and rubbed his thumb up to her star. She moaned loud and long, and when he stroked over her clit, she came apart with a moan.

"That wasn't nearly loud enough," Daniel said. "You used to shake the walls. I guess you need more."

"Oh, God," Ashleigh moaned when he added a third finger.

"There we go. Take what you need from me. Tell me what you want, Ash."

"Harder," she moaned, half-begging. "Deeper."

"How about your clit? Do you like me to play with it?"

"Yes," she whimpered.

He stroked over her clit and fucked her hard with his fingers. "And what about your ass, baby? Are you going to let me play there, too?"

"Oh, God, please," Ashleigh begged.

Daniel dropped to his knees and sucked on her clit. She rocked against his face. Then he toyed with her star, and she lost all control.

"Oh, God. Oh, God. Yes, Daniel. Oh, God, yes. Yes! Yes!" Her body thrashed as a monster orgasm raced through her. Her greedy body begged for more, and when Daniel kept going, she nearly whimpered in relief.

"More," he commanded, then sucked on her again.

She exploded, unable to stop the string of curse words and praises that fell from her mouth. She didn't care. Daniel had heard it all before.

"More," Daniel commanded once more. When he sucked on her once again, he pressed a finger into her ass and she screamed.

"Fuck, Daniel. Yes! Oh, God! Fuck, fuck, fuck, fuck, fuck!"

She was barely aware of him pulling away from her. As she started to come down, she was frustrated that he wrung her out, then walked away, then she felt him rubbing against her slit a second before he plunged into her.

"Oh, fuck," she moaned, her channel tightening around him and coming instantly.

"Fuck, yes. I love the way you come on my dick. Let me feel it again, Ash."

He grabbed her hips and slammed into her. She cried out when he hit her in just the right spot and she fell again. As she came, he fucked her hard, taking his pleasure from her body. She tightened around him and shifted back, chasing one more orgasm that felt just out of reach.

"Fuck, Ash. Fuck," Daniel groaned. "Touch yourself if you need to."

"You do it," Ashleigh said, knowing Daniel could make her come faster than she could.

He leaned over her and slid his hand between her thighs. "You're so fucking wet, Ash. So fucking perfect."

His breath was warm in her ear, his words rough with lust. She knew it was just sex, just mutual pleasure, but it was Daniel. It was the man she'd always compared others to. The man who drove her crazy in more ways than she ever knew possible. Daniel was the one who introduced her to sex. The one who showed her how amazing sex could be. And he was doing it again, reminding her of all the things she'd forgotten in the years she was with Frederick.

"Come, Ash," Daniel growled. "Let me feel you come."

"I'm trying," she whimpered, so close but not there yet.

A sharp pain between her thighs morphed quickly into unfathomable pleasure. She screamed his name and barely stayed upright as he fucked her so hard she rose up on her tiptoes.

"Fuck, Ash," he groaned as he swelled and came inside her.

Ashleigh's knees shook and her body trembled, but she didn't want to move. She locked her knees and prayed they could stay there forever, linked together with nothing outside the two of them.

But nothing lasted forever. It wasn't long before Daniel was lifting his weight from her back and withdrawing his hand from between her thighs. She nearly cried at the loss of his touch. He took a step back and slid from inside her. Cold air rushed between them, making her shiver.

Come slid down her thighs when she stood. Horrified, she looked at him. He pulled the condom off, and she breathed a sigh of relief. Then the panic set in.

She just had sex with a man who was virtually a stranger. She didn't know him anymore. He was familiar, but like an old sweater. Warm and comfortable, but didn't fit quite right. She wanted Daniel to fit, but she had to admit to herself that he didn't. They didn't.

She grabbed her clothes and raced down the hall to the bathroom. He called her name, but she didn't stop until there was a locked door between them.

She sucked in as much air as she could and slumped onto the toilet. She put her head in her hands and wondered what in the hell she was thinking. She woke up thinking she was married, and five seconds after she found out she wasn't, she jumped into bed with her ex.

She used the bathroom and washed her hands, then slowly redressed. All her clothes were what she packed for her business trip, so everything was business casual. The shorts she wore were long and black to hide her thick thighs. Her top was loose and light since she traveled to California. As she redressed, she wished Daniel had torn them to shreds, erasing the life she had before.

Ashleigh stared at herself in the mirror as her face flushed. She hadn't been fucked like that since the night before he told her he was leaving to be a SEAL. It had been far too long since a man made her feel like she was the only reason he was losing his mind.

Since Daniel.

DUNN WANTED to break down the fucking door. The second Ashleigh stood, he noticed the stiffness of her spine and knew she was getting ready to run.

Dunn dressed and waited. He couldn't break the door down, but she couldn't get far. Not unless she climbed out the window. He really hoped she didn't do that. Chasing her all over town once was enough for one damn day.

The door finally opened, and he breathed again. He didn't realize he was holding his breath, but when she walked into the room, she stole it all over again.

Then she looked up at him with those green eyes full of regret, and he wanted to kick his own ass.

"That never happened," she said firmly.

"Ash," he groaned.

She shook her head. "No, Daniel. I can't. I'm married. Or I thought I was. Just because my marriage isn't legal doesn't mean I'm ready to start something else with you. It's not fair to either of us."

Dunn nodded. What the hell else could he do? Her husband was bad news, which meant he needed to keep her safe. And that meant keeping her close while keeping his distance.

In other words, torture.

"How about some dinner?" he finally managed.

She nodded, chewing on the inside of her lip.

Instead of asking what she was thinking, he turned toward the kitchen and started dinner.

He managed to avoid looking at her until he finished cooking. She was sitting there, watching him the entire time. He set a plate in front of her, then carried his own to the table and sat across from her.

Dunn stewed through dinner, hating himself for touching her. If he'd kept his hands to himself, they would be talking. But he couldn't resist her. He had to put himself and his fucking needs above hers.

Again, she didn't want him. She still wanted her husband. Her fucking husband who cheated on her and stole children. Talk about a blow to his ego.

Dunn finished his dinner and put his plate in the dishwasher. He ached to go for a run to get rid of the pent up energy in him, but he couldn't leave her alone. He needed a good, punishing workout, though. The kind of workout that would be even better between the sheets with a warm, willing, curvy woman like Ashleigh.

But that wasn't going to happen.

Dunn walked down the hall, ignoring Ashleigh's stares, to his office. He rarely used the room. He hated being caged in, and he had an office downtown, but he needed one in his home, just in case. For the first time, he was happy he had it.

He went into the closet and pulled out the free weights he stashed there when he moved in. Even before he bought the place, he joined a gym, so he never bothered with the weights, but they were his only option if he was going to have any hope of sleeping.

Dunn put himself through a painful two hours of weight lifting, not taking a break between sets or reps. He was aware of Ashleigh walking down the hall past him to the bedroom, then returning to the other side of the house, but he didn't pay attention to her aside from that.

He needed a shower and to collapse into his bed. One out of two was going to have to work. He closed the bathroom door and stripped out of his sweaty clothes. He turned the shower as cold as he could stand it and got in, washing away the day and cooling his skin.

He adjusted the water to warm up and settle his body. He washed quickly, pushing all thoughts of Ashleigh out of his head when his cock threatened to rise. He got out and dressed quickly, then went back to the living room to get some sleep.

Ashleigh was sitting on the couch. Her feet were tucked under her. She was snoring softly. Instead of the buttoned up outfit she had on earlier, she was wearing one of his old

SEAL tees and a pair of black panties, the edge visible where his shirt pulled up on her hip.

"Jesus," he breathed, hard again. He stared at her, desperate to touch her again. His cock throbbed. Every inch of him ached. He needed to slide into her again, but she said no. She said it never happened. Being with him was a mistake. He was a mistake.

He walked over to the couch and nudged her shoulder. She jumped and scrambled off the couch. His shirt fell to mid-thigh, covering the panties and the delectable stretch of skin he wanted to lick.

"Sorry. I guess I fell asleep."

"Orgasms always did that to you," Dunn said before he could stop himself.

Ashleigh bit her lip and nodded, avoiding his gaze. "I guess I should go to bed." She glanced around. "I'll sleep out here tonight."

Dunn shook his head. "No. Go to my room."

"Daniel—"

"It's safer," he said firmly. "If someone breaks in, they're likely to come in one of the doors. The bedroom window is higher off the ground. You should sleep in there."

She sucked in a sharp breath, almost like she'd forgotten the reason she was at his house in the first place. She nodded once, whispered, "Good night," and left the room.

He waited until his bedroom door closed to sink onto the couch. He definitely wasn't getting any sleep again.

11

———

FREDERICK EDWARDS PACED HIS OFFICE, READY TO FIRE OR shoot anyone who told him they couldn't find his wife. She was his fucking wife. She wasn't smart. She wasn't savvy. She was a simple woman who never questioned anything. That was why he married her. She had a rack that made him drool and she was so desperate for love when they met that she didn't see who he really was. She was perfect for him.

And now she was fucking missing.

His phone rang, and he glared at the device in his hand. Blocked numbers were common in his business, but usually he expected the call. This one he was not expecting, which meant it could have something to do with whoever took Ashleigh.

"What," he barked into the phone.

"Are you missing a wife?" the man on the other end of the line said.

"Who the fuck are you?"

"Just a friend. I met this woman today, and she bears a striking resemblance to your beautiful wife. Dirty blonde hair, curves to make a man lose his mind, and an ex-boyfriend who protected her like she still belonged to him."

Frederick saw red. No man had the right to touch what was his. "Where," he growled.

"Oh, see, that information might cost you. I was thinking we could work out a trade."

"What kind of trade?" Frederick asked. Any person who stood between him and his wife was going to fucking die. He didn't care what he needed to promise, he'd swear to it, then murder the fucker with his bare hands.

"This man who had his hands all over your wife, he's someone I know. Someone who's in my way. He's keeping me from my wife, too. So, I thought we could work together to eliminate him. Then you can have your wife, and I can have mine, and we're good to go."

"Who is he?"

The other man laughed. "You don't get to know that yet. Not until I know you're not going to kill me."

"You're a smart man," Frederick said with a grin.

The man laughed again. "I am. And the only way for me to get my wife back is to stay smart, which means staying alive. So, do we have a deal?"

Frederick thought about it for less than a minute, then said, "Where do I meet you?"

"Niagara Falls. Observation Tower. Ten am tomorrow. I'll find you."

"I'll be there," Frederick said. He hung up the phone and glared at the man standing next to him. "My wife has an ex-boyfriend. She's with him right now. In Niagara Falls. Find out everything there is to know about him. Now."

The man scurried away. Frederick didn't have to tell him he would put a bullet in the man's head if he didn't do what was asked. The dead body in the corner of the room said that for him.

ASHLEIGH TOSSED and turned all night. Between the news she learned about her husband, having a gun jammed in her side, and the best sex of her life, she'd had a hell of a day.

She was angry with herself for giving in to her desire for Daniel. He was the kind of man any woman with a pulse would struggle to resist, but she was supposed to be married. She couldn't jump into bed with him every time he looked at her.

It didn't matter how much she wanted to. The throbbing between her thighs begged her to do it again, but she couldn't. She told him it wasn't going to happen again, and she meant it.

Ashleigh finally gave up on sleep when she heard Daniel in the kitchen. He was quiet, but she was awake and straining to hear anything that told her she could leave her confinement.

She was still wearing his tee, wishing she'd brought other clothes. She used the bathroom and splashed cold water on her face, then went to get some coffee and breakfast.

"Morning," she said softly when she walked into the room.

Daniel had his back to her. He didn't turn, but he did mumble, "Morning."

She hesitated, sensing his frustration left over from the night before. He was fixing breakfast again, but she couldn't tell what it was. He stopped and moved to the side, then turned and handed her a cup of coffee, fixed exactly how she liked it.

"Thank you," she whispered, giving him a smile.

His fiery gaze slid down her body and glided back up, leaving goosebumps in its wake. She squeezed her thighs together to stop the pulsing, but it didn't help.

Daniel went back to cooking breakfast, ignoring her again. She wondered how he did that. He existed in his space like she wasn't there, but she couldn't breathe without the reminder that she was in the same room as him.

She sipped her coffee and tried to figure out what she was going to do with herself. At some point, she had to talk to Frederick, but she wasn't ready to do that yet. She had to help the woman whose child he took. She had to expose him.

Daniel carried two plates to the table and set one down in what had become her spot. She sat on the cool wooden chair and tucked one foot under her. She stared at her plate and tried to figure out how to talk to him.

"Did you get any sleep?" she asked finally, figuring small talk was the way to go.

He grunted and shook his head.

"Are you used to being up early?"

He looked up at her, and she shrugged.

"You were up early yesterday, too."

"I don't sleep well." The finality in his voice said he wasn't open to discussing the matter further.

Ashleigh ate her breakfast in silence. When she was done, she added her plate to his in the dishwasher and asked if she could take a shower.

"Fine," was all he said.

She got halfway down the hall when she stopped. She could handle him being distant, but she couldn't handle him not talking to her at all. She spun and marched back to the living room and got in his face.

"What the hell is wrong with you?"

He raised an eyebrow and didn't respond.

"Are you seriously giving me the silent treatment right now? Because that's childish. If I'm going to stay here with you, you should at least talk to me."

"What exactly do you want me to talk to you about?"

She sputtered. "I don't know. Anything. Something."

He took a step toward her. "Like how your marriage was never real and you don't owe that son of a bitch another second of your time? Or how he never deserved you if you had to wait eighteen years to come like you did last night? Or maybe how if you get in my face again, I'm not going to be responsible for what I do to you?"

Ashleigh sucked in a breath. Daniel's eyes dropped to her breasts and held. Her nipples tightened, rubbing the rough cotton of his tee. Everything ached, desperate to find out exactly what he would do.

She took a step forward, bringing her breasts into contact with his chest.

"I'm not fucking around, Ashleigh," he growled.

She hesitated just long enough for him to shake his head and step back.

"Go take a shower so we can get out of here."

Ashleigh walked down the hall with her tail between her legs. She wanted to be bold and strong. She wanted to stand up to a man like Daniel. But she was scared. He already hurt her once, and her marriage was over, but that hurt, too. She was raw and sore... and not just between her thighs.

She closed the door and let the shower heat up while she looked for something to wear. All her clothes were far too fancy for a day at Daniel's office, but until she could go shopping, she was stuck with what she had.

Her panties were all dirty since she hadn't done laundry since before her trip, so she picked a pair of dark, cotton capris and a loose, green top. She carried the clothes into the bathroom and got in the shower.

The heat of the water slid down her curves and lit her up. Her body begged for a release, but she didn't want to hold Daniel up any longer than she already was. She showered quickly, using the last of her shampoo and soap, then slid his razor over her skin carefully. When she stepped out, she wrapped herself in one of his towels and got dressed.

Once she was ready to go, she left the room and gave him a wide berth as they traded places in the house. While Daniel showered, she tried to tell herself nothing was out of the ordinary. It was just another day. A day where she was wearing no panties and standing in her ex's living room while he showered before taking her to his job so they could catch her husband before a child disappeared for good.

Yeah, normal.

DUNN WALKED into the office with Ashleigh right behind him. He needed coffee and a few hours in the gym, but all he had time for was coffee. English was already there, and by the look of him, he hadn't gotten anymore sleep than Dunn.

"Ashleigh's husband is here," English said when Dunn joined him in the conference room.

"What?" Dunn blurted.

"I've been monitoring his passports. One of them was used to travel here through Canada overnight."

Dunn fell into a chair and set his mug down with a hard thunk. Hot coffee sloshed over the edge and covered his hand. He jerked it away, slinging coffee everywhere.

"Fuck." Dunn grabbed napkins and wiped up the table, then focused on English again. "Why didn't you call me and tell me this?"

English shook his head. "It didn't hit until he crossed back into the US an hour ago. We can't get records from Canada, you know that."

"Fuck," Dunn said again. "How the hell does he know where she is?"

"Does she have a phone?"

Dunn shook his head. "She ditched it before she got out of Detroit."

"Maybe he's been watching her? Some other kind of surveillance?"

Dunn shook his head and slammed his hand on the table. "Fucking Williams. That's the only way her husband could know. If he was tracking her, he would have been here by now. We saw Williams yesterday. He knew who she was, recognized her from her picture. He must have called her husband."

English held Dunn's gaze for a long moment, but he didn't say anything. Instead, he turned his focus back to the screen and started typing again.

"If he called Ashleigh's husband, we might be able to get a number for Williams. We haven't been able to track him. Get Ashleigh in here. She can give me his number."

"I thought we didn't want to tip him off."

"He's already tipped. He's here. It's time to use it," English said without looking up.

Dunn knew he was right, but it felt like they were using Ashleigh as bait. If they searched for the man, it was possible he had something on his phone to alert him to their search. He was conniving and smart, and if they told him they knew where he was, he wasn't likely to run and hide.

Dunn stomped out of the room and went in search of Ashleigh. He found her in the break room, talking to Dex. Laughing.

"You're joking," she said, wiping tears from the corner of her eyes. "That did not happen."

He nodded. "Oh, it did. Trust me. And it was not pretty."

She laughed again. Dunn just stood there and stared at her. All he'd managed to do was upset her. In less than forty-eight hours, she'd cried in his arms twice, slapped him once, and had a handful of orgasms that threatened his sanity. But he didn't make her laugh.

He cleared his throat, and they both turned to him. Dex smirked and leaned back against the counter. Ashleigh's smile faded. She looked away from him, then stared at his feet.

"Ashleigh, we need your husband's phone number," Dunn said simply.

"Not her husband," Dex said, winking at her.

Dunn clenched his fists, considering using them on his friend. "She still thinks of him that way."

Dex shrugged. "Time for a change."

Dunn was tense, his entire body stretched tight and ready to snap. He wanted to tell Dex that she was the one who reminded him she was married. After he made her scream *his* name. She needed that reminder. She threw it in his face.

Dex refilled his coffee and looked almost bored. He could have been on a hammock by the fucking ocean.

Nothing about the situation was phasing him. Ashleigh was just another client.

"It doesn't matter," Dunn finally growled. "We need the number."

"Then he'll know we're onto him," Dex said calmly. "Are you sure you want to do that?"

"He's here," Dunn said, keeping his eyes on Ashleigh as he spoke to Dex. Her head snapped up, eyes wide as she gaped at him. "Williams must have found him and told him where she was. Crossed the border a little while ago."

"Fuck," Dex mumbled.

"Frederick is here?" Ashleigh said softly. "He knows where I am?"

Dunn shrugged. "We don't know, but it's hard to believe it's a coincidence that he showed up this morning. Williams knew who you were yesterday."

"And I told him I was married," she said with a sigh.

Dunn nodded.

She straightened her shoulders. "I can't sit back and let him hurt people."

Dunn nodded and stepped aside for her to lead the way down the hall. He glanced back at Dex and found his friend checking her out. Dunn growled.

Dex smirked at him and shrugged. "I'm only human."

Dunn wanted to break his fucking face, but they needed him. He glared again, but Dex just smirked even bigger and jerked his head toward the hallway.

"Better go make sure English isn't hitting on her. He noticed how pretty she was before anyone else."

Dunn's head snapped back so fast his neck cracked. He closed his eyes and took a breath, then followed Ashleigh to the conference room while Dex chuckled in the break room.

Fucking assholes.

Ashleigh was rattling off her husband's phone number when Dunn walked back into the conference room. English keyed it into his computer and waited.

"How long will this take?" Ashleigh asked.

English shrugged. "It depends on what kind of software he has. If he has something advanced that scrambles his signal, we might not get him at all. We're hoping that doesn't happen."

"And this will help save the little boy? The one I saw the picture of?"

English glanced at Dunn, then focused on his screen again. Ashleigh followed his gaze and turned to him.

"We've already been in touch with the FBI. They looked into your husband, but the connection is tentative. We told them what you saw, but they still said it's not enough to give them justification for a warrant."

"What? But there's a boy's life in danger. How much justification do they need?"

Dunn shrugged. "I've never worked on a kidnapping case. I don't know what it takes. They did say if you remember anything else to call. English has a number."

"What if I give them permission? It's my house. If I tell them they can go in, does that help?"

Dunn shook his head. "It doesn't work like that. They have to have cause to enter a property, and you're not there."

"Neither is he. This is the perfect time for them to go."

"If there's something else you can tell them, we'll call them back, but otherwise, everything is speculation. Your word is not as valid because you caught him cheating. You could be a wounded spouse out for revenge," Dunn explained. He hated saying the words, but he knew they applied. They were probably the reason she slept with him, too.

Ashleigh stopped and looked up at him. "That's not why I did it," she said softly. "He's not... What happened has nothing to do with him."

Dunn nodded sharply and moved to the other side of the table. He needed distance between himself and Ashleigh. Otherwise, he might do something he regretted. Again.

"Did you find anything yet?" Dunn asked English.

English nodded. "He's in the area. Downtown. See?"

Dunn looked at where English pointed on the screen. "Is this live?"

English nodded. "It's an active trace on his phone. Since we have the number, we can watch it. As long as it's on, we have a signal."

"So we wait?" Dunn asked.

English nodded again. "We wait. And we watch."

"And hopefully we catch them," Dunn added.

12

ASHLEIGH WASN'T SURE WHAT SHE NEEDED TO DO, BUT SHE couldn't sit back and let a child be taken from his family. She tried to think of anything she could remember about Frederick and the woman, but nothing stood out. Especially not anything that could connect him to the kidnapping.

Still, she had to try.

"Can you call the FBI? Maybe they can ask me questions that will trigger something?" Ashleigh said to the room. She looked up and found Daniel and English staring at her.

"Did you remember something else?" Daniel asked.

She shook her head, feeling like a failure. "No, but I have to try to help."

Daniel glanced at English who shrugged. English grabbed the phone in the middle of the table and dialed a number. "Agent Marks please."

Ashleigh chewed on the inside of her cheek while she waited.

"Yes, sir, Ms. Edwards would like to speak to you. Are you available to come to our offices today?" English paused. "No, but she's hoping you'll ask her something that will trigger more information." English paused again. "I understand, sir. She wants to help. For the child." English paused a third time and nodded. "Thank you, sir. See you then." He hung up and looked at Ashleigh. "He'll be here at nine."

Ashleigh nodded, feeling slightly better. She was going to try to help.

Ashleigh spent the next hour running through everything that happened that night in her mind. By the time Agent Marks arrived, she wasn't sure she'd be of any help, but she would do her best.

Daniel led them into one of the smaller conference rooms and introduced them. Ashleigh shook hands with the agent, thankful for the way he smiled at her and the kindness in his eyes.

"Shall we get started?" he asked her.

Ashleigh nodded.

"If you'll excuse us," Agent Marks said to Daniel.

"I'm staying," he said firmly.

"This is an active investigation."

Daniel nodded. "I'm aware. One we are going to help you solve. I was the first person to see Ms. Edwards when she arrived in town. I can help her remember things if she needs it."

Agent Marks glared at Daniel, but when it was clear he wasn't going to win, he sighed. "Fine. But you stay silent unless I ask you to speak."

Daniel nodded and took a seat between them at the oval table.

Agent Marks focused on Ashleigh. "Are you doing okay?" he asked.

She smiled and shrugged. "As okay as expected after finding out my husband is not who I thought he was."

"Who did you think he was?"

"I thought he was a good person. He's always been wealthy, and I thought that was why he was so private."

"But you don't think so now?"

She laughed mirthlessly. "Um, no. It's obvious he's more than that."

"Do you feel that way because you saw him with another woman?"

His question surprised her. She expected it, but the casual way he slid it in reminded her that her marriage was over even if Frederick didn't kidnap that child. He was still not who she thought he was.

"I was mad when I saw that. It's not something I ever expected. He acted like he loved me, but he obviously doesn't. But—"

"Do you love him?" Agent Marks asked.

Ashleigh shrugged. "I thought I did."

"True love doesn't go away just because someone does something that hurts you. If you really loved him, you still should."

"I can't be with a man who cheats on me."

"That doesn't mean you don't love him, though. And if you're just mad at him, you could be accusing him of something to punish him. A way to get back at him for sticking his dick where it doesn't belong."

Daniel stood quickly, sending his chair flying against the wall. He got up close to Agent Marks and growled, "What the fuck is this?"

The agent barely glanced at Daniel. "Answer the question, Ms. Edwards. Do you love your husband?"

"No," Ashleigh breathed. A part of her was relieved to finally say it out loud, but another part of her was ashamed. She spent years with a man she liked, but she never really loved him. She told herself she did, or that she would one day, but she always held a part of herself back from him.

"Why did you marry him?" Agent Marks asked.

"I wanted to love him."

"Because he's rich?"

"She's not the one on trial here," Daniel barked.

"No one is on trial," Agent Marks said. "But if you won't let me do my job, you will have to leave the room. One more word from you, and I will remove you."

"I'm in charge around here. You're not going to remove me."

Agent Marks stood and faced Daniel down. The two of them were nearly eye-to-eye, with murderous looks in their dark gazes. Daniel was wider and stronger, but Agent Marks was younger and faster, judging by the way he moved quickly into Daniel's face.

"If you're in charge, then you know how things like this have to go. If I take her at her word, and she's just pissed off at her husband and shacking up with you, I lose valuable time I could be spending to find a missing child. The fact that I even came down here today says I'm willing to listen, but I need to do this my way, not yours. So sit down and shut up, or I will remove you."

Daniel held his glare for another second, then slowly lowered to his seat. Agent Marks turned his attention back to Ashleigh. She squirmed in her seat but knew she had to be honest if she was going to help.

"I never cared about money, but his money gave me an opportunity to do something I cared about."

"Helping adoption agencies," Agent Marks said with a raised eyebrow.

Ashleigh drew in a breath. "Yes. I helped with their finances. That's why I knew what the paper was when I saw it with Frederick's stuff. It was an adoption docket. A one-page sheet of information about a child that's up for adoption. Nothing identifying, but it's enough for most potential parents to make their decision."

"And you and your husband were looking into adoption yourselves, weren't you?"

Ashleigh nodded. "We were. I wasn't able to get pregnant, and we know how many children out there need homes. We were always open to it."

"How did you first hear about Anthony Madison?"

Ashleigh tried to place the name but couldn't. "I'm sorry, who?"

Agent Marks narrowed his eyes at her. "The missing child. You don't know his name?"

Ashleigh shook her head. "No. I saw the news, which had his picture up. It was online also. It seemed everywhere I looked, his face was there. Maybe it was because we were talking about children but his face was in my head."

"And the docket? You said it had his picture?" Agent Marks asked.

Ashleigh nodded. "It did. It wasn't the same picture as the news, but it was definitely the same child."

"My sister had a baby a year ago," he said with a smile. "Cute little thing. But when I went to see her in the hospital, I had no idea which kid was hers. They had all the babies in the nursery at one point, and I tried to pick out her kid, but they all looked the same to me. Isn't it funny how kids all look the same when they're little?"

Ashleigh nodded, smiling with him.

"So, if you think all babies look alike, how do you know for sure that the child you saw in that picture in your house was the missing child? You were tired from your trip. You were upset. You just saw your husband fucking another woman. Is it possible you made a mistake?"

Ashleigh sucked in a sharp breath. Before she could speak, Daniel jumped out of his chair again, moving toward Agent Marks.

Agent Marks held up his hand and smirked when Daniel stopped. "I told you I'd throw you out if you said another word, Mr. Dunn. Same applies if you throw a punch at me."

The fury pouring off of Daniel was palpable. Ashleigh wanted to sooth him as much as she wanted to slap Agent Marks.

"Are you perfect, Agent Marks?" Ashleigh asked him instead. "Have you ever made a mistake?"

He turned to her with a grin. "Of course."

"So is it possible that other people can as well?"

His grin grew wider. "Absolutely. Thank you for your time, Ms. Edwards. I'll see myself out."

"I didn't make a mistake," Ashleigh said before he reached the door. "Not with the child. There were two pictures, one that was released publicly and the one attached to the docket. I definitely made a mistake in marrying a man who wasn't right for me. I made excuses for his behavior for years, thinking I understood him. But I don't. He's in town right now. He's here because another man, a man I only met yesterday when he slammed a gun into my side, called him." Ashleigh stood and lifted her shirt to reveal the bruise on her side. "Am I angry with my husband? Or, the man I thought was my husband? Yes, I am. But more than that, I'm angry with myself. I feel stupid for believing his lies all these years. Things that I probably would have noticed if I actually cared to spend time with him. But I traveled. I spent as much time away as I could. So when things seemed off, I didn't press. When he didn't talk to me, I felt relieved. And when I walked down the hallway of my house and saw him jerking against that woman, I was hurt, but I was hurt because I felt stupid. I'm sure the affair was going on for a long time because she just accepted it, the same way I accepted sex with my husband for years. It was a duty, my payment for the roof over my head and the freedom to help others. Am I trying to punish him for cheating on me?" Ashleigh laughed. "No. Because I'd have to care about him or have any interest in going back to him, for that to matter. And I don't. Care or want him back. She can have him. You can have him. I don't really care what happens to him. But I care what happens to that child. His family shouldn't have to suffer. I can only imagine the other families that suffered like this, and it makes me sick to know if I'd paid better attention to my husband, I might have been able to stop something like this from ever happening."

Ashleigh choked back the emotion in her throat and swallowed her tears. Agent Marks didn't need them, and he didn't want them. He wanted the truth.

He moved back to his seat and sat. "Tell me everything you know, Ms. Edwards."

Ashleigh nodded. "Please, call me Ashleigh. I don't want any reminders of him."

DUNN SAT in the corner and listened to Ashleigh talk about her husband. Not her husband. The man she thought was her husband. He was still trying to wrap his head around all of it when Agent Marks stood.

"I think we have enough for a warrant. We couldn't have done this without you, Ms... Ashleigh."

"Thank you for listening, Agent Marks. I want him brought to justice, but I want that child found."

"We'll do our best. And thank you for sharing your information so willingly. Having access to your phone records and your account information will go a long way with the judge."

Ashleigh shook Agent Marks' hand. He turned to Dunn and nodded, then walked out the door. Ashleigh sank onto her chair and leaned forward, her elbows on the table and her head in her hands.

"I'm sorry, Ash," Daniel said softly. "I'm sorry for everything you went through over the last eighteen years."

She shrugged. "It was my life. I made the choices I made."

Dunn nodded. "About last night…"

"Don't," she said firmly. "I know I said it never happened, but that doesn't mean I regret it."

"Then what, Ash?"

She turned to him and smiled. "I don't know. But I know I'm a little bit broken right now. Just because I didn't love my husband doesn't mean it doesn't hurt that he slept with someone else. And the other stuff, I hate that I never saw it."

"He wasn't worth seeing," Dunn said harshly.

"Maybe, but people got hurt because of it."

"All of this isn't on you, Ash."

She smiled. "I knew if I ever told him about you, he would have been really jealous. He didn't like me having anyone else in my life. I got close to one of the people I worked with at one of my first companies. She was someone I considered a friend. I told Frederick about going out with her one night. We had some wine and dinner and we talked. I liked having someone to talk to when I was on a trip. The next time I visited there, she had moved to another division, and when I tried to get her to agree to a dinner, she blew me off. For months, she kept telling me we couldn't get together because she was too busy. I finally cornered her one day and forced it out of her. She said she got threats about spending time with me. She didn't know who they came from, but she had a family. She wasn't willing to risk her kids getting hurt."

"He was a controlling asshole."

"And I knew he was. I didn't know it was him. I couldn't have proven it if I tried, but I knew he didn't want me to be close to other people. When we talked about exes, before we got married, I mentioned I dated someone in college. He had this look in his eyes. I didn't tell him much about you except that we dated and it ended before college was over. He didn't push, and I played it off like it was no big deal. If he'd known..."

"I can take care of myself," Dunn said.

Ashleigh nodded. "I know, but you shouldn't have to. Not like that."

Dunn pressed his lips together. He couldn't listen to anymore about Ashleigh's husband. He never treated her well, and she was beating herself up about it.

"Dunn!" English yelled from down the hall.

Dunn and Ashleigh both turned and headed for English's voice.

"He's at the Falls. Right now. At the Observation Tower. Stationary."

"Let's go," Dunn said.

"Frederick?" Ashleigh breathed.

English nodded. "We think he might be meeting with Williams."

Ashleigh's eyes were wide with fear. "He could hurt someone."

"He already has. They both have, Ash. We have to go after them."

"What about the police?"

Dunn shook his head. "We work with Homeland. Your husband and Williams are both people of interest. We'll call them, but we need to go."

"Daniel," she said as he rushed out of the conference room.

"Yeah?" he said.

"Be careful."

He nodded once, then took three steps to her. He didn't think about it as he dipped down and captured her lips. She opened to him instantly, allowing him to sweep his tongue through her mouth. Her breath hitched, pressing her breasts tighter to his chest. He pulled her closer, one hand around her back and the other cupping her jaw, and deepened the kiss.

Ashleigh's arms slid around his waist. He wanted to stay there and hold her and kiss her all day, but he had a job to do. Dunn gentled the kiss and was relieved to find the conference room empty. He kissed her once more, then winked and left, ready to face his demons.

13

Dunn ignored the questioning looks from the rest of the team as they drove across town to the Falls Observation Tower. They needed to get their heads on straight, so even though they all wanted to know what was going on, he wasn't about to get into it. Not on a ten minute drive.

Dunn parked at the visitors center and checked his weapon before he got out of the SUV. They didn't want to scare the casual observer so they were dressed in street clothes, but all of them had at least three weapons on them at any given time.

They met on the sidewalk and headed toward the Observation Tower. Dunn, Jack, and Slade went straight toward the tower, but Dex, Rocky, Archer, and English hung back. There were too many paths for them to risk letting either man escape.

"Comms on," English said in their ears. "Be on the lookout."

"Copy," Dunn said, moving through the crowd as quickly as possible. Summer was always a nightmare at the Falls. People flocked from all over the world to see the spectacle. For two men trying to blend in, it was perfect. For the people trying to find them, it was a nightmare.

Dunn, Jack, and Slade made it to the Tower. "Search the area. I'm going in," Dunn said.

Slade put a hand on his arm. "No. If he comes out, you're faster. I'll go."

Dunn wanted to argue, but Jack nodded.

Slade disappeared into the building alone. Dunn and Jack scanned the area, trying not to look threatening to the families waking around and enjoying their day.

"You sure about getting involved with her again?" Jack asked after a minute.

"It's not the time," Dunn said.

"To get involved? I agree."

"To talk about this," Dunn replied. "We need to stay focused."

"Then why are you sleeping with her?"

"I'm not talking about this with you. It's between Ashleigh and me."

"Not if you screwing her gets us all killed."

Dunn ignored his friend and scanned the area again.

"No sign of them," Slade said through the earpiece. "It's crowded out here, though."

Jack looked at Dunn and said, "I'm coming in. Dunn can handle this."

Jack followed Slade inside, and Dunn was left alone to watch the door. He paced around, smiling at people as they walked by. He was still standing there when Slade and Jack came outside again.

"They weren't there. There's no sign of them," Slade said.

"The signal says he's there," English said.

"No, his phone is. They're onto us," Dex said.

"Fuck," Dunn barked. "And now we lost the one and only lead we had."

"Let's get back and regroup. Maybe Ashleigh can think of something," Archer said.

Dunn drew in a breath and started walking back to the SUV.

"Who the fuck was that?" Frederick demanded.

Williams rolled his eyes. "Well, the guy in charge is the one who's fucking your wife."

Frederick turned to him. The man was clearly not someone used to not getting what he wanted. And what he wanted was his wife back.

"Who the fuck is he?"

"That's the man we're going to destroy. You're going to help me."

"Why would I help you?"

"Because I know those men. I trained those men. And like I told you, they're keeping me from my wife."

Frederick narrowed his eyes at Williams. "All I care about is my wife. I don't give a shit if all of them take a turn with yours."

Williams wanted to shoot the guy in the head for even thinking something like that, but he saw the statement for what it was. A test. If Williams lost his cool with one threat, he was someone Frederick wouldn't trust. If he laughed it off, they could work together.

Williams shrugged. "If you don't work with me, I'll make sure they all get a turn with your wife."

Murder filled the other man's eyes, and Williams knew he had his attention.

"Now that we're on the same page, we need to talk details."

"What kind of details?"

"The details that allow us to kill all those men and walk away with the women who belong to us."

Frederick nodded and led the way to his rental. "Apparently, I'm at your mercy."

Williams smiled. He liked the sound of that.

ASHLEIGH PACED the office the entire time the guys were gone. They all rushed out so fast she didn't even think about being alone in their office, but once they were gone and the place went silent, it was all she could think about.

She didn't know where to go if someone came in. She didn't know what to do. She was trapped as far as she knew, and she didn't even know where she could hide.

She was walking up and down the hall, chewing on her cheek and wishing she had a phone so she could call Daniel, when the elevator door dinged.

She froze. When she rode up with Daniel, he used a card to gain access to the floor, but that didn't mean someone else couldn't have the same card, or a copy or something. She was starting to realize a lot of things she never thought were possible were very possible.

Before the doors opened, she raced into the nearest room. It was an office, but one she hadn't been in yet. She hid behind the door and waited, praying whoever was in the elevator was supposed to be there.

Footsteps walked toward her, but there were no voices. One set of footsteps. Not the team.

Ashleigh's heart throbbed in her chest, trying to get out

and run away. Her pulse roared in her ears as she strained to hear something, anything, that would tell her who was in the building.

The person, likely a man based on the thud his steps made, moved through the building, slowly like he was looking for something. He checked in every room, and when he walked by the door she was hiding behind, Ashleigh covered her mouth with her hand.

He was huge, taller than Daniel. He had a shaved head also, and shoulders almost as wide as the doorway. Ashleigh couldn't see his face, but it didn't really matter. The guy was twice her size and could take her down without a thought.

He walked back down the hall, but instead of leaving, he walked into the conference room.

"No one's here," he said. "How would I know?" He paused. "Do you really think that's better?" Another pause. "I need to get out of here." A pause and a sigh. "Jesus. Ashleigh. Ashleigh, are you here?"

She froze and squeezed her thighs together. He knew her name. She didn't understand why people peed their pants when they were scared, but she was about three seconds from doing just that.

"All right, you're on speaker," the guy said. "I'm walking down the hall. Talk so she knows I'm not here to kill her or something."

"Ash," Daniel's voice came out of the speaker. "Ash, this is Mason. He's a big, ugly shithead, but he's there to protect you. He was at my house the other night. When you got here."

Ashleigh pushed the door she was hiding behind and moved around it to the hallway. "Mason?" she said softly.

He turned and grinned at her. "Got her. She's okay."

"Thank fuck. I owe you, Mace. Thanks," Daniel said. "Ash, we're on our way back."

Ashleigh nodded and kept her eyes on Mason. He promised Daniel he wouldn't let her out of his sight, then hung up.

"Sorry," he said. "I didn't mean to scare you. Dunn told me to get over here right away when he realized no one had a way to reach you. He didn't want you here alone, but they don't always think about things like that."

Ashleigh nodded. "Thank you. I didn't think about it either. Not until the silence descended."

Mason forced a grin. "I know all about that." He turned and walked to the kitchen. "Want a water?"

Ashleigh shook her head and remembered her terror from earlier. "Actually, I'm going to use the bathroom real quick."

Mason nodded and grabbed a bottle of water from the fridge, ignoring her.

Ashleigh scrambled to the bathroom and dropped her head into her hands once her butt was on the seat. She couldn't believe she thought Mason was there to kill her.

He was still in the kitchen when she walked out, eating a massive cupcake that made her mouth water.

"Archer's wife, Lily, makes the best damn cupcakes. She also thinks it's hilarious to put pink frosting on them all the time. Joke's on her, though, because none of us care."

Ashleigh laughed.

"Want one? They're really damn good."

He waved the container toward her and she took a step forward, unable to resist. Frederick didn't like her eating sweets. He reminded her constantly that she needed to watch her weight. He was frustrated that she wasn't a single digit size, but she didn't care. Women were meant to be all shapes and sizes, and all of them were beautiful. Sure, there were times she hated her flabby thighs and large breasts, but when she looked at other women her size, she only saw them as beautiful.

Ashleigh selected a cupcake from the container and licked a swipe through the frosting on top. Mason laughed.

"Sorry," Ashleigh said. "I'm not fit for company most of the time."

Mason shook his head. "I find that hard to believe."

She smiled. "I'm sure Daniel's told you plenty about me."

Mason shook his head again. "Actually, I've only known him about a year. The only woman I've heard mentioned in connection with him is the one who betrayed him overseas. Got all of them in a tight spot and a few of the guys killed. Got herself killed from what they told me, too, so that's definitely not you."

Ashleigh sucked in a breath. She didn't know anything about the woman Mason was talking about. Obviously, Daniel was involved with this woman, but he hadn't mentioned her.

But why would he?

"Well, Daniel and I dated in college. Before he joined the SEALs. I haven't seen him in a long time."

Mason nodded. "I guess that's why the word around you is pretty hush, hush. Sorry about your husband, by the way. He sounds like a real son of a bitch."

Ashleigh waited for the anger or the pain to hit her, but all that hit was laughter. No one had been so blunt with her. They were all treating her like she was a wounded animal to be handled with care. But Mason called it like he saw it.

She burst out laughing and shook her head. "You're right. He is. It works out that he's not my husband. I wonder if I still get half of what he had, though? Then again, it's all probably blood money. I'd rather live with nothing than get anything from him."

"You were with him a long time, though."

Ashleigh shrugged. "It doesn't matter. All that means is I should have seen it coming."

Mason leaned against the counter and leveled her with a stare. "Do you really think we can see everything the people around us don't want us to see?"

Ashleigh opened her mouth to answer, but she closed it again when she realized she didn't have an answer. "I don't know."

Mason shifted and slid his gaze down her body. "For example, when I look at you, I see a woman who's pretty damn pulled together. Nice clothes, fancy shoes, expensive jewelry. Make up and hair done. You're not the kind of woman who is going to fall for a guy like Dunn." He paused, and a breath shuddered from her. "But when you heard his voice, you trusted him. It didn't matter that you didn't know who I was, you trusted him. That makes me think you might still love him."

Ashleigh wanted to deny it, but she couldn't.

"See, the thing I struggle with the most is that you two don't match. You're pressed and polished and he's so messed up he can't tell which way is up half the time. The guy who put a gun in your ribs yesterday? Dunn trusted him with everything. And the woman I mentioned? Dunn thought he loved her. The two of them betrayed him, within a year of each other. He's chasing ghosts." Mason pushed off the counter and moved toward the door, pausing when he was next to Ashleigh. "I don't know if he can handle someone else betraying his trust, Ashleigh. So, if you're not ready to go all in with him, keep your distance and let the man heal."

Before Ashleigh could reply, he was out the door and saying hello to the rest of the team as they walked into the office. Ashleigh just stood there, processing his words.

When Daniel walked in, he touched her back, letting his fingers linger. She jumped and moved away from his touch. She tried not to notice the way his face fell, but she saw it. And she saw when he pasted on a bland look and told her they didn't find anything at the tower.

"I thought they were there," Ashleigh said. The last thing she wanted to talk about was her ex and the man who wanted them all dead, but it was safer than talking about the way she felt.

Daniel nodded. "They were. We think they knew we were going to track the phone and ditched it. It's likely they were watching us the whole time."

"Seriously?" Ashleigh breathed.

Daniel nodded again. "Yeah. Unfortunately, it means we need more help from you. Thoughts about where he would go. What he would do."

Ashleigh shrugged. "We've never been here. I don't know of anyone he'd be in touch with."

Daniel sighed. "Okay, well, let us know if you think of something. We have work to do. Slade wants everyone to come to his house tonight. We try to get together outside work once a week. Unless you're not up for it?"

Ashleigh shook her head. "No, that sounds good."

Daniel nodded. "Good." He turned to walk away. "Oh, and we have extra phones if you want one. They're company numbers in case we lose one of ours. Obviously, you can't call anyone you know, but you can have a phone."

Ashleigh smiled. "Thanks. That would be good. Any good games? I need to do something to keep my mind off everything."

Daniel laughed and nodded. "I'm sure there are. Just ask English if there's something you want added. He'll take care of it. He's in his office."

Ashleigh drew in a breath. Daniel was distancing himself from her. Just like she was trying to do. After Mason's talk, she knew it was the right thing since she wasn't ready to jump into a new relationship. That didn't make it easy.

Daniel pointed to English's office on his way past, and kept walking. She pasted on a grin and turned away. She spent the last eighteen years without Daniel Dunn in her life. She could survive the rest.

DUNN BARELY LISTENED as Dex laid out his plan for Kate Maddox. He knew it was important, but he couldn't think straight. Just like the last time Ashleigh was in his life, nothing mattered to him except her.

"What do you think?" Dex asked the room.

Dunn pulled his head back to the conversation and glanced around. Everyone was looking at him. Not directly, but they were all waiting for him to say something.

"Looks good," he answered.

Dex held his gaze for a long minute, then walked over and closed the door to the conference room.

Dunn's fight-or-flight instinct threatened to kick in. Seeing as he was as far from the door as he could get, there was only one option, and he didn't feel like kicking his team's ass. Especially since he wasn't sure he could.

"Let's get it out there," Dex said calmly.

"What?" Dunn asked.

"Ashleigh. All this. Tell us what's going on," Dex said.

Dunn looked around the room at the curious and concerned faces and laughed. "Did we all hand over our dicks and I missed it?" He patted his crotch. "I still have mine, which means I'm not talking about my feelings."

"So you do have feelings?" Jack said. More like spat.

"Listen, all of you. I'm not going into this with you. Whatever happened with Ashleigh when we were in college ended the day I left for Coronado. She moved on, and so did I."

"Yeah, and got fucked up all over again," Jack said.

"I'm not fucked up," Dunn argued.

"Yeah, you are," Archer said. "Listen, I'm fucked up. We all are. The shit we saw and did over there was one thing, but Williams? That's a whole different level. And right after what you went through with Ashaki? Are you sure you should be sleeping with a client?"

"Isn't that how you got your wife?" Dunn threw back at him.

Archer nodded. "It is. And she's the best fucking thing that ever happened to me. Can you honestly say the same for Ashleigh, because I'm pretty damn sure you spent most of your first few years on the Teams regretting walking away from her."

"Who the hell told you that?" Dunn demanded.

"Williams. Do you really think you're the only one who talked to him?" Archer said. "He took my brother. He took my wife. He let me take the blame for killing my best friend. You're not the only one he betrayed."

"I should have seen it!" Dunn roared. "I was with him constantly. I asked him about his family. I talked to him about it, about every-damn-thing. And he cooked up this whole plan to fuck up the Navy and blow up half the fucking city. It was under my nose the entire damn time, and I never saw it."

"Sounds like Ashleigh," Mason said.

Dunn whirled on him. "What the hell do you know about her?"

Mason shrugged. "Not much, except she blames herself for her husband's actions. If anyone in this room knows who's to blame for something, it's me. Do you blame Ashleigh for her husband's actions?"

"What? No. Of course not," Dunn sputtered.

Mason shrugged again. "Then I'm not really sure why you blame yourself for Williams'. Or for that Ashaki chick. Both of them acted in their own best interest. They didn't give a fuck about you or anyone else they were hurting. So stick it up their fucking asses and let them deal with the damn consequences. It's not on you to do it."

Dunn stared at Mason. He made it all sound simple. Just put all the blame on them. Could he do it, though?

14

―――――――

DEX FINALLY MOVED THE MEETING BACK TO THE CONVERSATION at hand, and they all approved his plans for Kate Maddox. When the rest of them left the room, he took a seat next to Dunn.

"Can you handle all this?" Dex asked.

"All what?"

"Williams, Ashleigh, and Kate Maddox? It's a lot if it's just one," Dex said.

Dunn nodded. "I got it." He stood and picked up his notepad.

"Let me take Kate Maddox."

"You know she's getting married," Dunn said.

Dex rolled his eyes. "I'm not trying to get into her pants. Just because the rest of you got involved with the client doesn't mean I'm going to."

"I'm not involved with her," Dunn argued.

"Could have fooled me," Dex said, walking away.

Dunn stood there for another minute, unsure what he wanted to do. If it was a regular day, he'd go out for a run or punish himself in the gym. But it wasn't a regular day, and he had Ashleigh.

She was sitting in his office, shifting in her chair, when he walked in. She stilled and looked up at him with a distant smile.

"Listen, I feel like I've held you captive. Is there anything you need to do? People you need to call? You can use the office lines because they go through multiple towers and are untraceable."

Ashleigh shook her head and shifted again.

"Are you okay?"

She nodded. "Yeah. Um, actually, I wouldn't mind doing some shopping. Is that something you'd be okay with?"

"Shopping?" Dunn asked. She couldn't be serious.

"Yeah. You know, where people go buy things at a store," she said, her voice dripping with sarcasm.

Dunn groaned. "I know what shopping is. I just hate doing it."

Ashleigh shook her head and shifted again. "Okay, it's fine. Don't worry about it."

Dunn sighed and shook his head. He was definitely going to regret it, but he closed his eyes and said, "Let's go."

"Really?" Ashleigh asked, sounding far more excited than should be possible. "You'll take me?"

Dunn nodded. "Yeah, but one store. And we aren't staying long. Can you handle that?"

She nodded vigorously. "Yes, thank you. Yes."

She moved closer like she was going to hug him, then stopped and smiled at him. "I'm ready when you are."

God help him, he was going shopping. With Ashleigh.

THEY SNUCK out the back way so Dunn didn't have to tell anyone they were going shopping. He still couldn't believe he agreed to it. Ashleigh suggested Target, and thankfully, he knew where it was.

Ashleigh seemed to know where she was going, so he followed behind her inside the store. He looked around the entire time, watching for anyone who could be following them or watching them. He made note of where the cameras were and the employees, just in case.

The whole time, he watched Ashleigh. She was his job, so he told himself it was work, but it was more than that. The guys were right. He was in deep. And it was pulling his focus.

Ashleigh went to the women's section first. Dunn wasn't sure where he thought she would go, but when she headed for the casual clothes, he was definitely surprised. She'd been wearing nice clothes since she got there, and seeing her fingering the cotton shorts and everyday tees had him thinking about her in his tee.

And he was hard again. Dammit.

He thought about his mom and grandmother and willed his dick to settle down. Thankfully, it did the trick, and he could focus again.

Ashleigh chose three pairs of shorts and a pair of capris that looked soft and comfortable, then added a few plain tees and one that advertised Niagara Falls. She flashed him a sheepish grin, then pushed her red cart over to the intimates section.

Kill me now.

Dunn sucked in a breath and followed her. She was his responsibility, and where she went, he went. Dear God, help him.

She grabbed a modest pajama set, but her gaze lingered

on a sexy tank and shorts set. She chewed the inside of her cheek and gave her head a little shake.

"Why don't you get both?" he asked.

She shook her head again. "I don't need two."

Dunn shrugged. "Yeah, but if you like that one, get it."

She shook her head but glanced back at the set like she was considering it.

Dunn grabbed it off the rack and tossed it into her cart. "My treat."

She grabbed it and went to hang it back up, then paused. Her eyes went wide, and she dropped her hand back to her side. Her shoulders sagged, and she looked like she was going to fall over.

"Ash, what's wrong?"

She sucked in a ragged breath and put the pajamas back. Then put the other ones back.

"Ash, what are you doing?" he demanded when she started to walk back to where they were at first.

She finally stopped and looked up at him. "I just realized I can't pay for any of this. I always use cards, and I can't use them. I mean, he knows where I am, so maybe I can, but I don't want anything else from him. I'll just... deal with it."

Dunn sighed and bumped her out of the way. He steered the cart back to the pajama section and grabbed the two items she had.

"Daniel, I can't buy them."

"I'll buy them, Ash."

She shook her head. "I can't ask you to do that."

"You're not asking. I'm doing it because I have the money, and I don't mind."

"But—"

"Ash, just let me. It's the least I can do. Now, what else do you need?"

She chewed the inside of her cheek again and glanced around.

"Come on, Ash. Just tell me. I don't care what it is or how much it costs. If you need it, we'll get it."

"Panties," she said so softly he was sure he heard her wrong.

"What did you say?"

She sighed and looked up at him, giving him one of her annoyed looks. "Panties. I need panties. I didn't pack more clothes when I left my husband. I just ran out of there before he caught me. All the clothes I've been wearing were left over from my trip. And I ran out of clean panties yesterday."

Dunn's gaze fell to her center. He swallowed roughly and closed his eyes. "Are you telling me you're not wearing any panties? That you haven't been all day?" he forced out.

When she didn't answer, he opened his eyes. She shrugged and nodded. "I didn't really have a choice. I'd rather go without than wear dirty ones, and doing laundry wasn't my first priority."

Not even thinking about his mother or grandmother was going to eliminate that erection. His cock pressed hard against his zipper and begged to be let out. He thought about the squirming he caught Ashleigh doing all day and nearly embarrassed himself even more. In the middle of fucking Target.

"Get what you need," he growled, gripping the handle of the cart so hard his knuckles ached.

Ashleigh's cheeks flamed red, but she turned and walked toward the massive display of panties on the wall that divided the section they were in from the one behind it. Dunn followed her, praying she didn't pick something insanely sexy that he wouldn't be able to stop picturing her in.

Oh, hell, who was he kidding. Everything Ashleigh wore was sexy, and he was going to picture her in all of it. He was going to be lucky if he slept ever again.

Ashleigh looked through pack after pack of panties, searching for what, Dunn didn't know. When she sighed, he finally asked, "What's wrong?"

"I can't find my size."

"What size are you?" he asked, immediately hating the question. It was close. Too close. Intimate.

"Nine."

Dunn nodded and focused on the display in front of him. He never knew there were so many choices for women's underwear. He always bought the same thing. Boxer briefs, black. He didn't care what brand. But women's underwear came in about a dozen styles and more colors than the rainbow had. There were packs of three up to packs of twelve. If the section he walked through was right, you could also buy them one by one, but those were the sexy, lacy, silky ones. He wouldn't have made it out of the store if Ashleigh bought those.

He found a pack with a nine on the top and held it up to her. She shrugged. "That's fine."

"But it's not what you like."

She shook her head. "No, it's okay."

"What are you looking for?"

She sighed. "Those go up really high. The leg is high and the waist is high, and for me, they end up rolling down over my belly. It just annoys me. I usually prefer boy shorts or bikinis."

Dunn put the package back and crouched down again. He flipped through the panties again, wondering how in the hell men survived shopping with their wives and girlfriends. If Ashleigh was his, he'd have already demanded she try on about half the store and taken his time stripping her out of each item.

Fuck. He had to get his head back on straight. She wasn't interested. She made that more than clear.

Dunn found another option, and Ashleigh agreed to it. She said that was all she needed, and they headed for the register.

"Oh, wait. I need a few things for the bathroom. If it's okay."

Dunn nodded and followed her again. She went up and down the aisles until she found the razors. She grabbed a pack of disposables and a bottle of shaving cream, then added a poof ball thing and a bottle of body wash.

"Do you have shampoo?"

She shook her head. "I've been using yours. I guess I should get my own, though. Well, not really mine since you're paying for all this."

"It's all yours, Ash. Get what you need."

She added shampoo and a bottle of conditioner, then got in line at a register. She chewed on her cheek the entire time they waited their turn.

"What is it?" Dunn asked quietly.

She shook her head. "Nothing."

"It's not nothing. What's going on?"

She smiled up at him. "It's funny that you still know me so well."

Dunn shrugged. "You're hard to forget. And you're changing the subject."

She smiled again. "I just don't like any of this."

Dunn nodded. "Neither do I."

When it was their turn, Ashleigh made small talk with

the cashier. Dunn almost choked when he saw the total, but it was a small price to pay for Ashleigh's safety.

They carried the bags out of the store and were on their way back to his house when his phone rang. Lily popped up on the screen in the car.

He answered and said, "Hey, Lily. What's up?"

"Where are you?"

"On my way home. Why?"

"Are you bailing on tonight?"

"No, I'll be there."

"Do you promise?" Lily asked.

Ashleigh shifted in her seat again. Dunn glanced at her and caught her frowning at the screen.

"Yes, Lil. I'll be there. Archer told us earlier. Mason ate all your cupcakes, by the way."

Ashleigh's eyes widened, and she smiled to herself.

"Ah, jeez. I told Archer to make sure everyone got cupcakes. I thought the pink was particularly manly."

Dunn laughed. "Yep, definitely manly. Are you bringing more tonight?"

She sighed. "You know I will, since you asked."

Dunn chuckled. "Thanks, Lil."

"Is Ashleigh with you?"

"Is that why you're really calling?"

"Well, Daniel Dunn lets a woman into his house and goes all gaga over her, you know I want to meet her."

"Lily!" Dunn yelled, but it was too late.

"Uh oh. She's with you, isn't she?"

"Yeah, she is."

"And she can hear everything I'm saying, can't she?"

"Right again."

"Shit. I'm sorry."

"We gotta go, Lily!"

"Wait, but—"

Dunn hung up the phone with a tap to the screen. He gripped the steering wheel again and focused on the road, not looking at Ashleigh.

After a minute, Ashleigh cleared her throat. "So, she sounds nice."

"Lily thinks she's our mother."

Ashleigh laughed. "She cares."

Dunn nodded. "Yes, she does."

"Her cupcakes are delicious, too."

Dunn glanced at her with narrowed eyes. "How do you know?"

She smirked. "Mason shared with me."

"A cupcake better be all he shared with you," Dunn growled.

Ashleigh just smirked again.

SEEING Daniel jealous was a boost to her confidence. Ashleigh wasn't the kind of woman who usually had more than one man interested in her, but it was fun letting Daniel think Mason might have been.

They got to his house, and he carried her bags inside, closing his door with a hard slam and taking all her stuff to his room. He set the bags on the bed and started to walk out, but Ashleigh got in front of him.

"Do you really think I would do anything with Mason?" she asked.

He glared at her. "How the hell would I know? You've made it clear you don't want me. Maybe you want him."

She laughed. "Are you kidding me right now? You know you're being stupid."

"Gee, thanks."

He pushed past her, and she went after him. "The only reason I even talked to Mason today was because you were on the phone with him. I was hiding because I didn't know who he was, but I trusted you. And you said I could trust him."

"Yeah, I thought I could, too."

"You know what Mason and I did after he gave me a cupcake? We talked. And you know what we talked about? Me messing with your head. Mason told me I needed to walk away from you if I wasn't sure I was all in. And he told me about Ashaki. He said you can't handle another betrayal."

"Mason needs to stay in his own lane."

Ashleigh shook her head. "Every single one of the men I've met over the last few days looks up to you. They all look to you for guidance and direction. They trust you, and they will follow you through fire if that's what it takes. And all of them know I hurt you, so they're protecting you the only way they know how."

"They all need to stay out of my business."

"They care, Daniel."

"They have a funny way of showing it."

"Do they? Because I think you're doing the same thing to me. The only time since I've been here that we were real to each other was when we were yelling at each other."

"So you want me to yell at you?"

She smiled. "No, but I want you to tell me you hate me. Or tell me you wish I'd never shown up. Or tell me to go away. I don't know what you want to say, but I wish you'd say it."

"I miss you," Daniel said quietly, the words soaked in regret and longing.

"What?"

He sucked in a breath. "Jack and Williams know about you because they saw me when I was still trying to get over you. They were there. The others just heard about you. I never got over you, Ash. You were gone, so after a while, I just stopped thinking about you constantly, but I never stopped missing you."

"I missed you, too. That's why I kept in touch with your grandmother."

"I still can't believe she told you where to find me and didn't warn me."

Ashleigh laughed and nodded. "She always liked me."

Daniel closed his eyes and shook his head, laughing. "There were times I thought she liked you more than me. She was pissed when things ended between us."

She smiled sadly. "She wasn't the only one."

Daniel sobered at her words. "I'm sorry I kept it from you, Ash. I didn't tell you I wanted to be a SEAL, but every time I told you I loved you, I meant it. I wanted a life with you."

"But now it's too late," she said sadly.

Daniel sucked in a breath and took a step back.

"I'm sorry I messed up your life, Daniel."

"You didn't."

"Not just before, but now. I shouldn't have come here. I should have called the police in Detroit and let them handle it."

Daniel shook his head. "No, I'm glad you came. No matter what's happened between us, you can always come to me when you need something."

Ashleigh smiled. "I just don't want to make things harder on you. I was selfish to come here. The last time I felt truly safe was when I was with you. And I just couldn't imagine going anywhere else."

Daniel nodded and pulled her to him. He wrapped his arms around her and she sank into him, letting him take away all the fear and shame she felt when she thought about Frederick.

After a minute, Daniel pulled away and said, "You need to go put on some of those panties because if I have to spend all night knowing you're not wearing any, I won't be able to control myself."

She gasped, and he winked at her, then walked away.

Ashleigh chuckled and went back to his room. She closed the door and stared at the new clothes on his bed. She chewed on her lip and debated. She always loved pushing Daniel, and the flirty side of him was impossible to resist. Even if she knew better.

15

———————

Daniel's friends were hilarious. Between Slade's dog, Howler, barking loudly at everyone when they walked in to the affectionate ribbing they all gave each other, it was clear to Ashleigh that Daniel built a good life for himself.

She was happy for him. A part of her was a little jealous, but she was happy for him. She wanted him to have everything he wanted. He talked about doing good in the world and having a family of his own. She always thought he would have been an amazing father, but the idea of Daniel having kids with someone else hurt more than she was ready to admit.

"So, Ashleigh, tell us about Dunn in college," Archer said. "Did he always have a stick up his ass?"

Everyone laughed, and Daniel flipped Archer off.

Ashleigh shook her head. "I'm pretty sure that's something the Navy put in for him."

"Ohhhhh," they all chorused.

"No, Daniel was much looser in college. He was the one who approached me. He said he saw me on campus and basically stalked me until he got up the courage to ask me out."

Daniel rolled his eyes but didn't contradict her story. The rest of the guys gave him shit for it.

"The only way you could get a woman to date you was to stalk her?" Jack asked.

Daniel shook his head. "No. The only way I could get that woman to date me was to stalk her. She was the only one I wanted."

The woman said, "awww," and the men pretended to gag. Ashleigh looked at Daniel and smiled. He winked at her again, like he'd been doing most of the night.

She definitely should have worn those panties because every time he gave her one of those looks, she had to clench her thighs together. She really hoped she didn't have a wet spot on the back of her shorts when she stood.

"What about you, Ashleigh?" Archer asked. "Did you just say yes so he'd stop following you around?"

Ashleigh laughed with the group. "No. I said yes because he was cute. Of course, he didn't tell me about the stalking until after we'd been dating a few months. By then I figured he hadn't killed me so I was safe."

"Hey, hey," Daniel said above the noise of the group. "It wasn't stalking. I was just trying to find her again. I saw her once, then not again for a while. I tried to do recon, but I didn't know anything about her."

"No name, age, social security number, and mother's maiden name?" Dex asked.

Ashleigh snorted a laugh.

"You guys are horrible," Daniel said, dropping back in his seat.

Ashleigh was across from him on the couch. She stared

at him, enjoying how relaxed he looked. He'd looked more like the Daniel she remembered from college since they talked.

He glanced at her and caught her watching him. He narrowed his eyes in question. She shook her head. He tilted his head, and she just smiled, then turned back to the conversation.

The group talked and joked and picked on each other. There was a lot of love in the room, and not just from the three couples, although it flowed there, too. The ease they all had with each other was something Ashleigh hadn't witnessed or experienced since she and Daniel split up.

She couldn't help but wonder if she would be a part of this group if she and Daniel had stayed together. She also wondered if he would be. If she asked him to stay, he would have, and then he never would have met the people who'd become his family.

She wished she was stronger. That she could have been the woman he needed and stood by him and waited for him while he served their country. Military wives impressed Ashleigh, always had. She couldn't imagine having a spouse overseas, completely unavailable, and worrying about him while also having to maintain some sense of normal at home. They were heroes, too.

"So, Ashleigh, when all this is over, what are you going to do?" Pilar, Jack's girlfriend, asked.

Ashleigh shrugged. "I haven't even had time to think about it. I have a degree, and I've been using it, but I don't know."

"Are you going back to Detroit?" Lily asked.

Ashleigh's gaze strayed to Daniel. He was watching her, but when she glanced at him, he got up and went to the kitchen. Howler followed him and barked, making everyone wince.

"Howler, hush!" Slade yelled. The dog turned to him and howled again. Slade just shook his head and looked at Lily. "Those obedience classes suck."

Lily smirked. "It's not the dog who needs to be trained." Slade glared at her, but she just laughed. "You know it's true."

"Doesn't mean I like it."

Daniel gave Howler a piece of meat from the decimated food on the counter, and he finally quieted.

"Did you feed him?" Slade asked.

"Nope," Daniel said without hesitation. "I can't help it if a piece just fell on the floor."

"Nothing falls on the floor with that dog. Except him," Slade said lovingly. "He'll skid halfway around the room if food is free."

Howler looked up at Daniel, and he dropped another piece. The dog snatched it up before it got even close to hitting the ground.

"Stop feeding him!" Slade said loudly, which set Howler off again. "Oh, come on!"

Ashleigh laughed when Daniel dropped one more piece of meat and Howler stopped. Daniel looked up and winked at her, then pressed a finger to his lips. She locked hers and winked back at him.

"You two are pretty flirty," Kelsea said with a grin. "I've never seen Daniel like this."

Ashleigh liked Jaymes's girlfriend. She introduced herself right away and explained that she was a professor who studied depression and she was willing to talk if Ashleigh ever needed to talk to someone. She wasn't quite ready to open up to a stranger who wasn't really a stranger, but she appreciated the offer.

"He was always like this when we were younger. I hate that he's not the same man," Ashleigh said.

Kelsea shrugged. "We all change. He's older now, and he clearly has a lot more responsibility. But I think it's you that brings this side of him out. You're good for him."

Ashleigh pursed her lips. "Not everyone thinks so. None of the guys want us involved."

"Who cares what they think," Kelsea said. "It's not their lives. If you and Daniel care about each other, you're adults. You can decide what you want to do. Neither of you are with anyone else, and if you want to see if there's still something there, you should be allowed to do that."

Ashleigh smiled. She liked the way Kelsea thought. Getting involved with Daniel didn't have to be an all or nothing thing. They could get to know each other again. The chemistry between them was still off the charts, just like the sex, but they didn't know each other as people anymore. Having a chance to get to know him and see if they could have something was a good idea.

"Do you need another drink?" Daniel asked from right next to her.

Ashleigh nodded. "Yeah, thanks." She handed over her glass and held his gaze for a long moment. He smiled at her and when he walked away, he adjusted himself.

"You two definitely won't have trouble finding out if there's any heat left. I think I got scorched from those looks," Kelsea said with a grin. "Good for you. And him."

Ashleigh smiled and watched Daniel walk back to her. His gaze slid down his body then back up to his face. He smirked and shook his head. "You're trouble," he whispered when he handed her the cup.

She nodded and left it at that. He'd figure out just how much trouble she was later.

"MY TEAM IS GOING to think I was a loser in college," Dunn said with a grin when they were back in his SUV.

Ashleigh laughed, and he loved the sound. A night out with the team and the girls was exactly what she needed. She'd definitely been wound tight since she showed up, and a little wine and some girl talk seemed to be just the ticket to get her to relax.

"I think they all know you were amazing."

Dunn chuckled. "I'm not so sure about that."

"I am. You were magnetic. You still are. Everyone quiets down when you talk. They want to hear what you have to say. That's not a quality you got from the Navy."

"No, I just got the stick up my ass," he said with a smirk.

Ashleigh laughed again. "Well, you were a lot more relaxed when we were in college."

"So were you," he countered. "If memory serves, you were the one who wanted to streak through campus."

Ashleigh laughed. "Oh, my God. I forgot about that. I still wish I'd done it."

"You would have gotten arrested," Dunn said with a shake of his head.

"Probably," Ashleigh replied with a laugh. "But it would have been a hell of a story."

"We had some pretty great stories," Dunn said softly.

Ashleigh huffed a laugh. "Yeah, we sure did."

They were quiet for the rest of the ride. When they got inside, Dunn turned to Ashleigh at the same time she turned to him.

"You go first," he said.

"Um, I was just going to ask if you want to watch a movie or something. You probably have to be up early, well, I guess we both do, but I just—"

"I was going to ask you the same thing," Dunn said.

Ashleigh smiled, and the years since they were together slipped away. They stood there, staring at each other for a long moment. Dunn wanted to touch her, or kiss her, or something, but he couldn't be rejected again.

He broke the tension between them and walked to the couch. "Feel free to change into those pajamas you got earlier," he said with a grin.

Ashleigh gasped, then laughed. "What do you sleep in?"

Dunn looked back at her over his shoulder. "I sleep naked."

Her cheeks went red, but she said, "Are you going to change?"

Dunn chuckled and shook his head. She walked down the hall before he lost it. *Thank fuck.*

Dunn flipped through the channels and didn't find anything, so he flipped over to Netflix. Ashleigh never liked scary movies, but she was always up for something with a lot of action. He hoped she had the same taste in movies, since it was his favorite genre also.

He was debating between two movies when she walked back down the hall. "Hey, have you seen either of these?" he asked, then turned to look at her and almost swallowed his tongue. "Holy. Fucking. Shit."

She smiled and blushed.

She was wearing the tiny, sexy pajamas she didn't want to buy. Her full breasts pressed against the tiny tank top. The thin straps over her shoulders looked like they would snap without much encouragement at all. And Dunn really didn't need any encouragement.

The shorts were barely more than panties. Her curvy thighs were on full display, and the memory of burying his face between her thighs just twenty-four hours earlier scorched what was left of his brain cells.

"I wanted to see what you thought about it," she said softly.

"I think I'm going to need a cold shower before I get any sleep. Ever again."

She laughed softly. "I like it."

"Yeah, me, too."

She walked closer and sat on the other end of the couch, tucking her feet under her.

"What are you doing, Ash?" he managed to ask.

She looked at him and blushed again. "I'm being selfish again. I know I'm hot and cold. I'm not being very fair. I shouldn't do this to you. But..."

"But what?" he croaked.

"But I still care about you, Daniel. I want to get to know you again. To see if maybe we could have something again."

Dunn swallowed thickly. There was a part of him that wanted the same thing. Or really anything she wanted as long as she was dressed like that. But another part of him that knew he wasn't any good for her. He would ruin her, just like he ruined Ashaki.

"You said Mason mentioned Ashaki?"

She nodded, shifting to turn slightly toward him.

"Mason didn't know her. He didn't know the whole story."

"Do you want to tell me what happened?"

Dunn took a breath and knew he had no other choice. "Ashaki was our informant. She was a local, and over time, we developed a relationship with her and she started helping us. After months of feeding us information that led to the capture of multiple threats, she was given more freedom. Slowly, the powers that be allowed her access to the base and she could basically go wherever she wanted. I saw her in the mess hall and sat with her. She was funny and interesting. After a few weeks of having lunch with her, we ended up in bed."

Dunn glanced at Ashleigh, but her face was a mask.

"We knew it wasn't allowed, but we didn't care. I told myself she cared about me, and that we were building something. We talked about her coming back to the States with me when I was out."

He paused, realizing that what Ashaki did to him was the same thing he did to Ashleigh. He looked up at her, but she was looking away.

"She was a double agent. The people she gave us over the months she was an informant were small potatoes. We knew that, but we were getting closer to the bigger fish, so they trusted her. I trusted her." He drew in a breath and stared away, not seeing the room around him. "We had a mission. It was a big one. We were going after one of the big fish. She wanted to meet up with me that day, but I told her I couldn't. She asked why, but I just told her it wasn't an option. She figured out what was going on and told the man we were going after. They were waiting for us. We lost a lot of men that night, including the man Williams killed, one of our own. They did, too, and when it was all over, Ashaki was there. They'd beaten and raped her and left her for dead. They succeeded, and by the time we found her body, she was gone."

"Oh, Daniel," Ashleigh breathed.

He finally realized he wasn't there and shook his head to clear the fog. Tears streaked down Ashleigh's cheeks. "Ashaki was playing us the entire time. She worked to gain our trust so she could bring information back to the other side. She was only with me because I knew other things. I never figured it out, and I helped her bring down our Team."

"It wasn't your fault," Ashleigh said quietly.

Dunn scoffed. "Yeah, it was. I trusted her. I thought she cared about me. I let my feelings cloud the truth. When she started asking questions, I should have told my superiors. I should have never gotten involved with her in the first place."

"You loved her," Ashleigh said softly.

Dunn sucked in a ragged breath. "I thought I did."

"I know the feeling. I thought I loved Frederick. I told myself it was just different than when I was in love with you. For us, we were young. Passion and freedom and excitement ruled us. We had the world in front of us and nothing stood in our way. It was intoxicating. With Frederick, I was an adult. I'd already been living on my own and taking care of myself. I wanted stability and companionship, not blinding passion and endless excitement. I knew those things weren't real. Not forever. Passion fades and excitement dulls. I told myself I didn't need them, and that I'd grown up. After being here with you, I know all that was a lie."

"Ash," he groaned.

Ashleigh eased toward him. "You loved another woman, and I loved another man. We both made the wrong choice. But us together... that never felt wrong. Letting you go felt wrong."

"Ashleigh," he said again.

She shook her head and moved into his space. "I know the timing is horrible. I know getting involved is probably stupid. But I also know no one has ever made me feel the way you do. Like I can do anything. Like I'm beautiful and sexy and that I can have all those things I lost when we ended. That passion is still there, Daniel. I know you feel it, too. I don't want to let it go again. Not tonight. Please."

16

ASHLEIGH STOOD THERE WITH HER HEART ON HER SLEEVE, waiting for Daniel to say something. If he refused her, she had her answer. If he kissed her, she had hope.

Both options were terrifying.

Seconds ticked by with every beat of her heart, and she waited. She wasn't going to walk away this time. He needed to tell her to. Otherwise, she was staying.

In one swift move, he slid his arm around her back and drew her to him. He pressed his lips to hers before she could take a breath and licked his way into her mouth.

She moaned and threw her arms around his neck, smiling as he devoured her.

Daniel stood and set two large hands on her ass and carried her down the hall to his bedroom. He kicked the door closed and laid her on the bed, then stood back and looked at her.

"I'm still thinking about you walking around all day without panties on. From the second you told me that, I knew I had to have you again," he growled.

She smirked and said, "I never put my new ones on."

He groaned. "I told you I wasn't going to be responsible for my actions."

She grinned. "I was counting on it."

He stripped his shirt off, baring his chest to her. It was the first time she'd really seen him. Dark brown slashes across his skin and puckered spots showed the wounds he'd suffered. She wanted to ask him about what he went through, but they'd shared enough pain for one night. Pleasure was all she was interested in for a few hours.

Daniel came down over her and positioned himself between her thighs. He was hard and urgent with his strokes, even though they both still had clothes on. She moaned at the feel of him. He captured the sound with a kiss that had her grabbing on to him and praying the night never ended.

"Let's see how good you look in my bed," Daniel said roughly. The deep timbre and the rough need in his voice sent shivers through her. But it was his eyes, the endless black pools that watched her every move, that did her in.

"Please, Daniel," she begged, reaching for her shirt.

He put his hand over hers. "Let me." He eased her shirt up, kissing every inch of skin as he exposed it.

Ashleigh was so blissful she barely processed him touching and kissing her body. She'd changed since college. He'd seen her naked, but she had her back to him. Laying down on his bed with all her flabby parts flopping around was a different experience.

"You're beautiful," he whispered against her ribs. "Delicious."

She sighed happily at the needy tone of his voice. She ran her hand over his head and smiled. Daniel had short hair when she knew him, but the shaved head gave him a harder look. Rougher. More alpha.

"You're going to scream my name again tonight," Daniel said, lifting her to pull her shirt off. "But tonight, you're not going to tell me this can't happen again. Tonight, you're mine all night."

She trembled at the possessive sound of his voice, then moaned when he bit down on her nipple.

He shifted his hips against hers while he teased her breasts. She wrapped her legs around his narrow hips and let herself feel the pleasure Daniel offered so willingly. He was always the kind of man who made sure she was mindless and boneless before he let himself have anything.

"Tell me what you want, Ash. Talk to me."

"I want you," she said automatically.

"You have me, baby. What do you want me to do to you?"

"Kiss me," she breathed.

He obliged instantly, moving up to put his lips on hers. The kiss was sweet, painfully so. His hips continued to press against hers, but his kiss was borderline chaste with closed-mouth pecks traded between them.

"Kiss me," she begged again.

He finally got the point and pushed his tongue between her lips. She moaned and slid her tongue next to his, battling to see who could make the other lose control first.

His hand on her breast tugged her bra to the side, and he won the battle. Like he always did. Ashleigh broke their kiss to moan loudly when he rasped his thumb over her taut nipple.

Daniel kissed his way down her throat, then drew her nipple into his mouth and flicked it with the tip of his tongue. Ashleigh moaned and held him in place. He smiled against her skin and pressed his hand over the other bra cup.

The feel of his weight on top of her, his tongue and hand caressing her, and his erection pressing against her were like heaven. She let go of all her fears about not being enough for him and pleasure took over. Each stroke of his hips pushed her closer to the edge, and when he switched sides to take her other nipple into his mouth, she let herself fall.

"Oh, God, Daniel. Yes!"

Her orgasm triggered something in him, and he bit her nipple, sending another burst of flames through her body. She cried out again and trembled with an aftershock.

He yanked the straps of her bra down, exposing all of her, then put her hands on herself. "Touch yourself. I have somewhere else to be."

For a second, panic swept in. Then he kneeled between her thighs and drew her shorts down her hips. He groaned when cool air hit her core, exposing her bare skin to his view.

"You have the prettiest pussy, Ash. I've missed this." He let her shorts slide to the floor and pressed her knees apart and inhaled. "You're wet, baby. Have you been thinking about me?"

"All day," she admitted. "I haven't been able to stop thinking about you."

"Me, too, beautiful. One taste of you wasn't enough. It'll never be enough."

He looked up at her, his eyes meeting hers and locking on. She lost her breath at the heat in his eyes.

"How many times do you want to come tonight?"

She shrugged. "I... I don't know."

"Oh, beautiful. You're going to come until you can't

breathe. Then you're going to come some more. How does that sound?"

Her body shook with the loaded promise. Death by orgasm sounded pretty fucking spectacular, if she was being honest.

"Keep playing with those sexy tits, Ash. I love watching you touch yourself."

She picked up her breasts again and pinched her nipples, letting herself moan.

"Oh, fuck, yeah. I'm so hard right now I might not be able to wait. I might come before I get in you."

"No," she begged. "I want you inside me."

He slicked his tongue over her from bottom to top, and she moaned. "After I eat. I'm starving."

Ashleigh moaned and fell back onto the bed. He teased her with his tongue, licking her all over. She rolled her nipples between her fingers, starting slowly like he did. When he circled her clit and pressed his tongue flat to it, she cried out.

He teased her entrance with one finger, shallowly thrusting into her then tracing around her entrance until she was so close she couldn't breathe.

"Please, Daniel. I need to come. Please," she begged.

He sucked on her clit and slammed his fingers deep into her, and she lost her mind.

"Yes, oh, God, yes! Daniel, yes! Yes! Yes!"

He didn't give her a chance to recover before he added another finger and sent her right over the edge again. It was always like that with him. He made her come until she couldn't take it anymore and begged him to stop so she didn't die from lack of oxygen.

He slicked his tongue through her folds and brushed her clit with the very tip again. She sucked in a ragged breath as her pulse raced and her sanity left.

"Harder. Please, more. Now. Daniel."

The man, God bless him, listened. His fingers pumped into her in a rhythm that set her blood to boiling. He licked her at the same fast pace, everything lining up to push her into an orgasm that would shatter her. Then he pressed a finger into her ass, and she lost it completely.

She screamed and cried and begged him for more. Again, he listened, sending her from one orgasm straight to another and another until she was breathless and boneless, just like he promised.

"Stop, please, stop. Oh, God," she begged, nearly in tears from the pleasure he gave her.

Daniel stood and shoved his shorts and boxer briefs to the floor. Ashleigh pried her eyes open to watch him put on a condom then line up with her.

He looked at her and held her gaze as he pressed into her in one hard thrust. She cried out again, her entire body still sensitive from the pleasure he delivered. He didn't say anything as he withdrew, then slammed back into her. They watched each other, his eyes stormy and determined, hers heavy from lust and pleasure.

He held her legs up on his hips, spreading her thighs apart. He stood next to the bed, watching her the entire time. His gaze drifted to where they met, then back up her body to her face and down again.

"So fucking perfect," he groaned.

He hooked one knee over his arm and ran his hand up her thigh. When he pressed on her clit with his thumb, she screamed.

"Daniel!"

"That's what I needed to hear," he said roughly. He changed his angle, leaning forward over her, and slammed into her.

His punishing rhythm had Ashleigh's heart pounding and flames licking at her core. She gasped and moaned and chased her orgasm as he grunted above her.

"Need you, Ash. Need to feel you. Come for me. Scream."

She let go and did as he said, screaming his name again. Her body tightened and drew him in, and he followed her right over the edge, shouting her name just before he collapsed onto her.

Dunn didn't want to get up. He never wanted to get up. He just wanted to lie there forever, wrapped in Ashleigh. He felt like he was dreaming, but her breath tickled his overheated neck and her heart pounded against his. She was real. She was there.

His skin cooled, and he knew he had to get up. He kissed her neck and pushed off of her. He went to the bathroom, and when he returned, she hadn't moved.

"You doing okay?"

She smiled up at him. "You promised me breathless and boneless. It was a successful mission, sir."

He groaned. "I like hearing you call me 'sir.'"

She laughed huskily. "Don't get used to it. I'm not the taking orders type."

He grinned and climbed into bed, pulling her to him under the sheet. "Maybe one day."

She laughed and wiggled closer to him, brushing her bare ass against his cock. "Doubtful. Maybe you'll take orders."

"Any time, beautiful. Any time."

She laughed softly, then fell silent. He wanted to ask

what she was thinking, but the quiet was too peaceful to ruin with what he was sure would be a fight.

Eventually, she drifted to sleep in his arms. Dunn wasn't counting on any miracles, but after a while, he faded, too.

Ashleigh woke him a few hours later as she disappeared under the covers. He selfishly enjoyed her mouth on him, then fell back to sleep with her in his arms.

He was up well before dawn, feeling better than he had in years. He teased Ashleigh awake and made sure they both had a really good morning before they raced each other to the shower and used up one more condom.

Dunn was still flying high when they made it to the office. They walked in, holding hands and laughing. He kissed her on the elevator. For a few hours, it felt like they were a normal couple with a normal life together. He almost had himself convinced of it.

Then they walked through the front door.

"Where the fuck have you been?" Jack demanded the second they were inside.

Dunn blanched. Ashleigh tried to pull her hand from his, but he tightened his grip and glared at his friend. "Home. Why?"

"You don't answer your phone anymore?" Jack barked.

Dunn pressed his lips together and grinned. "Not when I have a beautiful woman in my bed." He glanced at Ashleigh and enjoyed the blush staining her cheeks.

"Yeah, well, the rest of us have been here working, trying to make sure the two of you don't end up dead like the woman in her house," Jack growled.

Fear. That was what it was. Dunn wasn't sure at first because they'd all faced more in their time as SEALs than they did as civilians, but fear was the reigning emotion in the office. And the one that had Jack in his face.

"What?" Ashleigh breathed next to him.

Dunn turned to her. Her face was stark white, and her hand was limp and cold in his. "Ash?"

"Do you know who she was?"

Jack shook his head. "We got a call from Agents Marks this morning. A courtesy call, really. He didn't have to tell us, but he wanted you to know that the information you gave him helped them get a judge to grant a warrant. They found the body. She'd been there a couple of days. He sent a picture, but I don't know if you want to see it."

"No," Dunn said immediately.

Ashleigh shook her head and squeezed his hand. "I have to. It might be someone I know. I have to help."

Dunn let go of her hand and turned to her, blocking out Jack and everyone else. He cupped her jaw and tilted her head back so she met his gaze. "You don't have to do this."

She gave him a sad smile. "I do, though. What if I know her? Or if I've seen her before? I've already done enough damage. I can at least give her family closure, if she has family."

Dunn leaned forward and kissed her gently. She was strong. He wanted to protect her, but she was right. He moved next to her again and grabbed her hand, then nodded at Jack to lead the way.

Jack paused at the conference room door to let the others know Dunn and Ashleigh were finally there, then led them to his office. He sat down and unlocked his phone. He clicked a few times, then handed his phone over.

"I zoomed in on her face. You don't want to see the rest, Ashleigh," Jack said firmly with a look at Dunn.

Dunn raised an eyebrow, and Jack nodded. The woman had trauma visible from the photo, more than just whatever the cause of death was. Judging by her bare shoulders,

Dunn had a few good guesses.

He turned the phone toward Ashleigh so she could see the picture. She looked at the picture and gasped. "Oh, God."

He handed the phone back to Jack before Ashleigh could see more and pulled her close. "Do you know her?"

Ashleigh jerked her head in a nod. "That's the woman he had sex with the night I left. I don't know her name, but she obviously works for him. He killed her."

"We don't know that," Dunn said firmly. He glanced at Jack for confirmation, and Jack nodded in agreement. "We don't know that he killed her."

"She's dead, and in my house. That was his office, which is where they were when they were having sex. She was clearly an assistant or something, and he killed her."

Dunn eased Ashleigh onto his lap and held her while she cried. Jack quietly left the room and closed the door. Dunn just sat there, trying to figure out how to help the woman in his arms move on from a betrayal she never imagined and never saw coming.

Maybe if he could help her, he could help himself.

"How could he do this?" Ashleigh asked a minute later. "How does someone kill another person?"

"Sometimes it's for survival," Dunn said quietly.

Ashleigh laughed mirthlessly. "This was not self defense. That woman was smaller than him and clearly his subordinate. He killed her for sport. How did I not know what kind of person he was?"

Dunn drew her against his chest and rubbed her back. "I've asked myself the same question many times. They don't want us to see who they are. They know we wouldn't be okay with it. So they hide it. They don't let us see. And they're good at it. He never wanted you to know. And you never would have found out if you hadn't gotten home early."

She shuddered. "I could still be there with him."

"But you're not," Dunn said firmly. "You're here. With me."

17

Ashleigh liked the sound of that. *With Daniel*. She knew better than to think it would last, but for however long she had him, she was going to enjoy it.

At least, as much as she could when her psycho ex was out there killing people.

"I want to call him," Ashleigh admitted. "Frederick."

"What?" Daniel blurted, pulling back from her. "Why?"

"Maybe he'll tell me something. Maybe he can explain who she is."

"Why do you keep putting yourself in harm's way?"

"I'm not in harm's way. I'm here. I'm with you. I'm safe. Especially compared to the woman who slept with my husband four days ago and is now dead in the same room."

"I don't like it," Daniel said.

Ashleigh cupped his jaw and brought his lips to hers. She could feel his tension even in their kiss. "I don't either, but if I don't try, no one will ever know who she is."

"They can run fingerprints or dental records," Dunn argued.

"Of course, but even I know that if she could have been

identified easily, she would have been by now. She's invisible. She was intimately familiar with my husband, and I didn't even know she existed until he was inside her. And even now, I don't know her name. I can't stand back, Daniel. You of all people should understand that."

He drew in a breath and nodded. "Okay. But you're using one of our secure phones and all of us will be listening in and recording the call."

Ashleigh nodded and let Daniel lead her to the busy conference room. English had his head down, focused on his computer. Jack and Dex were talking in front of a large whiteboard. Archer and Rocky were sitting together off to the side, both looking like they needed to hit something.

"Ashleigh wants to call Frederick," Daniel announced to the room.

Everyone stopped what they were doing except English. "He left his phone at the Observation Tower, remember?"

Ashleigh stepped forward. "He's had the same number for years. He might have left that phone behind, but he wouldn't get a new number. He never has."

English looked up at her. "You really think he didn't change it?"

Ashleigh shook her head. "No. I know him. He kept his number."

"Well, fuck. We need to run a trace right now," Dex said.

"Let her call him," Daniel said. "She wants to find out who the woman was."

Everyone averted their eyes. Clearly, Jack told them all that she was the one Frederick had sex with the night she left. Learning her name could help her family find peace, but it could also help lead the FBI to Frederick and the missing boy.

"You need to be careful. What are you going to say to him?" Dex asked, stepping forward.

"I was going to ask him who the woman was," Ashleigh said simply.

Dex shrugged. "Direct, but do you think he'll tell you?"

Ashleigh thought for a minute, then shook her head. "He never told me things. Not about work. We didn't talk much."

"Okay, so we need a new plan. He obviously knows you're here and you've left him. We don't know how much else he knows, though. Can you get him talking? Maybe ask him why he cheated on you. If he thinks you ran because he cheated, he might be more willing to talk. Then you can catch him off guard," Dex suggested.

Ashleigh nodded. "Okay. I'll try."

Daniel moved with her to sit at the table. English tapped on his keyboard before he looked up and nodded. Daniel moved the phone closer to her and handed her the receiver. "We will be recording the conversation."

Dex handed him something tiny. Daniel held it up for her to see.

"It's a communication device. We wear them all the time, and they're connected to the phone system. Dex will be taking notes while you talk, picking up anything he notices. Archer, Jack, and Slade will be helping him. English will be tracking the signal. And Rocky is going to sit right here with you and me in case you get too upset. We're a team, and you're a part of that," Daniel said with a smile.

Ashleigh smiled back and took the phone from him. She inhaled a deep breath and blew it out slowly, then leaned forward and kissed Daniel. "I'm ready."

She dialed the phone number she knew by heart and waited for the ringing to stop.

"What?" he barked into the phone. Her husband. The man she'd shared a bed with for years. The man she planned to have a family with.

"Hi, Frederick," she said simply.

He laughed. "Ashleigh. Now you call me. I've been trying to find you for days. Where did you run off to?"

Dex scribbled on the board, but she ignored the squeak of the marker and focused on the call.

"That's not what matters right now. I want to know why you cheated on me."

"Cheated on you? What do you mean?" he asked, sounding truly confused.

"I got home early, Frederick. An entire night early. And before I made it up the stairs, I heard you talking to a woman, then you went to your office and fucked her over your desk. I'd like to know why."

He swore quietly. "She's not important."

"Who is she?"

"She's no one. You don't have to worry about her anymore."

"Why not?"

"Because she's not in the picture. Where are you, baby? Let me come get you."

"Why? So you can kill me, too?" she blurted.

He swore again, louder, and something crashed. "Where the fuck are you?"

"I'm somewhere you can't get to me."

"Are you with him? Your ex? The one you never told me about? See, it's funny, because you mentioned someone once, but you told me he wasn't really important. That he didn't matter. And the first thing you do when you find out I fucked someone else is run off and screw him."

"He's twice the man you'll ever be," she growled into the phone.

Rocky tapped on her arm, silently reminding her that she had a task.

"I doubt that. I've heard all about Lieutenant Daniel Dunn. And his grandmother that you called. Maybe I should pay her a visit since you won't tell me where you are."

"No, don't. Leave her out of this," Ashleigh said, terrified. She was vaguely aware of Daniel getting up and leaving the room. "She has nothing to do with this."

"Well, she does if she's the one who helped you leave me."

"She didn't do anything. She's a friend."

"Then I think I should meet her. I always said you didn't have enough friends."

"Because you didn't want me to have friends, Frederick. You pushed them all away."

"You had me. You didn't need anyone else."

"What about a baby?" she breathed. "I wanted a baby. But we couldn't have one. Is that why you stole one from Anna Madison?"

"What did you say?" Frederick asked, his voice deadly.

"Anna Madison? The cleaning lady at Edwards Unlimited. The one who was all over the news because her son was kidnapped. I saw the adoption docket for him. You made it look like the boy was up for adoption. Were you going to bring him into our home? Wave him right under her nose?"

"You were the one who wanted a baby so badly. You didn't care where it came from. You just wanted to be a mother. You thought you could be better than your own mother, shove it in her face that you did something she couldn't do."

"Wanting to be a mother had nothing to do with my mother. I don't even know where she is. And I don't care."

"Oh, really?" Frederick said with disdain. "You don't care. It doesn't matter to you at all that your mother left your father, but she married someone else. Had more kids. Kids she loves and is there for. That she loves more than she ever loved you."

Pain Ashleigh didn't even know she could feel welled up. She'd stopped caring about her mother years ago, but knowing she rejected Ashleigh but loved other children was hard to hear.

"That's not true," she whispered.

"It is. She actually lives outside Detroit. Small community. She's going to be devastated when she finds out her daughter is dead."

"I haven't been her daughter in years," Ashleigh said firmly.

He laughed. "Oh, my love, I'm not talking about you. I'm talking about her other daughter."

Realization slapped Ashleigh in the face. "That woman was my half-sister?" she breathed.

"Like I said before, you don't have to worry about her anymore."

Ashleigh couldn't stop the sob that ripped through her throat and shredded her heart. She folded in half, pain and regret crushing her. Someone took the phone from her and said something, but she couldn't hear what or who. She didn't care.

A sister she never knew she had.

Ashleigh turned and thankfully found a trash can

behind her. She emptied her stomach into the can, praying she would die.

Her sister. How could he do that?

DUNN HEARD Ashleigh's sob from the hallway. He hadn't heard a sound like that since the day they told Pilar her brother was dead. That gut-wrenching, horrible sound that was pure pain.

He was on the phone with his grandmother, making sure she was safe, and he hung up with her to go to Ashleigh. By the time he got there, she had her head in the trashcan and Dex was on the phone. Dunn looked at Rocky. Rocky shook his head. So did every other man in the room.

What the fuck is going on?

Dunn put his hands on Ashleigh's shoulders, but she recoiled from him. She slumped to the floor next to the trashcan and kneeled there.

Dex hung up the phone quietly, barely making a noise when he set the receiver down. Dunn needed to know what happened, but he didn't want to leave Ashleigh's side.

He opened his mouth to ask when Dex caught his eye. He shook his head and pointed to Ashleigh, then walked to the board.

OTHER WOMAN = ASHLEIGH'S HALF-SISTER

Dunn closed his eyes and tried to breathe. When he opened them again, the words were erased, but it didn't make them gone.

Dunn sat in the chair next to Ashleigh and put his hand on her back. She didn't pull away from him again, but she didn't lean into him like he hoped she would. He didn't know she had a sister, and if he had to guess, she didn't know either. She would have recognized the woman if she'd ever met her.

Dunn understood why Ashleigh was sick. He felt like he was going to be, too, but he held it together. For Ashleigh.

After a minute, she fell to her backside and sat with her back against the wall. Her face was stark white. Her hair was sweaty at her temples. She looked up at him and offered him a weak smile.

"Did we get what we needed?" she asked, her voice hoarse.

Dunn nodded.

"Is your grandmother okay?"

Dunn nodded again. "She said to tell you hello."

Ashleigh breathed a laugh. "I'm sorry I involved her. If I'd known what he was capable of..."

"We're going to stop him, Ashleigh. He won't get away with this."

She nodded. "I can't..." Tears filled her eyes. She shook her head.

"You don't have to do anything. I'm sorry. I never should have let you call him."

She sucked in a ragged breath. "No, I needed to. I needed to hear that. To know he really is the monster I was starting to realize he was. He's even worse than I imagined, though. I just can't..."

Her face crumpled. Dunn dropped to the floor next to her and wrapped her in his arms. Rocky stepped over them and grabbed the trashcan, then left the room. The others weren't far behind them, giving Dunn and Ashleigh time.

"I didn't know she was my sister," Ashleigh said softly when she finally spoke. "I didn't know I even had a sister."

"She's your mom's I take it?"

She nodded. "That's what Frederick said. He knew. He

said my mom lives in Detroit. She has a whole other family, and he knew. All this time. And he used it. He slept with her, and he killed her."

"Yeah, but you said she seemed like she was familiar with him. Like the affair had been going on for a while, right?"

She nodded. "That doesn't make it better."

"At least you know he didn't take her to try to get to you or force her into something because of you," Dunn said.

She sucked in a breath and nodded. "True. I just... I can't believe I had a sister. And he took her from me."

"I'm sorry, Ash," Dunn said.

She forced a smile. "Thanks. I... it's a lot to process."

"And you don't have to process it right now. Take your time. We'll find him."

"I want him dead," she said with more venom than he thought she could possess.

Dunn nodded. "I'm with you, but we want to find him. Make him pay for what he did to her, and make sure we find the kid, and all the kids he might have taken."

Ashleigh nodded. "I just hope he didn't hurt the child."

Dunn nodded. He hoped so, too, but until they found him, they couldn't be sure.

WILLIAMS WAVED his key in front of the keypad outside the hotel room. The door unlocked with a soft click, letting him into the opulent hotel room his partner insisted on staying in. Williams didn't get the point, but the man he brought into the mission wasn't the kind of guy who got in the trenches. He was a suit and tie type, and a loose cannon.

But for the moment, he was smiling and sipping scotch from a crystal glass.

"Are you celebrating?" Williams asked, setting new newly purchased weapon on the glass coffee table in the living room.

The hotel room was bigger than the house Williams shared with his wife. With three bedrooms, a living room, a dining room that seated twelve, and a full kitchen, the suite was costing Frederick a fortune, but he insisted on it. The balcony alone, overlooking the Falls, was worth the price tag. Especially if Williams wasn't paying for it.

"I am celebrating."

"And what are you celebrating?" Williams asked. Talking to the man was like pulling teeth.

He smirked. "My wife just called me."

"What? Ashleigh? How did she get your number?"

"It's the same number I've always had. I don't change phone numbers."

"What do you mean?" Williams demanded. "We got rid of your phone."

Frederick shrugged. "And I got a new one with all my information on it. I can't lose my contacts just because someone thinks they know something."

"They don't think, they know. And if they have your number, they're going to know where you are."

Frederick laughed. "They only found my last phone because I let them. This one is encrypted. Not even your military can find me."

Williams clenched his teeth at the mention of military.

"Oh, right. I'm not allowed to mention that word in your presence." Frederick shrugged. "I forgot."

"What did Ashleigh want?" Williams demanded, ignoring the man's arrogant dismissal.

"She wanted to know who the dead woman in my house is."

"There's a dead woman in your house?" Williams asked. He didn't know that.

Frederick nodded. "I imagine the authorities have removed her by now."

"Who was she?"

"My assistant. Except she was only marginal at her job. She kept my transfers organized, but she was abhorrent at blow jobs. Always gagging. She was thin, though, and had an ass that could inspire a man. And she rarely complained when I needed her services. She was my wife's sister, well, half-sister. But neither knew the other existed. Until today."

"You were screwing your wife's sister and killed her?"

Frederick shrugged. "She was a good enough replacement for Ashleigh. Smarter, so she was good at the work stuff. It took a few beatings for her to perform well enough during sex. She cried the first few times."

Williams wasn't sure if the man was being serious or not, but it was best to assume he really was as batshit crazy as he sounded.

"Does Ashleigh know anything about what we're doing?"

Frederick shook his head. "No. She just wanted to know about the woman and the little boy. Fucking bitch. She was home before she came here. I didn't know it. She saw something she shouldn't have."

"What was it?"

"None of your fucking business," Frederick said with a glare that told Williams not to ask again.

"Fine. Are you set with everything you need?"

Frederick nodded. "I am. Nothing is going to stand in the way of what we need to do."

Williams nodded and smiled. "Good."

18

TIMING WAS EVERYTHING. DUNN KNEW THAT AS WELL AS HE knew the smell of Ashleigh's skin. But timing sucked when it wasn't in your favor. And that was what he was dealing with.

Two days after Ashleigh found out about her sister, they hadn't heard anything from Williams or Frederick. English had a constant trace running on the phone, but nothing came up. The man was smart, and if he was working with Williams, there was a good chance something big was going to happen.

Which was the worst thing possible since Kate Maddox was arriving that day. Her concert was in two days, but she and her new husband wanted a mini-honeymoon before her show. And the team was responsible for making sure nothing happened to them.

"She's on the way up," Dex said as he walked by Dunn.

Coffee was the drink of choice lately, as it always was when they were running on no sleep. Dunn was grateful Ashleigh was there. If it wasn't for her, he wouldn't get any sleep. Of course, if she wasn't there, he'd have time to get a lot more.

Dunn grabbed his coffee and checked in with Ashleigh. She was going to stay out of sight in his office, and she said she was content with the books she downloaded onto his iPad the night before. She needed the distraction from everything that had happened.

Once they notified Agent Marks about the supposed identity of the woman in the house, he was able to pass the information along to the Detroit FBI office. They went to see Ashleigh's mom and confirmed that the woman was, in fact, Ashleigh's sister. Knowing Frederick didn't lie about that didn't make it easier for Ashleigh to forgive herself, but Dunn did his best to help her forget for a few hours at night.

The elevator slid open and the stunning Kate Maddox walked out with her new husband right behind her. She smiled up at him, her brown eyes locked on his. His hand was on her lower back, and the look they shared was one of pure love. Newlyweds.

Dunn walked toward them, unlocking the secure door between the entrance and the rest of the office. They didn't normally let clients through the door, but she was Kate Maddox, after all.

"Good morning. It's nice to meet you both."

"Mr. Dunn. I'm so happy to finally see you in person. Months of video calls did not do you justice," Kate said, flashing him a bright smile that lit her brown eyes.

Dunn's cheeks heated with her praise. He nodded and extended his hand to her husband. They were nearly the same height, but he was the client, which meant he was the boss. "Mr. Young. Nice to meet you. Thank you for coming up here."

Dillon nodded and shook Dunn's hand. "Of course. Thanks for taking this job. We know it's not your usual thing, but it's hard to pass up the chance to have men like you protect my wife."

"Congratulations, by the way. I hope the wedding was wonderful."

They exchanged another one of those looks that had Dunn thinking of Ashleigh. Dillon slipped his hand around Kate's waist and winked at her.

"It was amazing," Kate said, brushing her light brown waves back from her face. "You'll have to come to the vineyard sometime. Dillon's family is so welcoming and friendly, and you would love it there. There's an inn, too. You can come stay with your... wife?"

Dunn shook his head, but before he could answer, Dillon said, "Katherine. Leave the man alone. Just because we're married, doesn't mean you have to marry everyone else off."

"Everyone except Ryan is married or headed that way. Even Quynn and my brother. I have no one else to pair up. Maybe Mr. Dunn can meet—"

Dillon silenced her with a kiss. He cupped her jaw and teased her lips apart, and Dunn started to wonder if he needed to walk away.

They finally pulled apart, and Dillon winked at Dunn. "How about we talk about how Mr. Dunn is going to keep you safe for the next few days."

Kate pouted, but rolled her eyes and nodded.

Dunn led the way into the conference room and introduced them to the rest of the team. Kate and Dillon were kind and friendly, taking a minute to speak to each man before moving to the next one. By the time she sat down, every man in the room was a little in love with her.

Dunn nodded to Dex and began, "There's been a slight change in our plans. Dex is going to be your primary contact through your stay. He's up on everything and very capable of handling anything and everything."

Kate smiled at Dex, but Dillon was not happy.

"Why the change? We've planned everything with the understanding we would be working with you. No offense to the rest of your team, but we're paying a lot of money and making changes like this wasn't part of our plan," Dillon said. It was obvious why he was a CEO. He commanded a room and managed to get his point across without being belligerent or rude, even when he kind of was.

"A lot has happened in the last few days. One of the many things is the new threat, that we mentioned before, and I feel it's in everyone's best interest to keep all of my focus on that," Dunn said calmly.

"That sounds reasonable," Kate said.

"Why does it have to be you that handles this other threat?" Dillon asked.

"The threat is personal. It's directed at us, and it's a man we all know well, but it's a man I know better than the others. I feel the best way to stop this threat is for me to focusing on him to keep you both safe," Dunn explained.

Dillon looked at Kate and tucked her brown hair behind her ear, lingering on her skin. She smiled up at him. "It's up to you," he told her. "You're the one who found them, and you're the one who wanted him."

She nodded. "I know, but I don't think it's possible to go wrong here." She smiled at the room. "It's okay with me."

Dex smiled at her. "I am aware of everything you and Dunn have talked about. I don't see any reason to be concerned. You two are booked into a suite, and I'll be in the extra bedroom. With earplugs and a noise machine."

Kate blushed, but Dillon puffed his chest up and

nodded. He was definitely the kind of man they would get along with.

"I don't think I'm going to be able to have sex at all on this trip," Kate said softly.

"Don't worry about me, Ms. Maddox. Mrs. Young?" Dex asked.

"Either is fine," Kate said.

Dex nodded. "I won't divulge anything that happens in the suite unless it's important to the case. And trust me, I could tell you plenty of embarrassing stories about all of us, and none of us have room to talk when it comes to sharing a bed with someone. There's nothing wrong with having fun on your honeymoon."

"We'll keep it in the bedroom," Dillon said, kissing the side of Kate's head. "Other than that, I can't make any promises when it comes to this woman."

They all chuckled and nodded. Dunn definitely understood the feeling. He felt the same about Ashleigh. He wasn't interested in sharing her with another man, but he wasn't going to stop enjoying her, either.

Shit. No. It didn't mean anything. It was sex. Good sex. No, great sex. And all the emotional stuff was left over from when they were together before. He wasn't in love with her again.

"So, do you have any worries about the concert?" Dillon asked, dragging Dunn's focus back to the conversation.

"We do," Dunn said. "But we're handling it. Nothing is going to be overlooked."

Dillon nodded and slid his hand into Kate's. Dunn watched them as Dex went into detail about their highest risk areas and how they were managing them. He saw love regularly in the eyes of his teammates. Archer, Jack, and Jaymes were head over heels with it. But Dunn was so used to seeing the dopey looks on their faces he didn't recognize it when he saw it in the mirror.

Watching Kate and Dillon, he saw it. He knew he could tell himself whatever he wanted, but he was in love with Ashleigh. Again, or maybe still. It didn't really matter. What mattered was he loved her. And he didn't want to screw it up this time.

ASHLEIGH WAS GETTING HUNGRY. The meeting was going on a lot longer than she expected. She was also getting frustrated that she couldn't move on with her life. Until Frederick was found, Daniel wouldn't let her out of his sight. And that meant she had to sit and do nothing all day.

Her book was boring, so she switched over to the internet. Daniel said it was secure and she could do whatever she wanted online, but all she really wanted to do was find a new job. Her current one was out of her reach since she didn't get paid. She'd love to do something like she'd been doing and keep helping companies who helped other people, but she wasn't sure how she could do it.

The first hurdle she came across was when the search asked her for a location. Detroit? No. She couldn't imagine going back there. Niagara Falls? She wasn't sure about that one either. She tossed the iPad on the desk and groaned.

She needed to get out of the office and find something to eat.

Knowing better than to leave the building, she headed to the lunch room hoping someone brought in food she could share. A box was on the counter and looked suspiciously like more cupcakes from Lily. She opened the box and moaned at the sugary scent that infiltrated her nose. She lifted out the one with the most frosting and carefully peeled off the wrapper, making sure she didn't pull any of the frosting off.

She tossed the wrapper and took a bite, then turned to sit and realized she wasn't alone.

"I didn't want to interrupt you. Before I met my husband, I had the same reaction to cupcakes. Well, I still do, but I have that reaction to him, too."

"Sorry," Ashleigh said through her chocolate crumbs.

Kate Maddox didn't appear put off at all. She moved into the lunch room and straight to the box. "Mr. Dunn sent me down here for a water, but I don't know if I can resist one of these. Is it okay if I have one?"

Ashleigh shrugged, her mouth still full.

"Oh, I'm sorry. I figured you were their assistant or something. Are you one of the SEALs?"

Ashleigh snorted a laugh and gestured to her body.

Kate grinned and gestured to her body. "I'm with you. The most exercise I get is lifting cupcakes to my mouth. That and sex. Oh, my God, I'm so sorry. I think it's the whole getting married thing. Dillon's sister and cousin and cousin's wives told me getting married would make sex better, but I didn't really believe them because it was always amazing. But it really is, and I think it's melting my brain. I don't even know your name, and I'm telling you about my sex life."

Ashleigh finally swallowed and said, "Ashleigh. I'm a... friend of Daniel's."

"A friend? Is that with or without benefits?" Kate slapped a hand over her mouth. "I'm so sorry."

Ashleigh grinned. "It's okay. I get it. And with, I guess. We dated in college, but he joined the Navy and we weren't in touch for a long time. We've only recently reconnected."

"Good for you. I love stories like that. I'm Katherine, by the way."

Ashleigh chuckled. "I know who you are."

Kate, or Katherine, grinned. "Sorry. I'm still not used to it. I met my husband one night when he didn't know who I was. I didn't know who he was, either. I ended up at his vineyard the next day, and his sister played matchmaker and got us together. None of them knew who I was for weeks."

"Wow, seriously?"

Katherine nodded. "Yeah, but I worked hard to keep my identity private. Now, I don't care. There are always people after me, but the town we live in is really protective. We haven't had any issues, but Dillon was worried about me going on tour again."

"I don't blame him. I'm actually here because my husband, or the man I thought was my husband, is not who I thought he was. Daniel is doing the same thing your husband is. Keeping me safe."

"You're lucky to have him," Katherine said.

Ashleigh nodded. "I am."

"There you are," a gorgeous man said, walking into the kitchen. Katherine smiled up at him and accepted a kiss.

"We were just chatting. This is Ashleigh. She's with Mr. Dunn," Katherine explained.

"And she has cupcakes," the man added.

"I'm trying to talk her into sharing." Katherine winked at Ashleigh. "This is Dillon, my husband."

"Nice to meet you," Ashleigh said. "And they're not my cupcakes. I'm stealing, too."

"Then steal fast," Dillon said to Katherine. "We need to go get checked into the hotel. Dex said he's already been over there to look at the room, but he's going to go with us now, too. No one knows we're in town yet, so he won't be with us full time until tonight. That gives us a few hours to go sightseeing."

"Or not," Katherine said, licking the frosting off the cupcake.

Ashleigh's cheeks warmed. She wondered if she could steal a few more cupcakes and lick them off Daniel later. Or have him lick them off her.

Dillon laughed and pulled Katherine in for a hug. "You're insatiable, my wife."

"Mmmm, I love hearing that," Katherine said, tilting her chin up for a kiss.

Dillon obliged and pulled back just enough to whisper, "I love you."

Ashleigh felt like she was intruding on a personal moment, but they were between her and the door, so she couldn't escape.

Katherine took a breath and stepped back. "Okay, go back to the conference room. I'm going to eat my cupcake and I'll be there in a minute."

Dillon shook his head. "They're done with us. I think they're working on something else. The other threat maybe."

Katherine scrunched up her face. "Are you worried?"

Dillon shook his head again and slid his arms around her waist. "I'm not. These guys have an amazing track record, and they all seem to be pretty great at what they do. If there's a threat, they'll handle it. They have it."

Katherine nodded. "If you trust them, then I'm good."

Dillon grinned and wiped frosting off her lip. "As long as you're good, I'm good. Let's go do some sightseeing."

They grinned at each other. "Or not," they said in unison.

"Nice to meet you, Ashleigh," Katherine said before they walked out the door.

"You, too. Good luck at your concert. And congratulations."

"Thank you. Hopefully, I'll see you at the show."

Ashleigh nodded. She wasn't sure about that one, but it was nice to imagine she could have a normal life.

Maybe one day.

SLADE JERKED his head to the side once Dex left with Kate and Dillon. Dunn wasn't really in the mood for whatever Slade had to say, but he couldn't ignore him either, even if he knew what was coming.

"Was that the best call?" Slade said with no preamble.

Dunn could play dumb, but he knew exactly what Slade was referring to. "Are you questioning my ability to lead this team or Dex's ability to keep two people safe?"

Slade glared at him. "I'm not asking if Dex can do it. We all know how to protect people."

"So, you're only questioning my decision."

"I'm worried Ashleigh is distracting you and going to compromise this team," Slade said firmly. Quietly, but firmly.

Dunn crossed his arms and rocked back on his heels. When there was an issue under Williams, it was always buried. No one was allowed to question him. Dunn did so multiple times, but Williams always had an answer. He never put himself on the line.

If Dunn learned anything from his former CO, it was not to do things the same way. He glared at Slade and stepped away from him, then knocked on the table to get the attention of the rest of the room.

"Slade has brought to my attention that he thinks I should not have assigned Dex the job of watching over Kate Maddox, and he is concerned that Ashleigh is clouding my judgement. This isn't the first time her presence has been brought up in reference to my ability to do my job. Instead of having all of you talking behind my back or questioning my decisions, I'd like to get it all in the open right now."

Archer and Jack traded a look, then Archer stood and peeked into the hallway. He pulled his head back in and closed the door, sealing off their conversation from Ashleigh.

Jack was the first one to speak. "From experience, I know what you're going through. It sucks. It was hard to try to protect Pilar and focus on the job at hand. I hated walking away from her, knowing someone was out there and after her. That said, I also know there's no way in hell you'd let any of us watch Ashleigh."

Dunn narrowed his gaze. "Does that mean you agree with Slade or not?"

Jack shrugged. "Both. My hesitation with Ashleigh has more to do with the threat she is to you personally, but I know you're not willing to listen to me about staying away from her. The thing is, she came to you, not the rest of us. She feels the safest with you. Yeah, Kate Maddox wanted you to be with her, but Dex isn't some guy off the street. We all have the same training, and Dex is smarter than the rest of us. He'll keep them safe. And, you don't have history with Kate Maddox. Changing things with her is easier than unloading Ashleigh onto someone else."

Dunn nodded, agreeing with Jack's assessment.

"It concerns me," English admitted. "I haven't liked it when any of you were involved with our informant. I think you need to be honest with yourself about how this is all going to work. There isn't one threat out there. Ashleigh's husband is here. Williams is here. And we have no idea if the people who threatened Ms. Maddox are honest. We have at least three threats, that we know of, and it's reasonable to assume all will take place at the concert. If you're going to do your job, someone else will have to be with Ashleigh. That can't be avoided."

Dunn nodded. "Thank you."

"There's nothing about this job that's easy. Every day, I walk out of my home and wonder if my wife is going to be alive when I return. Williams already proved he can get to her. He's smarter than I am, and he can do anything he wants. If he wanted to take Lily again, he could. But I have to put that out of my head when I come here every day. Every single one of you knows if Lily is ever in danger, I'll be there, and I'll never leave her side, but you have to be able to separate. Only you know if you can do that. Only you can decide what's right," Archer said.

Dunn nodded. "I think I'm good. We never deal with one thing at a time. It's always one fire after another. This is no different."

"Good," Jack said. "Then we're settled. Let's move on and catch these motherfuckers."

19

———

For the next two days, everything was quiet. Too fucking quiet. It was driving Dunn crazy because he knew things were happening, he just didn't know what they were.

English had a trace running on Frederick's phone constantly, but it never turned up anything. He had to have high-tech software that prevented them from finding out anything. They had access to his phone records, but the number Williams used to call him was a burner phone that was ditched.

Everyone was on edge. Dex said nothing was happening with the newlyweds, but with the threats in the area, it was going to be all hands on deck for the concert that night.

"Lily, Pilar, Kelsea, and Jaymes have tickets. They were planning to go to the show," Archer told Dunn that morning. "They want to know if they can still go."

Dunn sighed and leaned back in his chair. "All right, let's go through everything. We know Kate Maddox had threats a while ago. Someone said they couldn't wait to meet her and had pictures of her with her face ripped out. Then Williams tells us his family is going to be at the show. Then Ashleigh's not-husband shows up, and we assume he's working with Williams. That's three potential threats."

The rest of the men in the room nodded.

"And do we think this show is the most likely target?"

Again, the others nodded.

Dunn closed his eyes. "I can't answer your question. I can't tell you if they should go or not. I don't have any clue."

Archer took a breath and blew it out slowly. "Is Ashleigh going to be there?"

Dunn nodded. "Her not-husband is still here as far as we know."

"Why hasn't he come for her?" Slade asked. "We assume Williams knows where we all live. Why wouldn't he tell her husband where you guys are?"

"Williams doesn't show all his cards. He must need something from him. That's the only thing I can figure," Dunn said.

They nodded. The tension in the room rose. They were missing something, and until they figured out what it was, none of them was going to feel settled.

Dunn sent the guys home for the rest of the day. There was no telling what their night was going to be like, so he told everyone to try to get some rest.

He followed his own advice and took Ashleigh home, hoping they could get a few hours of quiet, too.

"Do you think he's going to be there tonight?" Ashleigh asked.

She was silent and still before she asked the question, and Dunn had hoped she was asleep. Neither of them had slept much since the night they went to Slade's. The night they decided to let their desire for each other lead the way.

"I do," Dunn answered her honestly.

"Do you think he's going to kill me?"

He tightened his grip on her and kissed her shoulder. "We'll keep you safe."

"So you think he'll try," she said in a shaky breath.

Dunn turned her onto her back so she was facing him. He cupped her jaw and caressed her cheek with his thumb. "These men will do anything to get what they want. I think if he is still here, it's not because he wants you dead. He wants something far worse than that."

She shuddered and closed her eyes. A tear escaped from under her closed lid.

Dunn slid his arm under her neck and turned so they were facing each other. He tucked her under his chin and kissed the top of her head. "I'm going to do everything in my power to keep you safe, Ashleigh. I will be with you the entire time."

"You have to stop Williams," she whispered.

Dunn slid his hand down her back. "I'm not going to let anyone hurt you," he said roughly.

Just the thought of anything happening to her had his entire body tense. Williams could hurt her to get to him. Her not-husband could hurt her to get revenge on her. Anything could happen, and would, if she wasn't protected. He'd die before he let anything happen to her.

"Daniel," she breathed, her hand sliding between them. "Will you help me forget for a few hours?"

Her hand wrapped around him. He hardened quickly, needing her just as much as she needed him.

He tilted her chin up and took her mouth in a kiss while she stroked him. Each slide of her hand up and down his cock sent him spiraling. He licked his way inside her mouth and threaded his fingers into her hair. She moaned when he tugged lightly.

He teased his way down her body with his fingers, caressing and pinching and teasing until his fingers slid between her wet thighs. She opened for him, and he pressed a finger into her.

"Oh, Daniel," she moaned softly.

"You're so fucking beautiful," he said against her neck. "So beautiful, Ash."

She kept stroking him until he gently pressed her to her back and positioned himself between her thighs. He would never get the sight of her, spread out and ready for him on his bed, out of his mind. Her skin was flushed with desire, her pussy wet and pulsing. He couldn't resist stretching out over her for a kiss.

She opened to him instantly, plunging her tongue into his mouth and wrapping herself around him. His cock slicked through her wetness, her heat begging him to slide inside.

He pulled back from their kiss and grabbed a condom. He rolled it on and pressed her thighs wider apart. She dropped her knees to the bed and looked at him.

The look in her eyes was the same as it had been eighteen years ago. Before he blew up their world with his confession. Love. Trust. Faith. Hope.

"I love you," he said.

Surprise curled her lips up into a smile. "You do?"

He nodded and swallowed. "God, Ash, I do. I always have. I'm sorry I ever let you go. And I don't expect you to say it back, or want you to. I just had to tell you."

"Daniel—ohhhhh, fuck," she finished on a moan when he thrust into her.

He didn't want her to say she loved him just because he

admitted how he felt about her. He wanted her to tell him when she was ready, but he couldn't hold the words back any longer.

Telling her how he felt unleashed everything inside him. He thrust into her with fast, shallow strokes that had her speaking gibberish. Once she moaned his name, he leaned back and propped up her hips, sliding into her with slow, deep strokes that had her eyes rolling back in her head.

She gasped and shouted her way through it, and Dunn leaned forward again, holding himself up with hands on either side of her head. He watched her as he drove into her, sliding deeper with each hard stroke. When she thrashed beneath him, her entire body tightening on his, he reached between them and pressed his thumb to her clit and sent her flying, screaming the entire way.

As she pumped him, he let go of all his fears and desires and let what he was feeling take over. Ashleigh. His Ashleigh. The woman he loved. Nothing would be better than her. Nothing could replace her. She was it for him. His. Forever.

He came hard, blacking out as he poured himself into her. She wrapped him in her arms and held him while he tried to breathe again. And when he did, she was whispering the words that would carry him through.

"I love you, Daniel. I love you. So much, Daniel. I love you."

ASHLEIGH NEVER THOUGHT she'd fall asleep, but when she woke up hours later to Daniel getting dressed, she knew she had. Not only did she sleep, but she slept well.

But reality was an evil bitch and slapped her in the face as soon as she was awake again.

Ashleigh slipped out of bed and went to get in the shower. She'd hoped Daniel would join her, but he was heading to the kitchen when she was heading into the bathroom.

She showered quickly, taking extra care between her thighs where she was sore. Spending almost a week with Daniel was great for her ego, but it was taking a toll on her body. She was sore inside and out, but it was the most delicious kind of sore. The kind you only got when you were thoroughly fucked and deliciously sated.

She was definitely both.

When she got out of the shower, Daniel was sitting on the bed waiting for her.

"About what I said earlier," he began, "I don't expect anything from you. I meant what I said, and I'll always love you, Ashleigh, but I don't expect you to uproot your entire life and move here or anything."

Ashleigh felt more exposed because of the conversation than because she was still naked. She wrapped her towel around her body and dared to meet his gaze. "If I wanted to move here, would you have a problem with it?"

He shook his head. "No, but I want you to know you aren't bound to me because of what you said."

She nodded. "Okay."

He offered her a half-smile and got up. He paused when he got to the door and said, "We need to leave in about ten minutes."

Ashleigh nodded, but he was already gone. She did laundry the night before, so she had plenty of clean clothes, but she didn't know what to wear. What did you wear when you were going to face your not-husband who killed the half-sister you never knew you had? She was pretty sure there wasn't a section on Pinterest that had recommendations for that.

She chose her new capris because they were comfortable but easy to move in and rifled through Daniel's drawer until she found one of his NAVY tees. If nothing else, it would piss Frederick off. And it smelled like Daniel.

When she walked out of the room, her long hair braided so it was out of her makeup free face, he looked her up and down. His lips quirked at his tee but he didn't comment. "Are you ready?"

She nodded and tied on her sneakers, then followed Daniel out of the house.

They didn't talk on the way to the concert, but Daniel held her hand tightly in his. It was still early, well before the concert was going to start, but Daniel and the rest of the team needed to be there before anyone else.

Daniel flashed his badge at the guard and signed them in, then parked in a parking lot for employees only. He got out and walked around to her side, then held her hand as they walked into the arena where the concert was going to be.

Daniel led them through hallways until he came to a door marked *Storage*. He knocked on it once, then someone knocked back in a complicated rhythm. He knocked again, and the door opened from the inside.

"Hey," Archer said as he let them in. "We're ready."

Ashleigh almost laughed when she walked in. If the situation weren't so tense, she would have. Lily, Kelsea, and Pilar were sitting on overturned buckets in the corner. The men were pacing, staring at the door.

"Thank God you're here," Lily said. "Can we go now?"

"No," Archer said firmly. "The show doesn't start for a while. You're not even supposed to be here yet."

Lily groaned. "We just don't want to be sitting on buckets for hours. Is there somewhere else we can wait?"

"This is the safest place right now," Daniel said. "We are going to take a look around and make sure the place is safe. Jaymes is going to stay with you."

Lily huffed, but Kelsea and Pilar nodded. Ashleigh held Daniel's gaze and tilted her chin up for a kiss. He wrapped their joined hands behind her back and pulled her in close. He treated her to a kiss that had her cheeks and thighs heating, then pulled back and disappeared with the rest of them.

"I'm going to marry that man," Ashleigh said to no one in particular.

"I don't think it'll take much to convince him," Lily said. "It's nice to see him happy."

"Agreed," Pilar said. "I wasn't sure he was ever going to smile again. He's had some tough times."

"You're good for him," Kelsea said. "And obviously he's good for you, too."

The others cackled, and the four of them sat together on the buckets and talked about the men in their lives, embarrassing and terrifying Jaymes in the process.

Ashleigh thought she finally found where she belonged.

"HE'S TOO SMART FOR THIS," Rocky insisted. "There's no way this is all he has planned."

Dunn couldn't shake the same feeling. Williams was one step ahead of them the entire time. Everything he'd done since before they left the Navy was calculated and planned to the finest detail. He almost got away with all of it.

It didn't make sense that they would be able to figure it all out so easily. Especially since he was the one who told them what he was planning.

"Did anyone see him here?" Dunn asked.

The other men shook their heads.

"It doesn't mean he's not," Archer said.

"Agreed. He knows how to be invisible. We have to stay vigilant," Dunn said.

"Do you really think the rest of us don't want him?" Slade barked.

Dunn drew in a breath and closed his eyes, ignoring Slade. They all wanted Williams. They all lost something because of him. But the rest of the men didn't lose a piece of themselves. They didn't lose all the faith they had in their abilities.

This was Dunn's last chance. If he couldn't stop Williams before other people got hurt, he had to walk away. He owed it to his team to let someone else lead them. If he wasn't good enough, if he was the failure he believed he was, it was better for everyone if he left.

Williams slipped through his fingers too many times. Between deceiving all of them when they were SEALs to masterminding everything a year before, Williams made it clear to Dunn that he was the better man. Dunn felt the pressure from the other men he stood with and knew this was their chance. For whatever reason, Williams wanted them to know he was going to be there, and if it was another trick and he got away one more time, Dunn couldn't look the men around him in the eye and promise them he was right for the job.

"Rocky, I need you with Ashleigh," Dunn said.

"What? Why?" Slade asked.

Dunn ignored him again and focused on Rocky. Rocky nodded.

"What the fuck?" Slade asked.

Dunn finally turned on him and got up in his face. "Last I checked, I still make the decisions around here."

Slade's eyes hardened. "Yes, sir."

Dunn knew that tone. Slade would be the first one to say Dunn was to blame if things went south. And the burning in hit gut said they would before the night was over. Especially if he couldn't get his head on straight. That was why he wanted Rocky with Ashleigh. She trusted Rocky, and so did he. Dunn could walk away from her and know Rocky would keep her safe so he could focus on stopping Williams.

"We have an hour before the show starts. Dex is with Kate and Dillon. The rest of us need to make sure this crowd is safe," Dunn said.

The others nodded. The tension between Dunn and Slade had everyone on edge, but they were soldiers before and above everything else. It didn't matter who called the shots or what had to be done, they'd make it happen. They had no choice.

The team paired off to go to their assigned spots. Dunn and English walked back to the storage room with Rocky. They unlocked the door to laughter on the other side and a very uncomfortable looking Jaymes.

"Please tell me you have a job for me," he said.

Dunn looked at the four women and shook his head. "I thought you were going to watch the show."

Jaymes shook his head. "I don't think I can handle it. Ashleigh can have my ticket. Anything."

Dunn almost laughed at the look of fear in Jaymes's eyes. He could only imagine the conversation that took place while the rest of them were gone. The women clearly didn't have any qualms about sharing intimate details of their sex lives, and with Jaymes's girlfriend and his sister-in-law in the room, the discomfort level was likely sky-high.

Dunn turned back to Rocky and English. "I don't like putting them in the crowd. Not without protection. We have no idea what to expect here."

"It's likely the safest place, boss," Rocky said. "If they're in the crowd, they're protected by everyone around them."

"Not if Williams sneaks up and presses a gun to their side," Dunn spat. It hadn't even been a week since Williams did exactly that to Ashleigh in a room full of people.

"I don't think any of us will blend in. We can position ourselves in the crowd near them, but we won't be subtle," Rocky said.

Dunn nodded. "It might be for the best. His family will be up there. We all agreed he isn't likely to harm his kids."

"I can help," Jaymes said. "I'll go with them, but I can't be the only one with a penis around these women. It's shriveling as we speak with all the talk about feelings."

Jaymes winced, and Dunn fought the urge to laugh at him again. He shook his head and said, "You two, take the women to their seats. The crowd is coming in, and if you get them up there, we will know where they are."

Jaymes and Rocky nodded and told the women it was time to go. "You, too, Ashleigh," Rocky said.

Ashleigh stood and gave them all a questioning look.

"Jaymes is giving you his ticket. He and Rocky will be close by all night if you guys need anything. It'll be easier to keep all of you safe if you're all together, and with two people to watch the four of you, it'll be fine," Dunn explained.

"Where are you going to be?" Ashleigh asked.

"Making sure no one gets hurt."

She walked over and threw her arms around his neck, drawing him down for a kiss. He slid his arms around her back and hauled her close, needing to feel her. She gave him strength. She believed in him. And she was his. Once Williams and her not-husband were taken care of, they could finally start a life together.

He hoped.

20

———————

Dunn watched Ashleigh walk away with a heavy feeling in his gut. Nothing about the evening was right. He couldn't put his finger on it, but nothing was right.

"You gonna be okay?" English asked.

Dunn shook off the feeling and nodded. "Yep, let's go."

They followed the path from the storage room to the dressing room Kate Maddox was using. Two hired guards were standing outside the door. They nodded at English and Dunn as they walked by. Dunn wanted to check the path from the dressing room to the stage, so they followed the corridors until they ended up under the stage where Kate was going to wait until she was lifted up.

Everything looked like it was supposed to. Nothing was out of place. There were no packages sitting around or big signs telling them where to look. Dunn was getting frustrated.

"It doesn't feel right, does it?" English asked.

Dunn shook his head. "No, it doesn't."

"Why did he tell you he'd be here?"

Dunn stopped and looked around. "I don't know."

"Well, the only thing I can think is he wanted all of us here."

Dunn nodded. "Makes sense, but we were talking about that, anyway."

"True," English said, "but he had no way of knowing that. So, if he wanted us all to be here, there are two options. He wanted us out of the office for some reason, or he wanted everyone in one place."

"Most likely the second one. The security you set up at the office is more than he can handle."

English nodded. "That's what I think, too. He was never interested in all the tech stuff. So, if he wanted us all here, it's safe to assume he really does have something somewhere."

"Yeah, but where. And what?"

English shrugged. "I don't know. That's what I can't figure out. We've had this place locked down for days. We've run dogs through it. We've searched and searched again. It doesn't make any sense to me."

"Which is why we're still looking when Kate Maddox is," he paused and checked his phone, "twenty minutes from taking the stage."

Dunn stood and looked around. The roar of the crowd was audible through the walls, but it was quiet enough that they could still talk. Solid walls. He turned and looked at the walls. Concrete. Likely cinderblocks.

"What are you thinking?" English asked.

Dunn shook his head slowly. "I don't know." He ran his hand along the wall. "This is an old building. The walls are solid, though. This place isn't likely to come down. But it wasn't built as a concert venue. Not with walls like this under the stage."

English moved to stand beside him. "True. Most venues have walls like this along the exterior."

"Yeah, but what does it mean? Is it significant?" Dunn felt like something was just outside his consciousness. Like the truth was right in front of him.

"Wait. We've been looking at this whole thing as a potential attack on Kate Maddox, right? A threat to her and to us. But what if this isn't about any of us? What if it's still about his family?"

"What do you mean?" Dunn asked.

English put his hand on the wall again. "Do you feel that?"

Dunn touched the wall. A slight vibration shook his hand. "Yeah."

"What if he's after them? The crowd? We looked through the venue, but what if he's in the crowd? What if he bought a ticket and walks right in?"

"There are metal detectors, though. He can't bring anything with him," Dunn said.

English shook his head. "He doesn't have to. Not if everything he needs is already here somewhere. How many times have we created an explosive from random things? Cleaning products and trash. He knows just as well as we do how to do that. All he has to do is get inside."

"Do you think...?"

English shrugged. "I don't know why not. He wants his family. All he has to do is create chaos, and he can walk up to them in the crowd and disappear."

"Son of a bitch," Dunn breathed. "We have to get cameras in there. And search all the bathrooms and storage rooms that the people inside can get to."

"And we need to do it fast," English said.

Dunn drew in a breath and nodded. "We need to warn Dex."

English pressed the comms in his ear. "We think Williams is building an explosive device inside the venue. A bathroom, maybe a service area. Somewhere that would make a scene so he can go unnoticed and get to his family."

"Would he go through all this for that?" Slade asked.

"He kidnapped me for them. Why not?" Jaymes said in reply.

"It's worth looking into," English said. "Dunn and I are heading up now. We'll check the south side."

"We'll take west," Mason said.

"Guess that means we have north," Slade grumbled.

"Do we want to delay?" Dex asked softly.

Dunn looked at English. English held up his hand with all fingers splayed. Dunn nodded. "Five minutes."

"Ten-four."

Dunn and English raced through the maze until they came to a door that let them out onto the public side. Most of the crowd was in their seats, cheering for Kate Maddox. A few stragglers were wandering around in groups. At first, nothing looked out of the ordinary.

Dunn tried to tell himself they figured it out, but until all the people there were safe, he couldn't think that.

One by one, he and English tried doors and searched bathrooms. One by one, they found nothing suspicious.

"Any luck?" English asked through the comms.

"Negative," Mason replied. "One more to search."

"Negative here, too," Slade said. "Wild goose chase."

"Sorry, everyone," English said. "I really thought we figured it out."

"It's on me," Dunn told the group. "I made the call. Slade, any ideas since you don't like anyone else's?"

Silence met his question.

"Bingo," Mason said. "Slade, west side, far south end. Door is marked 'Employees Only' and has a busted lock. No timer, but definitely an explosive device."

"Could be a trigger," Dunn said. "Clear the area."

"Clear the building," Slade said. "I'm on my way."

Dunn and English took off running toward the spot, too.

"We're on the move," Dex said calmly. "Going out the back."

"Good move. Rocky, Jaymes? You still have eyes on the ladies?" Dunn asked.

"Ten-four. Cackling like old bitties," Rocky said.

"Move, out of the way," Dunn shouted as he and English rushed through the crowd. It was thicker with the delay, and more people stood around, grabbing refreshments before the show.

English bumped a woman who spun and fell to the ground. Dunn stopped, but English waved him on while he stopped to help the woman up.

Dunn made it to the door seconds before Slade and Jack. Slade didn't hesitate before pushing through the door and kicking everyone else out. He shut the door behind him.

Archer slammed his hand on the door. "Let us in, you crazy asshole."

Through the comms, Slade said, "That door is steel. If this goes wrong, it'll protect everyone outside." He paused for a second, then breathed, "Fuck. Evacuate the building. Right now."

"That includes you," Dunn growled at him.

"No, it doesn't. Get the building clear," Slade said.

"We clear it, then you get the fuck out of there," Dunn said.

"I can take care of myself."

"Stubborn son of a bitch," Dunn mumbled.

"I can't focus with all of you out there. Go. Now."

Dunn slammed his hand against the wall next to the door and spun to the rest of his team. They all looked at him. They needed instructions. They needed to find a way to keep the crowd calm while evacuating the building quickly. Did such a thing exist?

ASHLEIGH LAUGHED WITH LILY, Kelsea, and Pilar. She had forgotten how good it felt to have friends. Real friends who talked and laughed and picked at each other. It had been far too long since she'd had that.

"I had no idea Jack was involved when we met," Ashleigh admitted.

"He hit on you, didn't he?" Pilar asked with a smirk.

Ashleigh shrugged. "Not blatantly, but he was flirty."

"That's the only way Jack knows how to speak to a woman," Lily said. "The day we met, he tried to stake his claim because I cooked for everyone."

"Wow, I feel left out. Jack never hit on me," Kelsea said. "Then again, I was in Jaymes's lap when we met. And I thought he was trying to kill me."

Ashleigh snorted a laugh. "You're kidding right?"

Kelsea shook her head. "I was being stalked and kind of freaked out. It's a long story, but Jack let himself into Jaymes's apartment and I honestly believed he was going to kidnap me."

"He still feels bad about that," Pilar said. "And I'm sure he'll hit on you, eventually."

The women laughed again.

"I thought the concert was supposed to start by now,"

Lily said. She looked around at the rest of the crowd. "I wonder what's going on."

Ashleigh looked around, too. She lost track of time and didn't think about the show since she was enjoying her time with the others. "Where are Rocky and Jaymes?"

Everyone looked around.

"There," Pilar said, pointing. "They're coming this way."

The women stood together, waiting for their protectors to reach them. When they finally did, Jaymes reached for Kelsea.

"We need to go," Rocky said. "They're evacuating the building."

"What? Why?" Ashleigh asked.

"We have no choice. Let's go before the announcement is made," Rocky said.

Jaymes led the way, with Kelsea holding his hand. Lily and Pilar were right behind them. Ashleigh followed, and Rocky hung back to make sure they were all together.

They were low in the stands, not on the floor, but only three rows up. The entire venue was crowded with people waiting to hear Kate Maddox sing. Ashleigh looked at the people around them as they passed, hoping they would all make it out of there before something happened.

They made it halfway up the stairs to the walkway that would lead outside when a voice came over the PA system.

"Good evening, ladies and gentlemen. We apologize for the delay. Unfortunately, at this time, we need to extend the delay even longer. We need everyone to leave the building. Please take all personal items with you as you go. Follow the attendants' instructions to evacuate the building imme-diately."

The groans were quickly drowned out by gasps of fear and shouts of terror.

"Go," Rocky said from right behind Ashleigh. "Faster. We need to get out of here."

Ashleigh tried to run up the stairs, but other people blocked her way. She couldn't push by them as they tried to get out.

"Ashleigh, go," Rocky said loudly. He put his hands on her back and pushed her forward, urging her up the stairs.

They finally made it to the top, and it was even more chaotic. People ran in every direction, knocking into each other without a concern for anyone around them.

Ashleigh lost sight of Jaymes and the others on their rush up the stairs, but she saw them a little ahead of her when she made it into the open space around the concession stands.

Someone rushed by her and knocked her into the wall. She slammed into the concrete wall and cried out.

"Are you okay?" Rocky asked, putting his arm around her shoulder and pulling her away from the wall.

Ashleigh rubbed her arm and nodded. "Yeah, I think so. Startled me more than anything else."

"Can you keep moving?" Rocky asked.

Ashleigh nodded. "Yeah. Let's go." She stayed close to Rocky as he guided her through the crowd. Everyone seemed to be going the opposite way they were, but she kept moving, trusting that Rocky was taking her where she needed to go.

They made it to the first ramp that would take them back downstairs to the ground level, outside the arena. Rocky still had an arm around her, making sure they didn't get separated. Ashleigh didn't know what was going on, but she felt better knowing they were almost out. And she was safe with Rocky. She was close to hyperventilating, but she was going to be okay.

"Help me!" a woman shouted from behind them.

Rocky stopped and turned.

"Help!" she screamed again.

Rocky turned back to her and started moving, but the person called out again.

"Brady, stop!"

Rocky froze. "Ashleigh…"

"Go," Ashleigh told him. "Jaymes and the others are right in front of us. I'll be fine. I'll catch up to them and stay with him. Go save whoever that is."

Rocky hesitated for a long moment. He looked over the edge of the ramp and nodded. "There's no way on or off this other than right here and at the ground. Keep going down. I'll tell Jaymes you're on your way so he knows to stop and look for you."

"Brady, please stop!"

Rocky looked up again. "Brady is Williams' first name, Ashleigh. If it wasn't… I have to go."

"Go," Ashleigh said, feeling the same fear that overwhelmed her when she sat next to the man in the booth. When he stuck a gun in her side. "Help her, Rocky. Save her."

Rocky nodded and turned away. He touched his ear as he left, and Ashleigh drew in a breath. She was on her own. But she could do it.

She turned and let herself get swept into the crowd. Everyone was rushing down the stairs, eager to get away from whatever happened that was making them evacuate the building. Ashleigh's head spun with possibilities.

She wound around the ramp, circling the concrete with thousands of other people. Someone above her shouted, and all of a sudden, the crowd rushed at her. They started running, and she started running, and before she knew it, she was outside.

Darkness settled around her. She was in a crowd of people, but she couldn't see anyone's faces. It was past sunset, and they were in the shadows of the building, making what little light that existed in the night sky invisible to them. All she could see was darkness.

People started grabbing their phones and turning on flashlights. One after another, they shone in her face, blinding her with each pass.

Ashleigh shielded her eyes to try to see around her. Jaymes, Kelsea, Lily, and Pilar had to be close. She wasn't far from the building, and she didn't see them inside when she ran out with the others. They couldn't have gone far, not if they knew to look for her.

She moved through the crowd quickly. She turned people to face her, startling them. She didn't care. All that mattered was finding Jaymes, Kelsea, Lily, and Pilar. They were her lifeline. She didn't bring a phone since she was supposed to be with Daniel the entire time. And now she was alone.

She reached the edge of the crowd and turned back. People flowed out of the arena, stuffing the outside until she could barely see through the crowd, let alone search for four people.

Ashleigh couldn't give up, though. She pushed her way back through, working her way toward the entrance. Maybe she ran past them. Maybe they were still inside looking for her.

She got to the door, straining to hear someone calling her name. Voices shouted for other missing people, but no one called her name. She waited for a break in the rush of people coming out, and let herself into the building. The only way to go was up. She looked around, but she didn't recognize anyone. Faces rushed by her in a blur, but no one was standing there, waiting for her.

She was alone.

People came running down the stairs, and someone plowed right into her. She fell to the side, stumbling over her feet, and almost caught herself before she hit the concrete wall.

Almost.

Pain exploded in her head. She blinked and saw stars. She sank to the ground, unable to tell which way was up.

Hands reached around her and lifted her. "Are you okay? Are you hurt?"

Ashleigh just groaned. Moving her head caused more stars to blind her.

"Come with me. I'll get you to safety."

Ashleigh had no idea who was helping her, but she was grateful there were still good people in the world.

21

DUNN PACED IN FRONT OF THE STEEL DOOR BETWEEN HIM AND Slade, ready to break it down if need be. He sent the rest of the team to help with the evacuation, but he wasn't going to leave his teammate behind.

"Talk to me, Slade," he said quietly through the commotion around him.

"There's a phone trigger. An old phone. Rudimentary, but effective. It could go at any time now that they know we're onto them."

"He always knew we were onto them. He told us to be here," Dunn said, still struggling with the whole thing.

People rushed by, racing to get out of the building before they got hurt. Dunn would have preferred a more controlled evacuation, but he didn't get a vote.

Dunn paced, wanting to give Slade as much time as possible but ready to get moving and get Ashleigh back in his arms. He wanted to call Rocky and Jaymes and make sure she was safe, but he trusted them. Nothing was going to happen to her with them protecting her.

A few minutes later, Slade opened the door between

them, holding an old flip phone. "We still need to get rid of it, but it won't go off."

Dunn nodded, feeling marginally better. "Now what?"

Slade clapped him on the back. "We get this to English and see if he can do any magic. Where's everyone else?"

"I sent them to help. We're meeting on the north side, away from the blast zone."

Slade nodded. "Let's go."

The two of them pushed their way through the crowd, helping people where they could and simply encouraging others to keep moving. A few stragglers were standing around like they didn't hear the evacuation announcement, so they stopped and asked them to keep moving.

They made it to the ramp that would take them down to the exit where the others were meeting when the phone in Dunn's hand rang. The one that was supposed to be connected to the bomb.

He and Slade stopped dead in the middle of the hallway. People grumbled as they moved around them. "Answer it," Slade said.

Dunn flipped the phone open and put it to his ear so he could hear above the crowd noise. "Yeah?"

Laughter echoed through the other side of the phone. "Well, this couldn't have gone better if I planned it. Oh, wait, I did."

"Williams," Dunn growled. "What the fuck do you want?"

"I just wanted you to say hi to someone. Say hi to Daniel."

"Daniel," Ashleigh whimpered. "Daniel, I'm so sorry."

"Ashleigh!"

"That's enough for you two. I just wanted to give you a chance to say goodbye to her," Williams said with a snicker.

"Where are you, you worthless son of a bitch? I'm going to fucking kill you!"

Williams outright laughed. "Why would I tell you that? Besides, we'll be gone by the time you get here. Ashleigh's husband is on his way. He's really missed her."

"No!" The phone beeped in his ear and went dead. Dunn pulled it away and stared at it. "Ashleigh."

Slade took the phone from his hands and guided Dunn down the ramp. He barely noticed they were moving until they were outside, and the cool night air hit him in the face.

"Ashleigh. We have to go back in and find her," he said, pushing away from Slade.

Slade grabbed his arm, but Dunn shook him off. "Listen, you're not thinking, and rushing around this place blindly is not going to save her. Let's find the team and find out how she got separated from them. Then we might have a better idea of where to look."

Dunn didn't want to listen to him, but he knew Slade was right. If he raced inside, he had no idea where to go. All he knew was Williams wouldn't have her out in the open.

Slade nodded once and pointed toward the crowd gathered outside. They started walking and found the group to the side near the exit.

"Everything okay?" Archer asked. His arm was around Lily.

Slade shook his head. "Williams called the burner he used as a trigger. He has Ashleigh. He's going to give her to her husband."

"Fuck," Archer said.

"Where are they?" Mason asked.

Slade shook his head again. "We don't know. We were hoping you guys would be able to tell us what happened. Why she's not with you."

"She was with me," Rocky said. "We were walking out when the announcement was made, and we got separated from Jaymes and the girls. We made it to the top of the ramp," Rocky pointed up to where the ramp was visible through the glass enclosure, "and a woman called for help and said the name Brady."

"What?" Slade asked.

Rocky shook his head. "It was a kid. They were walking out, and the kid got away from his mother. She spotted him through the crowd and called out for him to stop. I thought..."

"It was Williams," Slade finished for him, and Rocky nodded. "Okay, so what happened to Ashleigh?"

"We were at the top. I told her to go straight down and look for Jaymes. He was going to wait for her," Rocky explained.

Slade turned to Jaymes. "And?"

"She never showed. We were standing just outside the door because the crowd was rushing down the ramp. We waited, and we never saw her. We were looking, all four of us," Jaymes said.

Dunn just stood there. He was numb. The love of his life disappeared somewhere between the top and bottom of a ramp with no way off.

"Is it possible she made it past you?" Mason asked.

Jaymes shrugged. "I guess. We were looking, but there were a ton of people."

"Well, we know she's not out here wandering around. Chances are he wouldn't have her out here because there are too many witnesses. It doesn't really matter how she disappeared, what matters is she's with Williams, and we need to find them. Now," Slade said.

"Split into teams. Move through the building. It's mostly

empty now, so it'll be easier to search. We'll take the south side," Archer said, slapping a hand against English's chest. English nodded.

"We'll go north and west," Mason said with a nod to Jack.

"That leaves us to search backstage," Slade said, glancing at Rocky. "You two stay out here with Lily, Kelsea, and Pilar," he told Jaymes and Dunn.

"Fuck that," Dunn said. "I'm not sitting on my hands. I'm going with you."

Slade and Rocky exchanged a look. "Fine, you're with us. Jaymes, stay with them. If you hear anything or see anything, let us know."

Jaymes nodded, and the others turned back to the building. They walked inside with guns drawn, ready for anything. All of them went up the ramp together, hurrying anyone walking down out the door. At the top, they went in different directions, spreading out to find Ashleigh and Williams.

Hopefully, before she disappeared forever.

ASHLEIGH'S HEAD throbbed where she slammed it into the wall, but that was the least of her problems. Frederick was coming. She had to find a way to get out of there, but she didn't know how she was going to do that.

She tugged at her hands, but the zip ties were tight and dug into her wrists when she pulled. She looked around the room, but moving her head sent bursts of pain through her brain.

All she knew was she was in a small room, likely one of the rooms behind the stage.

"Why are you doing this?" she asked softly.

Williams turned to her with a smirk. "Do you think you're going to get me to talk?"

She shook her head, then winced from the pain. She clamped her eyes shut and took a deep breath. She was going to throw up, but since she was tied to a chair, she would only manage to cover herself. She had to choke it back.

A few deep breaths later, and the feeling passed. Thank God.

"That was a pretty nasty blow you took," Williams said with a smile in his voice. "Bad luck."

She glared at him, but it lacked heat because of her head injury. She closed her eyes with a sigh and prayed whatever he was going to do to her would be over soon.

"Your husband will nurse you back to health, I'm sure," Williams said.

"He's not my husband," Ashleigh growled.

"Really? Because you told me you were married when we first met. At JB's Subs. Don't you remember? You did take a nasty spill."

His laughter reverberated through her skull and made her head hurt worse, something she didn't think was possible.

Someone pounded on the door. Again, it felt like her head was going to split open, but hope blossomed. Daniel was there. He found her. He was going to save her.

She looked up as Williams went to the door and tapped back. Daniel hit the door again, and Williams turned the knob to let him in.

Except it wasn't Daniel who stepped into view. It was Frederick. And he was furious.

"What the hell is she doing tied to a fucking chair?"

Williams gave him a look that said he was only mildly concerned about Frederick's tone. "Uh, so she doesn't run away."

Frederick glared at Williams. "Why does she look like that? Why is there blood in her hair?"

"She fell," Williams said flatly.

"How?"

Williams shrugged. "I had to get her here."

Frederick grabbed Williams by the collar. Williams was broader, but Frederick was taller. Williams rose up onto his tiptoes with Frederick's hands dragging him up. "What the fuck did you do to her?"

Williams' eyes widened for a split second, then turned malicious. Neither man was going to back down. "I made sure I had an excuse to carry a woman through a crowd of scared people."

Ashleigh had never seen her husband so angry. His brown eyes looked black. Every inch of his body was tense and ready to snap beneath his three-piece suit. He was pressed and polished, like always, but there was a danger to him that she'd never felt before. For the first time, she witnessed the man who could take a child from his family or put a bullet in her sister's head.

All Ashleigh could feel was fear. The pain in her head subsided, the soreness in her ribs that hadn't healed went away. Nothing mattered except finding a way away from both men.

"I told you not to hurt her," Frederick growled, spit flying from his mouth to land on Williams' face.

Williams pushed Frederick back and narrowed his eyes at him. Williams wore a pair of jeans and a concert tee. He looked like everyone else who'd been in the crowd. Ashleigh could see how he would have blended in and gone unnoticed. She blamed herself for going with him, but she had no idea he was the one being so nice to her when she fell.

She pulled at her wrists again, and the zip ties cut into her skin. Her wrists were raw, and probably bleeding, but she couldn't think about either. If she could get free, maybe she could sneak past them.

"Where's my family?" Williams demanded.

"They're safe."

"What the fuck does that mean? Our agreement was you were going to bring them here. To me."

Frederick shrugged. "I decided I needed a little more insurance that you were going to do as you promised."

"I did! Your wife is here. Where the fuck is mine?"

Frederick got in Williams' face again. "Do you have any idea who you're speaking to?"

Williams backed up a half a step, just enough to put some distance between him and Frederick. Ashleigh could tell he was scared.

"I put this whole thing together. I made the threats against Kate Maddox so she would hire the team. I made sure my family was here. I got your fucking wife. I made all this happen. All you had to do was hold up your end of the bargain." Williams pulled a gun from behind his back and pointed it at Frederick. "Now, it's your choice." He swung the gun toward her and pointed it at her face. "My wife or yours."

Frederick's eyes were murderous. He didn't look at Ashleigh. He just glowered at Williams. If they made it out of there alive, he wouldn't give up until Williams was dead. Ashleigh knew that as well as she knew she'd never see Daniel again. She would be a ghost by the time Frederick was done with her. If he didn't kill her, he'd tell everyone she was dead and she'd never see the light of day again.

Ashleigh closed her eyes and prayed for a miracle. She didn't know how she'd get one, or even if she deserved one, but she prayed for one.

The door squeaked, and she opened her eyes. Frederick looked out into the hallway and nodded to someone. He reached for something and was handed a phone. Frederick turned the screen toward Williams.

A woman and two teenage girls were sitting on the floor next to a man. He was slumped over and could have been dead. Ashleigh was definitely going to throw up.

"Where the hell are they?" Williams growled.

"I told you, they're safe. And as soon as you give me my wife, I'll tell you where yours is. And your daughters. Although, all three of them would fetch a good price for me." Frederick looked at Ashleigh and shrugged. "If you don't want them, we can trade. My wife has been tainted. I'll happily teach her how a married woman should act." Frederick sneered at Williams again. "I could teach yours, too."

Williams roared and rushed toward Frederick. Before he made it two steps, Frederick pulled out a gun and fired. It happened so fast, Ashleigh was sure she imagined it, but Williams stopped in his tracks. He crumpled to the ground at her feet.

Ashleigh screamed.

Frederick just stood there for a long moment. Then he slid the gun back into his pocket and moved to her. He touched her arm, and she jumped.

"You'll get used to my touch again. Of course, it won't be gentle for a while." He kissed her shoulder. "I need to erase the man who've been fucking behind my back."

"You're not my husband," Ashleigh said quietly.

Frederick laughed and something cold and firm pressed against her skin. A snip and the zip ties binding her wrists fell away. She moved to stretch her arms, but Frederick wrapped a firm hand around the sore parts and growled in her ear, "Never fucking say that again. I'm your husband. You shared my bed. You sucked my dick. You came for my touch. It doesn't matter what my name is, you let me take care of you while you fucked around, and you embarrassed me and ran off with another man. Never again, Ashleigh. Never fucking again. And if you mention his name in my house, I'll kill him and you."

Ashleigh whimpered against the pain. She wanted him to get it over with and kill her, but she wasn't strong enough. She couldn't stare death in the face and say fuck you. All she could do was cry.

Frederick released her wrists and grabbed her under the arm, dragging her to her feet. She tripped over Williams, and he groaned.

Frederick glared at him, but continued dragging Ashleigh to the door. They were almost out of the room when Williams called his name.

"Hey, Frederick," he said.

Frederick stopped and turned back. "What the hell do you want?"

Ashleigh looked back. Williams had a phone in his hand.

"Fuck you." Williams pushed a button.

Frederick dropped her arm and pushed her against the door frame. He took off running down the hallway. Ashleigh's head throbbed as she tried to understand what just happened.

Then she heard the explosion, and everything went dark.

22

—————

Dunn was almost to the door that led backstage when the first bomb went off. The ground shook, and Slade shouted, "Take cover!"

He dove for the side and crouched down near the wall, as low as he could get.

The door in front of them burped, like the bomb was right on the other side. If they'd been just a few seconds faster, they could have been in the middle of the explosion.

"Everyone okay?" Slade asked.

Dunn pushed to his feet and brushed off his pants, then was knocked on his ass by the second explosion. Definitely bigger, likely closer. As he fell to the ground, he slammed his elbow against the wall and pain splintered away from where it impacted. He cradled his arm and curled up, praying the ground beneath him didn't give way.

He was still on the ground when another explosion shook the building farther away. On the other side.

"Three," Slade said. "One more! Don't move!"

Slade just got the words out when there was another explosion from inside the arena. The stage, maybe?

Dunn couldn't see his hand in front of his face. He choked on the dust and debris floating around them. Every part of his body hurt. He wanted to just lie there. Rest for a while.

"Got him," he heard through the fog. "Get him up."

Two hands reached under his arms and heaved Dunn to his feet. His feet didn't want to work, and his arm screamed with pain. He fought against the people holding him.

"Dunn, we have to get out of here. It's unstable. We need to go. Now."

Something filtered through the fog. "Ashleigh."

"We'll find her, Dunn. Right now, we need to get outside."

Outside sounded good. He let them lead him, half-drag him toward outside. Fresh air. He liked that.

"He's fading," the voice said. "Hurry."

They started moving faster, but Dunn's feet weren't working right. They put his arms over their shoulders, but he cried out from the pain.

"Broken arm," the voice said.

"I got him." Was that a second voice? He couldn't figure it out.

The room spun as Dunn was tossed up and over someone's shoulder. His gut landed hard on the shoulder, and the little he'd eaten earlier threatened to take a return trip.

"Don't feel good," he murmured.

"Almost there. Don't fall asleep."

"Sleep. I like sleep."

"Not right now. We need to find Ashleigh."

"Ashleigh? Where's Ashleigh?"

"We don't know, but we're going to find her. You're going to help us."

He nodded and tried to think. Something wasn't right. He didn't know what, but something wasn't right.

The jostling didn't help. His stomach grew more and more queasy, and his head was starting to hurt. His lungs burned for fresh air. And his arm was going numb.

"Let's get him down," the voice said. "I need to take a look at his head."

"My head hurts," Dunn said.

"Shit. Almost there, Dunn. Just hang on a little longer."

Finally, the cold air hit him. Just for a second, then it was snatched away again. He choked on the air, trying to take a deep breath and filling his lungs with dust. He coughed and tried to put his hand to his face, but it hurt. Jesus, everything hurt.

"We know. We're almost there. I'll take a look at you in just a minute."

"There. Over there."

Dunn groaned as he was shifted again and put on the ground. The grass felt good beneath his body. Soft. And the fresh air was like a gift from God. Until the pain sank in.

"Why the hell do I hurt so much?" he asked.

"You got hit," the voice said. "Don't you remember?"

Dunn shook his head, trying to piece it together. "No. The first one was on the other side of the door. The second, I stood up, and it went off, but I heard the other two."

"There were three, Dunn. Three more. Five total that went off. Williams always set five charges. I thought we were good after four because we found one. He must have counted on that and set another one to catch us off guard. It worked."

Dunn sucked in a breath, coughing when his lungs protested.

"Shallow breaths. Get that shit out of you instead of moving it deeper."

Dunn nodded and groaned at the pain.

"What did you hit?"

He shrugged, and the pain spiked in his elbow. "Right elbow. Head. Not sure what else."

"Your right arm is definitely broken. Concussion, probably worse than mild. Maybe not severe, but I can't be sure yet. Can you hear us?"

Dunn nodded.

"Open your eyes, boss."

Dunn didn't realize he hadn't opened them. He struggled to pry his lids up, but they wouldn't budge.

"Hang on," the voice said.

Something splashed on Dunn's face. He winced, but it loosened whatever was holding his eyes closed. He blinked up at Rocky and Slade. "I never thought I'd be so happy to see your ugly faces."

They both grinned back at him. "We never thought we'd be so happy you aren't bigger. Fuck, you're gonna owe us a few days off and a few weeks of physical therapy," Slade said with a groan.

"Trust me, I'd have much rather walked out of there on my own power."

A crackle through the comms had all of them sobering. Dunn awkwardly pushed himself to a seated position. Rocky helped him up, being careful of his arm.

"Check in. Radio check in."

Archer.

"Shit, it's good to hear your voice," Slade said. "Where are you guys?"

"South side. Near the location of the last explosion.

We're alive, but we're stuck where we are. He took out the ramp closest to us."

"The ramp on the north side is open. Can you make it there?" Slade asked.

"Negative. English has a broken leg. He can't walk that far. I dislocated my shoulder. There's no way I can carry him."

"We're on our way to you. Stay put," Mason said through the comms. "We were far enough away to take cover. Jack and I will get you guys out of there."

"Meet on the grass. North side, due north from the ramp. Stay safe, and work fast," Dunn said.

"Ten-four."

Dunn felt better knowing his team was alive and would heal, but none of them said anything about Ashleigh.

"We'll find her," Rocky said, reading his mind. "Let's regroup, and we'll get back in there."

"We'll get her," Slade reiterated.

Dunn hoped they were right.

The crowd that felt suffocating earlier was nearly gone. Sirens screeched into the parking lots, surrounding the arena. Slade went to brief them on what happened and what they were dealing with while Rocky worked on fitting up a sling for Dunn's arm.

Slade returned about the same time that Jack, Mason, Archer, and English made it out of the building. The local police turned on them, demanding they put their hands up. They did as they were told, but Slade smoothed it over and explained they were part of the team.

"Lieutenant Dunn," Captain Patrick from the local PD said, walking over. "I didn't realize you were working here."

Dunn nodded. "Yes, sir. We were hired to work private

security for Ms. Maddox. She received threats a few months back and wanted to have extra eyes on her."

"You didn't think something like this warranted a head's up?"

Dunn shook his head. "We didn't expect anything like this, sir. If we had, I assure you we would have encouraged Ms. Maddox to cancel the show and brought you in. We had dogs sweep the building. We don't know what happened or how it happened at this point."

"Do you have a suspect?"

"Yes. Two. Brady Williams and a man we know as Frederick Edwards."

"Who is that?"

Dunn handed over his phone with a picture of Edwards. "Agent Marks has been investigating him in connection with a kidnapping case in Detroit."

"And he got mixed up with you guys?"

Dunn shook his head again. "Not intentionally."

"Were they working together?"

Dunn nodded. "We believe so."

Captain Patrick blew out a breath and looked at the rubble that used to be the arena. He handed back the phone. "I need those pictures. This is a damn mess."

Dunn nodded and texted the photos. "Yes, sir, it is. If you'll excuse us, we have to get back in there. Someone we were protecting is believed to still be in there."

"What? Who? No one survived that."

Dunn shook his head. "I refuse to believe that until I find her body. I have to look for her."

Captain Patrick narrowed his gaze and nodded sharply. "If you need cadaver dogs, let me know."

Dunn nodded. "I hope it doesn't come to that."

"Me, too. Good luck."

Dunn turned back to the team. They looked like he felt. Broken, bruised, and beaten. But they were all on their feet, even English, who was leaning on Jack.

"Archer and English. Head over to those ambulances and get checked out. You two are done for the night. Everyone else, if you're not up for this, you can go with them. I imagine we all took in a shit-ton of dust from those bombs. Ashleigh is... my responsibility. None of you have to do this," Dunn said.

The others exchanged a glance and stepped forward. "We're with you. Always," Slade said for the group. "But I'm in charge right now."

"No, I—"

"Have a serious head injury, a broken arm, and are not an explosives expert. I can send you with English and Archer, or you can let me take lead on this."

Dunn wanted to argue, but his head told him he didn't have the power to fight Slade. He was still fuzzy, and if he moved too quickly, his arm reminded him he wasn't one hundred percent. Not even close.

"Good. Now, we're all going together. We can't risk something else happening and being separated. The danger appears to be over. Williams and Edwards might be in the wind, but they won't get far. Everyone will know their names and faces within minutes. The police will talk to everyone here and find out if anyone knows anything. Finding Ashleigh and any other survivors is up to us."

"We didn't see anyone inside when we were making our way through," Mason said.

"Neither did we," Slade agreed. "But we're going to make sure we didn't miss anyone."

The others nodded and moved toward the door to the ramp. The explosion blew out some of the windows, so fresh air filled the space. The rest of the dust settled in the time they were outside, leaving them with mostly clear air to move through.

Slade went in first, gun raised. Mason was right behind him, with Dunn, Rocky, and Jack at the end.

"Is Pilar okay?" Dunn asked on their walk up the ramp. The building was eerily quiet.

Jack huffed. "As okay as she can be right now. They're all pretty shaken up. And worried about Ashleigh."

Dunn nodded. He was, too.

"We'll find her," Slade said with a confidence Dunn didn't feel.

They stopped at the top and looked back and forth. "Where to?" Rocky asked.

Slade glanced at the four of them. He drew in a breath and nodded his head to the corridor that led away from the backstage area. "Let's take a walk this way. Those of you who came this way with Archer and English, lead the way. We'll follow. Everyone keep your eyes open."

Mason went first, with Jack at the end. Dunn cradled his arm, the sling Rocky crafted for him helping, but the pain was settling into his bones. His adrenaline was wearing off, but he couldn't give up. Not until they found Ashleigh.

The explosion at that end of the building knocked a wide hole in the wall, but the building was intact. Thankfully, they'd evacuated before the bombs, and didn't pass anyone on the way by.

"The ramp on the south side is a full loss," Mason said. "There's no way to tell if anyone is in there."

They all looked at Dunn. He shook his head, immediately regretting the decision. "He wouldn't have had her in the open. He would have had her somewhere no one else could see. She was hurt. It would have drawn attention to them."

He hoped.

"Let's go back the other way and get backstage. At least one of the explosions took place back there. One on stage, maybe, and one backstage. On the north side," Slade said.

Fatigue and doubt settled into Dunn's body as they trudged back the way they came. He could barely keep his eyes open, and guilt gnawed at him. If anything happened to her, he would never forgive himself. He put finding Williams above protecting her, and she paid for it. He failed both missions. He didn't catch Williams, and he didn't keep Ashleigh safe.

They made it to the door when Slade's phone rang. He held up his hand and answered it. "Yeah?"

His shoulders sagged with relief. "It's Dex. He was at the hotel with Kate and Dillon when the first explosion occurred."

"They're okay?"

Slade nodded. "They're good. He's been trying to reach us." He held up a finger. "Yeah, okay. We'll keep you posted." He hung up the phone and tucked it back into his pocket. "They're fine. He said it was all over the news that there were multiple explosions. People are flooding the local hospitals looking for missing loved ones. Social media is blowing up. Kate's people have released a statement, and she's pledging assistance to anyone who needs it. Outside these walls, things are going nuts."

"Inside isn't much better," Jack muttered.

"Agreed. Let's keep moving. We need to find out what's on the other side of this door," Rocky said.

Slade nodded and turned to the doors. One door was bent toward them and the other looked like it was swollen.

He tugged, and the door swung free. In front of them looked like a gravel yard with pieces of rubble and rocks everywhere.

"Fuck me," Jack breathed.

"Yeah," Slade agreed. "Let's move. Watch your step. Anyone stumbles, we all stop. Dunn."

"Yeah?"

"You don't make a move without someone in front and behind you," Slade said.

"I'm not a child."

"No, but you are hurt. You fall and try to land on that arm, it'll only get worse. My better judgement says not to let you even try to walk through here, but I know you won't stand down. You will listen, though," Slade said.

Dunn held his friend's gaze and nodded once. He knew Slade was right, but that didn't mean he had to like it.

Slade went first, stepping over the first large block of concrete. Mason followed him, then reached back for Dunn to take his hand. He wanted to slap it away, but he needed the help if he was going to keep going. Mason half-pulled him over the block and Jack and Rocky were right behind him, just in case. They kept moving, pushing doors open and glancing into rooms as they walked by.

No one spoke as they walked. Mason helped Dunn over the large and uneven spots, but no one said anything. It wasn't long before they came to what was clearly the site of one of the explosions.

"Holy shit," Slade murmured. "I don't think this is stable. We might need to come back some other time."

"Fuck, no," Dunn said. "I'm not leaving her in there. I'll go by myself if you're done."

Dunn tried to move past them, but Slade stopped him. "You go, we go." He looked up at the ceiling above them.

"Move slowly and touch as little as possible. Watch each other, help each other. Move together."

The others nodded.

Slade looked up and down, then chose a path, although Dunn had no idea why. Silence settled over them once more. A crater in the floor showed where the bomb was. The wall under the stage. Blown out on one side. There was no doubt the explosion would have killed the people closest to the stage if the bomb went off during the concert. It would have killed Kate Maddox and her band, too.

They moved past the site and down the hallway. The blast zone wasn't big, but what was left of it was a mess. Twisted metal, exposed rebar, and chunks of concrete littered the area, making it harder to move through.

Dunn was careful, but he still lost his balance. Jack grabbed his good arm before he went down. The pain in his head echoed through his skull.

"Dunn," Slade said.

"I'm fine," he barked, hating feeling weak.

"Dunn."

"What?"

"There's someone here. And they're not moving," Slade said.

Dunn spun to look and fell to his knees. "Ashleigh."

23

———

"GRAB SOMETHING AND PULL," SLADE BARKED. "WE NEED TO move all this off her. Now!"

Dunn sank to the floor while everyone else moved toward the still figure on the ground. Dunn couldn't explain how he knew it was her when all that was visible was the sole of a sneaker, but he knew it was.

His team lifted the first block off her, and she still didn't move. They pushed more debris away until all that was left was one large rock.

"We need to lift this as a team. With the wall here, we can't get a good handle on it, so we work as one," Slade said.

Dunn sat while Mason, Slade, Rocky, and Jack moved to the piece of concrete. They grabbed and Slade counted them down. They lifted, but they couldn't get the block high enough.

"She's still trapped," Slade growled. "We need another plan."

They stepped back and looked around. Dunn dropped his head in his hands. He didn't know if she was alive. If they didn't get to her quickly, it wouldn't matter if she was, she wouldn't be.

Slade and Rocky were talking quietly, but the silence around them meant Dunn could hear every word.

"Can we slide her out?" Slade asked.

"I don't know. I can't tell if this is resting on her or not," Rocky replied.

"Should we try? If we feel any resistance, we stop."

"We can try it," Rocky said.

Dun lifted his head and watched. They each grabbed one of her ankles, and she kicked.

"What the hell?" Dunn asked, scrambling to his feet. "She's alive."

"She's awake," Jack said.

"Ashleigh," Slade shouted. "Ashleigh, we're going to try to pull you out. Stop kicking, Ashleigh."

She groaned and stopped.

"Hurry," Dunn shouted, moving closer. He'd grab her himself if they didn't hurry the hell up.

"One, two, three," Slade said. He and Rocky pulled, but almost instantly Ashleigh cried out.

"Stop, stop!" Dunn shouted. "Stop."

They stopped pulling and set her feet down.

She whimpered.

Dunn moved closer. "Ash, I'm here. We're going to get you out. I promise you."

She tapped her foot on the ground three times, and he grabbed her ankle.

"I love you, Ash. I'm not going anywhere. We're going to figure this out."

She tapped her foot again.

"How are we going to do this?" Slade asked.

"Maybe we can help," someone said from behind them.

They spun and found a pair of firefighters. One of them had a jack in his hands.

"Yes, perfect," Slade said. "Over here. She's trapped, but we might not need to get this very high before we set her free."

Dunn released Ashleigh's ankle and moved out of the way so they could work. It felt like it took forever for Slade and the firefighters to decide how to position the jack and start lifting the massive rock from Ashleigh.

Once they started, she squirmed. Rocky and Slade moved to her and put their hands on her legs so she didn't kick the jack. They pulled gently, and finally, she was free of the prison.

Dunn crawled over to her, wrapped his good arm around her, and pulled her close. She sobbed when she was finally in his arms, her head on his chest. As far as he could tell, she wasn't hurt other than cuts and bruises, which was a small miracle.

"You're safe now, baby. I'm not letting you go. I got you, Ash," Dunn murmured over and over again.

She just held him and cried.

They lowered the large block back to the ground, and Slade said, "Holy shit."

Dunn looked up. He couldn't see whatever it was Slade saw, but he could tell by the looks on their faces it wasn't good.

Jack walked over. "Williams is dead."

"He's over there?" Dunn asked.

Jack nodded. "Yeah."

Dunn was surprised by the pain that hit him in the chest. He hated that man. He hunted him, but he was his brother before that. He hated him, but once, he loved him. A part of Dunn always hoped Williams could be saved. Without that hope, he felt the loss.

And it fucking hurt.

ASHLEIGH BLINKED her eyes open and looked around. Hospital. She wasn't surprised, but everything was more than a little fuzzy. Her head hurt like hell, and most of the rest of her ached, but she was alive, which was the best news.

"Hey," a familiar voice said.

She searched the room until she found Daniel sitting next to her. He looked as broken and beaten as she felt, but he was alive.

A sob choked her when she took in the sling over his shoulder and the bandage on his head.

"I'm okay," he assured her, even though he winced when he leaned forward. "I'll be okay. So will you."

She nodded. "Williams is dead."

He ducked his head and nodded. "We know."

"I saw him. When I was trapped under the rubble, I saw him. He was right in front of me when I woke up."

"I'm sorry, Ash. I should have taken better care of you," Daniel said, meeting her gaze.

There was immeasurable pain in his. She felt it to the very core of herself. He blamed himself. "Daniel..."

"I'm leaving the team. I haven't told them all yet, but I'm leaving. I can't be their leader when I make decisions like I did this week."

"Because of me," she said softly.

He shook his head. "No, not because of you. Because I wanted to stop Williams. I... I thought I could save him. I wanted to stop him, but I thought if we caught him, he would turn his life around. I believed in him."

"He was your mentor. You should have believed in him," Ashleigh said. "There's nothing wrong with that."

"There is if it costs people their lives. There are still people missing. Employees and a few attendees. I caused this."

"No, you didn't," Ashleigh said, pushing herself up to sit. "None of this was your fault."

"She's right," Rocky said, walking into the room with a cup of coffee. He smiled at her and came to her bedside. He handed the coffee to Daniel and asked her, "How are you feeling?"

She shrugged. "Like I was blown up."

Rocky grinned. "Sounds about right. How's the head? You have a pretty nasty bump, so they want to keep you a few days."

"It hurts, but I'm alive thanks to all of you."

Rocky nodded. "Are you up for visitors? Lily works here, so she talked them into letting everyone come in here, but only if you're up to it. It was a long night dealing with the fallout, and everyone wants to see you."

Ashleigh nodded, her eyes welling with tears. She couldn't remember the last time she had people who cared enough about what happened to her to show up at a hospital for her.

Rocky disappeared around the curtain and said something, then the others filtered into the room. Ashleigh smiled at them all and thanked them for coming as each one approached and patted her leg or hugged her. The men circled Daniel, and the women centered around Ashleigh.

"I'm so sorry we didn't keep you with us," Lily said to Ashleigh. "We had no idea we got separated."

"It's okay. You guys were safe. That was what was important," Ashleigh told her.

"Keeping you safe was important, too. I failed at that," Rocky said.

"We all failed," Slade said. "But we don't give up. No one is going to go through life without making mistakes."

The other men in the room nodded. All except Daniel.

"I'm not sure I want to ask, but Frederick...?" Ashleigh asked.

"They found his body," Slade said. "Not far from where you were. Thankfully, he hadn't made it to you yet."

"He did," Ashleigh told them. "He killed Williams. Well, he shot him. Williams brought me down there and I guess they were going to trade me for his family. Frederick didn't bring his family, and then he shot Williams. He was dragging me out when Williams called someone. Frederick shoved me down and ran, then everything went dark."

The men exchanged looks, and the entire room went still.

"What does that mean?" Ashleigh asked.

"Williams had the explosives wired to a cell phone as the trigger. When he called someone, he was setting off the bombs. Frederick must have known that and tried to get away, but he didn't make it," Slade explained.

She laughed mirthlessly. "So, if I didn't already hate him, the fact that he left me to die should definitely seal the deal. I can't believe I never saw who he was."

"Frederick stashed Williams' family away from all the blast sites. We don't think he knew where they were, so the police found them. They're all okay. And, more good news, the FBI found the missing boy you told them about. Everything you gave them helped them find him. He'll be back home with his family today," Dex told her.

Ashleigh couldn't stop the flood of emotion. She helped. She did what she could, and it helped. A family was reunited because of her. Even though they were torn apart by her husband, she helped bring them back together. "That's great news."

Dex nodded. "Yeah, it is."

"I'm sorry for everything he put all of you through. I'm sorry about Williams, too," Ashleigh said.

Daniel stood at her words and moved toward the door.

"Where are you going?" Slade asked.

Daniel stopped and looked around. His gaze landed on Ashleigh's then drifted away. "I failed all of you."

Dex got in his way and shook his head. "No, you didn't."

Daniel moved to go around him, but Slade stepped up. "You made this a successful mission."

"I fucked it up. You made it clear you thought I would from the beginning," Daniel argued.

Slade shook his head. "I wanted to save Williams, too. I think we all did. I wanted to believe he could be the man we knew, and the closer we got, the more clear it became to me that it wasn't possible. It got to me, and I took it out on you. But him being gone doesn't mean you need to be gone, too. We lost one leader, we can't afford to lose another."

Daniel glanced at Rocky. Rocky just shrugged. "So I was eavesdropping and told them what you said. We were all thinking it."

"Dex is a better leader than I am," Daniel argued, ignoring Rocky.

Dex shook his head. "I don't want it. I won't take your job. I'm here because of you."

"You're here because of Jaymes. We all are. We came here last year because of Jaymes," Daniel said.

"And we stayed because of you," Dex told him. "We

saved Jaymes. We got him back. And Lily and Kelsea and Pilar, and all the other people we've helped over the last year. But we did all that because we had you to follow."

Daniel looked around at the men surrounding him. Ashleigh's heart swelled. He didn't want to believe them, but his eyes softened. He nodded and reached for Dex. They hugged, slapping each other on the back, then he did the same with every other man in the room.

"Thank you," Daniel finally said.

"We mean it, boss," Dex said. "You know Slade isn't going to bullshit you. He'd be the first to kick you out the damn door if he thought you weren't up to the job."

Daniel laughed. "True."

"Hey," Slade said.

"All right, gentlemen," a nurse said, walking into the room. "I think we need to give the patient some time to rest. Five more minutes, then I'm going to ask everyone to leave."

"Thanks, Kelly," Lily said. "We appreciate you letting us all in here."

Kelly nodded and pointed at the men. They all held up their hands and pointed to each other. Kelly rolled her eyes and walked out chuckling.

"Will you make sure he doesn't make a run for it?" Dex asked Ashleigh.

She nodded. "I'll do my best, but I have a feeling I won't be much help."

"Just flash him. He'll stick around for that," Rocky said with a wink.

"Hey," Daniel growled.

Rocky laughed and hugged Ashleigh. "So glad you're okay. I'm sorry I left you."

She shook her head. "You were doing your job."

He nodded and moved to the door. Dex hugged her next.

"Next time, I'll be your personal bodyguard. I got my target out of the building."

Ashleigh laughed. "I really hope there isn't a next time."

"True," Slade said, squeezing her calf. "I thought I was going to have to break his other arm to keep him safe."

Ashleigh looked at Daniel. "You didn't tell me your arm was broken."

He nodded. "I'll be out of work for a while."

"Maybe I can pick up a few tips from Kelly and nurse you back to health," Ashleigh said. As soon as the words were out, she realized what she said. "I mean, um…"

"Sounds good to me," Daniel told her with a wink. "Although I don't have an extra bed. You might have to share mine."

Ashleigh sucked in a breath and couldn't stop her smile. She nodded. "I can live with that."

Lily hugged her and promised they'd be back, with cupcakes. Kelsea and Pilar hugged her, too, and promised they'd help Lily carry the cupcakes. The rest of the guys waved and filtered out the door until it was just Ashleigh and Daniel.

"I wasn't trying to put you on the spot," she told him.

He smiled. "I didn't mind. I was hoping you would stay. Not just to help me heal, but because I love you, Ash."

She nodded. "I love you, too."

He leaned in and kissed her softly. She could tell he was holding back, so she pressed her tongue against his lips, urging him to open for her. He did, taking over the kiss with a groan. Then he winced and pulled back.

"Are you okay?" she asked when she opened her eyes and saw the pain on his face.

He nodded. "I forgot about my arm. This fucking sucks."

"I'm sorry," she said softly. "But we'll heal. And I'm not going anywhere, apparently."

He smiled. "Apparently."

She yawned widely, and he kissed her forehead.

"You need some sleep."

She nodded. "Will you stay here with me?"

He smiled. "Always."

Dunn watched Ashleigh sleep. She looked so peaceful. He wished he had the same peace she did. That he could replace love with hate and forget the person who changed everything inside.

Dunn leaned back in his chair and rested his head. Everything hurt, but he refused to have his own bed. He wanted to be with Ashleigh, and if he was a patient, too, he couldn't be there for her. Kelly and the other nurses were keeping an eye on him, and were going to bring him a bed for the night, but he needed a little rest first.

He felt the movement in the room and bolted upright. When he saw it was English, he settled back in his chair again.

"How's the leg?" Dunn asked him.

English made his way to the other chair on his crutches and lowered himself down. "Better now. It'll heal. We sure took a beating in this one."

Dunn nodded.

"Williams came to see me a few months ago," English admitted.

Dunn sat up straighter in his seat and turned to him. He wasn't sure how he felt, but he was definitely curious. "Why didn't you tell us?"

English shrugged. "I wasn't sure how anyone would feel about it. He almost seemed like our old CO. I was running by the gorge. It was early. There weren't a lot of tourists out yet, and I had music on. He was right there before I realized it. He said he just wanted to talk to me."

"What did you talk about?"

English shrugged. "Life, I guess. He said he wished he'd made different choices. He still had a lot of anger, but it almost seemed like he regretted the things he did, too."

"Do you think he…?"

"Would have turned everything around?" English asked, and Dunn nodded. "I hoped so. But now?" English shook his head. "We knew him as well as he knew us. I think he wanted us to find that first bomb. It was easy, you know. In a closet with a busted lock? Hard to miss it. And it was easy for Slade to diffuse."

"And it meant we would evacuate the building," Dunn said, leaning forward. He slid a hand over his face as English nodded.

"Exactly. Everyone else was out. We cleared the building. Kate Maddox was gone. All the fans. Even almost all of the employees were gone. But we went back in."

"Because he had Ashleigh," Dunn said, looking at her. "He was going to let her not-husband have her, and he was going to get away and blow us all up."

English hesitated for a second, then nodded. "That's what I think, too. We thought we got the bomb, so we went in, but he had five rigged to blow. And the last one was a delay from the others, like he knew we'd come out before it went off. He was after us."

"Shit," Dunn said. That pain in his chest ached when he looked at Ashleigh. She almost paid for it. If Williams had succeeded, he would have killed her.

"He couldn't be saved, Dunn. There was nothing we could have done to save him. But we saved his family, and we saved Ashleigh. We did our jobs."

"I can't believe he hated us that much," Dunn murmured.

English sucked in a breath and nodded. "I agree, but I also know there's no reason to mourn him. He wasn't the man we knew. Not anymore. We need to move on, and leave him where he belongs. In the ground."

Dunn nodded. He reached for Ashleigh's hand and squeezed it. She was still asleep, but touching her brought a calm to him he hadn't known in years.

"I'm happy you two found each other again," English said. "I'm looking forward to getting to know her, and to know this other side of you."

Dunn grinned. "Me, too."

English clapped him on the back, gently, and hobbled out of the room. Dunn couldn't go back to sleep, but Kelly came back in the room before long, anyway.

"She's doing okay?"

Dunn nodded. "Sleeping. She's been out for about thirty minutes."

"I'm not sleeping," Ashleigh murmured. "Not now." She blinked her eyes open slowly. "My head still hurts. Can I take something? I don't know how concussions work."

"The best thing is rest and quiet. I'm going to restrict your visitors for a few hours and put a sign on the door to keep the lights off. It'll be the best for both of you. But some more of your bloodwork came back," Kelly said.

Dunn sat up straighter. "Bloodwork? Is everything okay?"

Kelly nodded and grinned. "As long as an elevated hCG level is okay."

"What?" Ashleigh asked, her breath stuttering.

Kelly nodded. "It's very early based on your levels, but it appears as though you're pregnant."

"What?" Dunn said. "Pregnant. How?"

Kelly smirked. "Well, you see, when two people love each other..."

"We used condoms. Is it...?"

Ashleigh shook her head. "There's no way. It's yours, Daniel. I know this wasn't what you wanted."

Kelly smiled and quietly backed out of the room.

"I... um... wow," Dunn stuttered.

"You don't have to do anything, Daniel. I know children aren't in your plan."

He laughed mirthlessly. "Yeah, but neither were you, Ash. Now, I have two people I can't let go instead of just one."

"Yeah?" she asked.

He nodded. "Hell, yeah. We're having a baby."

She grinned. "We're having a baby."

"You know what that means, right?"

"What?"

"It means you need to marry me, Ash. Make an honest man out of me."

She shook her head. "Daniel, it's been a week!"

"And I knew the moment I saw you that walking away from you was the worst decision I ever made. I'm not letting you go again, Ash. Marry me. Today. Tomorrow. Next week. I don't care as long as you say yes."

She shook her head again and grinned. "Yes."

He leaned down and captured her lips, sliding his tongue between hers to seal their promise. When he pulled back, he said, "I love you, Ash."

She grinned again. "I love you, Daniel."

"Hooyah."

ASHLEIGH AND DUNN'S wedding was a quick ceremony in Slade's living room, complete with a slippered bride and the SEALs in full dress uniforms. Lily and the other women teased them all relentlessly that they were too hot and would melt all the snow falling outside the sliding doors.

"I should have started dating a soldier years ago," Pilar teased Jack.

"Frogman, not a soldier," Jack corrected her.

"Sexy. That's all that really matters," Pilar said.

"Right? If I'd known this was what you'd look like, I might have followed you years ago," Ashleigh told Dunn.

Dunn was the same serious guy he always was, but Ashleigh softened him. He reached for her and whispered something in her ear the rest of them couldn't hear.

"No secrets," Lily said.

"You don't want to hear what he just said," Ashleigh told her. The blush creeping up her cheeks said enough.

Lily hooted and nodded. "Good for you. It's your wedding, and when that little one comes, life is going to change."

Ashleigh ran a hand over her belly. She was just barely starting to show, one more person coming into their family. Their team had grown in a year. It no longer included Rodney or Williams, but they added Lily, Jaymes, Kelsea, Mason, Pilar, and Ashleigh. And soon, Baby Dunn.

Family was always important to Slade. Being able to see their found family get a little bigger was exciting for him. It reminded him how important it was to enjoy every moment because you never knew when it would be your last.

"So, who's next? Mason?" Lily asked, examining the single men one by one.

Mason snorted and shook his head.

"Not me. Don't even think it," Dex said. "No way in hell."

"I think it'll be Rocky," Pilar said before anyone else could protest.

"Nope, I vote for English," Kelsea said.

"Slade," Ashleigh voted with a lift of her glass.

Everyone laughed at that one. Slade didn't mind. He knew none of them expected him to ever settle down. He wasn't looking for a relationship. He was open to one, but he hadn't been looking for a relationship since he walked away from his high school sweetheart to join the SEALs. It was the right decision, for both of them, and Slade had no regrets, but he missed being the person someone else looks for when they walk into a room.

After being held as a POV, Slade struggled to let anyone close. His teammates were there for him, but opening up to another person wasn't something he was ready for. It was something he envied his teammates for. Something he wasn't sure he'd ever get over.

Howler farted loudly before Slade could reply to Ashleigh, both startling himself awake and making everyone else in the room laugh. Howler looked up at everyone with the fog of sleep still lingering.

"Howler," Slade said, drawing his dog's attention. He whistled.

The dog loped over to Slade and settled on his feet, leaning his weight against Slade. He reached down and scratched the dog's head.

"Slade's already taken," Kelsea said. "He has Howler."

Slade looked over at her and nodded. She was right. He had everything he needed. His family, his friends, and someone who always looked for him first. It didn't matter that the someone was a dog. Slade didn't need a woman. He was all good.

THANK **you** for reading Dunn and Ashleigh's story. This was a hard one to write because even if we've never faced something like they did, we all know what it's like to feel like we failed. To lose hope. To lose an idol.

The series continues with Slade's story. Slade blames himself for people getting hurt during a bank robbery. When one of the other captives applies to be the new F-BOMB office manager, he pushes to hire her so he can help someone. What he didn't count on was how attracted he would be to her or how hard it would be to resist the curvy new manager. But she just wants to be friends. Read Friends today!

ARE YOU READY FOR MORE? Newsletter subscribers get *exclusive* bonuses like short stories, bonus scenes, and a first look at everything new. Sign up for my newsletter today so you never miss a thing!

LOVED KATHERINE AND DILLON? You can read their story now. She's a superstar hiding her true identity. He's a CEO who thinks everyone wants something from him. All they want from each other is one night, but when she turns up on his doorstep the next day, neither of them can resist. Read Walk Of Fame today!

ABOUT THE AUTHOR

USA TODAY Bestselling Author Mary E Thompson spent most of her childhood wishing she had a few less curves. She hid in the pages of books because her favorite characters never cared what size her clothes were. Now, neither does Mary, and she writes stories that celebrate women like her. Real women who have curves, chase dreams, and find love, because we should all be happy, no matter our dress size.

Mary spends her non-writing time with her husband and two kids, watching too much TV, cheering for her hometown football team (Go Bills!), and hiding chocolate from her family.

Visit https://MaryEThompson.com/ to sign up for Mary's newsletter, **Romancing the Curves.** Subscribers get free ebooks and other fun stuff, like exclusive, members only content and giveaways, plus are the first to know about new releases and sales!

9 781944 090753